The rogue cop looked Jessica up and down

"Please don't make my day by telling me some sweet kid has been wrongfully arrested," he growled.

"Consider your day made then," Jessica returned. "My client's not a kid, but I think he's innocent."

Casey smiled. "I seem to have left my violin at home. You'll just have to proceed a cappella."

Jessica couldn't ignore his presence, his muscular body, his striking eyes. Instead, she tried to ignore his taunts. "I do not appreciate being toyed with when a man's freedom is at stake."

"*Toyed with.* Now *there's* an interesting expression. Conjures up all sorts of images, doesn't it?" Casey grinned, moved toward the door and blocked her exit.

"Save the intimidation routine for your suspects," Jessica said. "It won't work on me." *But it was.*

Dear Reader,

The verdict is in: Legal thrillers are a hit. And in response to this popular demand, we give you the first of Harlequin Intrigue's ongoing "Legal Thrillers."

In this new program we'll be bringing you some of your favorite stories. Stories of secret scandals and crimes of passion. Of legal eagles who battle the system...and undeniable desire.

Look for the "Legal Thriller" flash, for the best in romance suspense!

Sincerely,

Debra Matteucci
Senior Editor & Editorial Coordinator
Harlequin Books
300 East 42nd Street
New York, NY 10017

In Self Defense

Saranne Dawson

Harlequin Books

TORONTO • NEW YORK • LONDON
AMSTERDAM • PARIS • SYDNEY • HAMBURG
STOCKHOLM • ATHENS • TOKYO • MILAN
MADRID • WARSAW • BUDAPEST • AUCKLAND

ISBN 0-373-22286-6

IN SELF DEFENSE

Copyright © 1994 by Saranne Hoover

Printed in U.S.A.

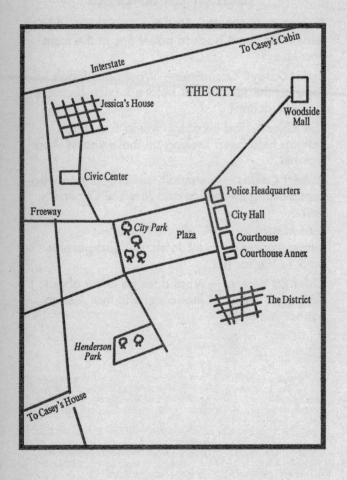

CAST OF CHARACTERS

Jessica Aylesworth—Had the past she couldn't remember come back to haunt her in the form of a killer?

T. S. "Casey" Casimiricz—Would this tough cop find the serial killer before Jessica became his next vicitim?

The Killer—Had he at last found the one woman he'd been seeking all these years? And was he...

Robert Collins—A mentally disturbed man who kept eluding the police and Jessica? Or was he...

Joel Matthews—The gentle hippie's reminiscences brought Jessica's dead parents back to life for her.

Chief Ed Waters—What does he know about the tragic events at that commune that Jessica cannot remember?

Prologue

He watched from deep within the shadows of a recessed doorway. This city was new to him, but there was a connection here, a link to the past that had beckoned him.

How many cities had he seen in his long years of wandering? Too many to count—except that he *did* count them in his own way.

So much of the time it seemed that he lived in darkness. But he could still remember the light: golden days and a golden woman. Her laughter rippled through his memory—laughter that had made him laugh, too, and even now could bring a smile to his face.

Always he saw them walking through a field of sunflowers, the big, heavy blossoms drooping and nodding in the warm breeze of a long-ago summer evening. He could never recall what they'd talked about—only the sound of her voice, the tilt of her head, the self-assured grace of her walk.

A sudden burst of laughter from across the littered street jerked him out of his reverie. He watched the group of women stroll past, their high heels clicking noisily on the pavement as they cut through here to get to lower Main. None of them held any interest for him, so he slipped once again into his memories.

She'd had a way of tossing her head that sent her golden hair flying to catch the light, and a way of saying his name that had sent shivers of pleasure through him and made him feel special.

So long ago. Golden days and a golden woman who had, in the end, turned out to be tarnished brass. He could still taste the bitterness of her betrayal, her unwillingness to understand what they had, what they *could* have had.

He could feel the darkness closing in on him again, surrounding him and obliterating the good memories. Then a sound intruded on his thoughts—and he saw her! He knew it wasn't really *her*, but there was always that brief moment when he believed, that moment when past and present merged. And now the darkness was upon him.

Chapter One

Jessica backed off to the doorway of her office, smiled and then laughed outright. The two small plants and the posters *did* improve things, but not by much. Ah, if only her former associates could see her now. From oak-paneled walls, Oriental rugs, damask drapes and original art to cracked plastic partitions, scuffed tile, bare, grimy windows and unframed posters.

She continued to chuckle as she sat on the squeaky desk chair and surveyed the battered desktop. She'd taken home her elegant leather desk set after the first day.

"Hey, what's that I heard just now? Didn't anyone tell you that we don't allow laughter in this place? Public defenders are serious people, Jessica Aylesworth."

Jessica smiled at the short, heavyset woman who appeared in her doorway carrying a bulging old leather briefcase.

"Millie, I think I'll take a picture of this office to send back to Smith, Hamilton & Wethersby. It'll confirm all their suspicions—that I've totally decompensated, as my shrink friend would say."

"I agree with them." Millie nodded. "I'll sign the commitment papers myself. I don't see how any sane person could give up a partnership in a prestigious firm for this."

"I wasn't a partner, only an associate."

"But you would have been. They told Mac that. You had it made, girl." She peered at the walls. "What happened to your degree?"

"I took it down." Jessica grinned. "Harvard's asked to have it back."

"I don't blame them. You sure aren't doing much to further their prestige." Then she heaved a bosomy sigh.

"Well, I'm off to a fun-filled day in juvenile court. One dealer, two possession and a trio of twelve-year-old muggers. With justice for all." She sketched a salute and disappeared. "Have a good day" floated back over the partition.

A good day, indeed, Jessica thought with a glance at the five new cases she'd just been assigned. There had been no easing into things in this office; from day one she'd been assigned a full caseload. She glanced at her watch. She had exactly seven minutes to prepare for her first appointment of the day.

Joel Matthews, age forty-six, was charged with mugging an elderly woman and stealing her Social Security money. He'd been apprehended near the crime scene and had in his possession a sum of cash that matched the amount stolen. The victim was hospitalized and had identified him from a mug shot.

Jessica sighed. This one had "guilty" written all over it, as did most of the cases she was handling. Where, she wondered, were the innocent people she'd thought she would be defending? She was reminding herself that her job was to defend them regardless of their guilt or innocence, when Joel Matthews appeared.

After introducing herself and asking him to take a seat, she stole a quick glance at the report. It was hard to believe that he was forty-six; she would have guessed him to be in his mid-thirties. Furthermore, if there was such a thing as a stereotypical mugger, he wouldn't have been on anyone's list.

She recalled now that Millie, who had appeared with him at the arraignment, had described him as being a "latter-day hippie;" it was an accurate description. He was tall and lean and walked with a slight hunch to his back. His medium-brown hair fell to his thin shoulders, and he had a rather longish face with dark eyes that could only be called soulful. Not only did he have the look of a sixties' flower child, he also had a manner of speaking that harkened back to that time.

He insisted upon his innocence, and as they talked, Jessica began to believe him. He'd been running away from the crime scene when he was caught by the police, but he claimed that he'd been running to catch a bus because he had a job interview. The money in his possession, according to his story, was the result of gambling winnings. He'd been playing the numbers.

At times, Jessica found the intensity of his stare disconcerting, but she liked him. Ever since discovering that her own parents had been hippies, she'd had a fascination for that lifestyle. She admired anyone who could choose to reject material success and do their own thing.

Joel Matthews was a carpenter and a folksinger, earning his living at either trade as he drifted around the country. He'd never made much money, he told her, but he liked his life.

He was a strange, intriguing character who stayed with her after he'd gone, intruding on her thoughts as she finished her morning's appointments. The man seemed to be very laid-back, yet somehow terribly intense at the same time. He had good reason to be intense right now. He was quite likely to end up in jail unless she could find some way to break the case against him. She had precious little time and for that reason had already been warned not to let herself become too involved with any of her cases, but she wanted to help Joel Matthews. She picked up the arresting officer's report and her notes and went off to find Mac.

George MacDuff, chief public defender and possessor of the only true office in their cramped courthouse annex space, was sitting with his feet propped up on a desk overflowing with papers and dirty ashtrays. He was nearing fifty and looked it; what he *didn't* look was intelligent—but he was. He'd spent his entire legal career in an office where the pay was low and the work load and turnover were high. He did it because he believed in the system. Jessica liked him very much.

She made a pretense of knocking on his open door and he waved her to a chair. Then she explained the situation.

"So he's got an explanation for running and for the money. But can I get it to work? He says that this Patsy, who runs the illegal gambling operation out of his bar, won't talk. After all, what he's doing is illegal."

Mac grunted assent. "It doesn't look good, Jessica. Is this that hippie type I saw earlier?"

She nodded. "I believe him, Mac. He just doesn't seem like the violent type, and the victim is an old woman who identified him from a mug shot in the hospital. She could have been wrong. There's nothing outstanding about his looks, except for his long hair, and he was wearing it back in a ponytail at the time. Do you think that there's any chance the arresting officer would help?"

"Maybe, but not likely. He's got an arrest and that's all he wants." He peered at her consideringly. "Since it happened in the District, there *is* someone who could help—if he's so inclined. Who's the arresting officer?"

Jessica frowned at the scrawled signature. "I can't make it out. The initials look like T.S., I think, and the last name starts with *C* and ends with *Z*."

Mac frowned and took the report from her to examine it. "Hmph! He must have just happened on the scene. He won't usually let himself get involved with paperwork."

"You know him?" she asked hopefully.

Mac grinned, then leaned dangerously far back in his swivel chair and laughed outright. "I'm surprised you haven't heard of him by now. Hasn't anyone mentioned Casey to you?"

"I think someone did mention him," Jessica admitted, recalling that the context had been anything but flattering. "Who is he?"

Mac glanced at his watch and stood. "I've got to be in court in fifteen minutes, and it would take four times that long to answer your question properly. Casey is Casey, our fair city's rogue cop. Idolized by the ordinary citizen, who thinks he's the only one standing between them and anarchy. The mayor's poster boy. The press's darling. And his fellow officers' favorite cop."

He started out of the office and she followed in his wake. "What do you mean by rogue cop? Are you saying that he's crooked?"

Mac shook his head and chuckled. "You know that old joke about where does a nine-hundred-pound gorilla sit? Anywhere he wants? Well, this gorilla *does* anything he wants."

He paused at the doorway to the reception area. "He might help you, especially if you go to see him in person. He's at headquarters occasionally, has an office there somewhere. If he agrees to help you, you tell him he owes me one."

He walked away chuckling, leaving Jessica to puzzle over his last remark.

She called police headquarters and asked for T. S. Casimir-icz, doing the best she could with the pronunciation.

"Casey isn't in."

"When do you expect him?"

"When he comes in. Would you like to leave a message?"

She did so, mentioning that she was with the public defender's office.

CASEY PARKED in a No Parking zone and got out, his eyes already busy scanning the dark, littered streets. A group of kids came around the corner, saw him and quickly moved off in another direction, vanishing into the darkness. Most of the streetlights were out, as they usually were in this neighborhood. A vandalized fire hydrant gushed water into the street next to a phone booth with an empty, dangling cord.

Then a trio of women appeared, greeting him with easy familiarity.

"Evening, ladies. Froggy warned you, didn't he?"

They nodded. "We know about it," one of them said. "We knew Jewel, too. She liked to work alone. We told her she shouldn't."

Casey nodded. "Yeah, so did I. Any rough trade around lately?"

They shook their heads. "Is it true he cut her up real bad?"

An image of the murdered prostitute crawled across Casey's mind. No one knew it, nor would anyone have believed it, but he was squeamish about violence.

"Yeah, it was bad," he admitted. "Could be we've got a real psycho out there."

"We're bein' careful," they chorused.

Right, thought Casey as he continued on his way. A careful hooker was an oxymoron if he'd ever heard one.

He continued his leisurely stroll down the street, past boarded-up shops and others with heavy iron grilles. A small crowd was gathered outside a bar, but they parted quickly for him and he walked inside, peering through the thick haze of cigarette smoke. Heads turned his way. A few greeted him, but most quickly averted their eyes. The bartender spotted him and hurried over.

"I heard about Jewel," the man said. "She came in here sometimes, but she wasn't one of the regulars. I heard she was really cut up."

Casey nodded, getting another unwelcome flashback of that brutalized body. "You had any weirdos in here lately?"

"Nah, pretty much the usual crowd."

"Call me if you hear anything," Casey told him. "I think we've got a real nut case out there."

"Will do."

He left the bar and made a circuit of lower Main, then headed back to where he'd left his car. Along the way he paused to check several dark alleyways. Then, just as he reached his car, he thought he saw something move in the deep shadows of a dead-end alley between boarded-up stores. He unzipped his leather jacket and turned in.

"Police!" he shouted. "Come out where I can see you, hands on your heads!"

Shadows moved in the darkness. He reached for his gun, at the same time moving deeper into the shadows himself. Then the kids he'd seen earlier came walking toward him, their hands up.

"We wasn't doin' nothin', Casey. Honest!"

He put his gun away and gestured to a wall. "Sit down against that wall, hands under your butts, and don't move!"

They muttered rebelliously, but did as told. Casey checked behind a dumpster and saw what at first looked like a pile of rags. Then he knelt and felt for the man's carotid artery. Dead drunk probably, but not dead. He went back to the kids.

"Okay, slimeballs, hand it over."

Two of them looked nervously at the third, and he finally emptied his pocket. "It's *my* money! I didn't do nothin'."

"Uh-huh." Casey counted it. It was the fifth of the month—a good time to roll drunks. "I suppose you got this working at McDonald's, right?"

Without waiting for an answer he went over to his car, reached in and pulled out the mike to call dispatch. "Send a garbage truck down to Torrence and Ninth, Bobby. I've got a pickup."

"You can't do this to us, man!" the leader cried as Casey walked back to them. He was pausing between each word to sniffle.

Casey walked into the kid's space and stared down at him. "What'd you say? I didn't understand you. Must be that coked-up nose of yours."

The kid backed off quickly and kept quiet. While he waited for the wagon, Casey lit a cigar. He didn't bother to handcuff them.

The wagon finally arrived and relieved him of the kids. He went back into the alley, carefully picked up the unconscious drunk and put him into the wagon, too, then handed over the money.

"When Nick sobers up he might be able to identify them. They've all got records. Nick's a diabetic, so you'd better have the doc take a look at him."

He turned back to the wagon and grinned at the kids. "Have a nice night, pond scum." Then he slammed the wagon's doors and locked them.

Fifteen minutes later he was on the freeway ramp, headed home. Jewel was on his mind again, but this time he wasn't thinking about her battered body. What he was seeing instead was her long blond wig. She'd been proud of that wig. She'd told him it cost her a fortune, but the johns liked blondes.

The wig had been torn from her head and then ripped apart. Tufts of honey blond hair were all over the place, almost as if the killer thought he'd been cheated.

Casey definitely had a bad feeling about this one.

THE MYSTERIOUS CASEY DID not return her call, and neither did he return the other two calls she made over the next two days. Then Jessica remembered Mac's statement that he might help her if she went to see him in person. Maybe the man *never* returned calls. She was getting worried. Joel Matthews's pretrial hearing was only a week away and he'd been in twice more to see her, still protesting his innocence. So she left her office and walked the two blocks to police headquarters, determined this time to find some way to reach Casey. Surely he must carry a pager if he was never in his office. What good was a cop who couldn't be found?

The veteran cop on the desk told her Casey wasn't in and she was about to inquire how she could reach him when a younger officer standing nearby interrupted her.

"You're looking for Casey?"

Jessica nodded hopefully.

"He just came in. I saw him at the coffee machine. He's probably down in his office. I'll take you."

"He's not answering his phone," the desk cop grumbled. "He never answers his phone. Tell him the chief would like to see him if he can fit it into his schedule."

"Last time I was down there he didn't even have the phone plugged in," the younger cop said with a grin as he gestured to Jessica to follow him. "He says he comes here for some peace and quiet and the noise bothers him."

He led her through a maze of hallways and large rooms filled with uniformed and plainclothes officers. Then they went down a set of dimly lit stairs to the basement. After the noise upstairs, the silence down here was almost deafening. As she followed the officer down the hallway, Jessica could see that the area was obviously used for storage. A faint trace of cigar smoke hung in the air.

The young officer was a short distance ahead of her and he suddenly stopped at an open doorway. "Casey, there's a lady here to see you."

"If it's that P.D., tell her to get lost," a deep male voice responded.

"She's right here," the young cop replied, with a grin at her.

The man inside the office muttered something Jessica couldn't hear—and probably didn't want to. Her hopes of gaining this Casey's assistance were sinking rapidly.

The officer turned to her, still grinning. "Don't worry. It's not true that he eats P.D.'s for breakfast. Sometimes he's almost human."

He stepped back and Jessica moved into the doorway, drawing herself up to her full height and putting on her best professional smile. But the smile wavered as the man inside the tiny office stood to greet her.

They stared at each other in a silence that seemed to charge the very air between them. Jessica felt very strange. Shock gave way to fear, which in turn was almost instantly transformed into something else. Warmth? A feeling of safety? A vague memory seemed to tickle her mind. But then all of it was lost in the overpowering presence of T. S. Casimiricz.

He had to be six and a half feet tall, with impossibly wide shoulders and a body that, while far from being lean, was scarcely flabby, either. His hair was very black with a trace of gray threaded through its slightly wavy thickness. She supposed he must be in his late thirties.

But for all his physical presence, it was his eyes that held her captive: pale, ice blue eyes that were very busy appraising her as she stood there trying to cope with her strong reaction to this man.

There was no way he could be called truly handsome, she thought, but that description seemed irrelevant in any event. He defied such descriptions; he simply *was*.

Casey wasn't happy about being cornered by a P.D., but the minute he saw her, he forgot all about what she was and instead thought about how long it had been since he'd had a woman in his life.

She had all the right stuff in all the right places: tall, curvy even in her conservative suit, long, honey blond hair, wide gray-green eyes and a great mouth, the soft kind of mouth that . . .

He glanced down at her left hand, thinking that no P.D. could afford clothes like that. But there were no rings, which definitely pleased him.

She put out her hand and he took it, liking its softness and the firmness of her grip. Most women had limp handshakes.

"I'm Jessica Aylesworth, Mr., uh. . . ."

"Casey." He forced himself to let go of her hand, then gestured to a battered chair, remembering only at the last second that one of its legs was loose. He didn't generally encourage visitors down here.

She was about to sit down when he reached out and grabbed her, hooking one long arm around her waist. She stumbled against him with a startled cry and her hands came up quickly to push him away. He didn't want to let her go. He liked her perfume, too: subtle and classy. After dragging out the moment as long as he could, he dropped his arm.

"Sorry. I forgot that chair has a bad leg."

She gave him a doubtful look, then turned to examine it.

"Honest. I haven't attacked a woman down here in years— or months, anyway. Sit here."

He motioned to his own chair, then waited until she'd taken it and sat on the edge of his desk, too close to her. She moved the chair back, but since it was already near the wall she couldn't get very far.

"You're new," he said, taking the opportunity to run his gaze over her long, trim legs. She had a cool poise that he liked. He knew how intimidating he could be and was tempted to push it a bit more to see if he could shatter that aplomb.

"Yes, I started last week. I'm sorry to have come here without an appointment but, as you can see, I've been trying to reach you for several days."

She gestured to his wastebasket, where several pink message slips were clearly visible. He leaned over and looked, too.

"Huh! Well, the wind gets bad in here sometimes. I guess they just blew off my desk."

The tiny office had no windows. She laughed, and he *really* began to like her.

"Mac said you might help me," she ventured.

"He did?" Casey narrowed those striking eyes on her. "Did he suggest that you come over instead of calling?"

"As a matter of fact, he did." And now she was beginning to understand why.

His wide mouth twitched with amusement. "Okay, tell Mac I might owe him one. What's your problem? And please don't make my day by telling me that some sweet, cute kid has been wrongfully arrested."

"Consider your day made, then. He's not a kid, but I think he's innocent."

He groaned and rolled his eyes.

"Do you think you could at least hear me out?"

He made a show of looking around the office and even opened a desk drawer. "Damn! I seem to have left my violin at home. I guess you'll just have to proceed a cappella."

Jessica ignored his taunts and began to explain about Joel Matthews. But there was no way she could ignore his presence. She tried not to stare at his muscular thigh that rested on the desktop too close to her. She avoided those striking eyes that were fixed unwaveringly on her. She struggled not to watch his big hands that were toying with a pen.

Then she leaned back in the chair to put some more space between them—and straightened up quickly when she felt the hardness of a gun in a shoulder holster beneath the jacket he'd slung over the back of the chair.

"I really think he may be telling the truth," she finished. "But for obvious reasons, it's going to be difficult to prove that."

"I'd say that's a fair assessment, Counselor."

"I was hoping that perhaps you could look into it a bit more."

"I could. Would you like me to have the bookie testify on his behalf? I'm sure I could persuade him."

She heard the slight emphasis on "persuade" and saw the glint of amusement in his eyes. Whatever craziness she'd felt before was rapidly being swallowed up by anger over his behavior. "I'm not asking you to do anything unethical."

He grinned. "Me, unethical? Perish the thought. Didn't Mac tell you that I always go by the book?"

"Mr. . . . Casey, do you think you could take this matter seriously? I do not appreciate being toyed with when a man's freedom may be at stake."

"Toyed with. Now *there's* an interesting expression. Conjures up all sorts of images, doesn't it?"

Jessica picked up her bag and stood. But he stood, too, then moved to the office door, blocking her exit. She glared at him.

"Save the intimidation routine for your suspects, Casey. It won't work on me. Thank you for your time."

He chuckled. "Yeah, you're right. Sometimes I just feel compelled to live up to my reputation."

They stood there for a moment, staring at each other intensely. Jessica was still angry with him, but her treacherous body was sending some very mixed signals.

"This place needs better ventilation," he muttered. "The atmosphere seems awfully close."

She heard the slight huskiness in his voice and felt an embarrassing flush begin to creep through her fair skin.

"Too warm, too." He smiled. "Okay, Ms. Aylesworth, I'll look into it. It probably won't cost you more than an evening in the pleasure of my company. You can even bring your boyfriend along, but like you said, I can be pretty intimidating."

"I certainly don't doubt that, but I'm sure he can hold his own." She moved toward the door and he stepped aside this time. "Thank you."

By the time she'd found her way out of the building Jessica had half convinced herself that none of it had really happened. He was surely nothing more than a very large hallucination, brought on, no doubt, by her failure to eat lunch.

BUT THE HALLUCINATION that was T. S. Casimiricz was still on her mind when she met her old friend Susan for dinner that evening.

Susan and Jessica had been friends ever since elementary school in Philadelphia. Then Susan had come to this midwestern city of five hundred thousand to do her graduate work at its prestigious university, the same school Jessica's parents had attended and the place where they'd met.

When Jessica had decided to make a change in her life, she'd found herself being drawn there, as well. Since her arrival, she'd several times gone for walks on the lovely campus, imagining her parents as young lovers strolling beneath the trees.

Over excellent Japanese food the two women talked about their respective jobs. Jessica had many juveniles on her caseload and Susan was a child psychologist, so although their professions were different, they saw many of the same problems.

Still, the client who was uppermost in her mind at the moment was Joel Matthews, and she told Susan about his situation.

"The only hope I have is the officer who arrested him, and I'm not at all sure that he's going to help." She paused as an image of Casey filled her mind once again. The impact he'd had on her was downright scary.

"He's the most extraordinary man, Susan. I've never met anyone quite like him."

"Who? You mean this hippie?"

"No, he's unusual, too, in a different way. I was referring to the cop."

Susan stared at her for a moment, then rolled her dark eyes. "Casey!"

"You know him?" Jessica asked in surprise.

"I've met him. He dated a friend of mine for a short time."

"Well? What do you think of him?" Jessica found herself wanting another opinion. She'd spoken to Millie at the office about him. Millie detested him, and Jessica had thought at the time that she should, too, given the way he'd acted.

"Actually," Susan said with a smile, "I try *not* to think about him."

"What do you mean?"

Susan sighed. "Did you ever stare at the sun and then end up with this black spot before your eyes afterward? That's Casey—except that the image never quite goes away."

"Are you saying that you're attracted to him?"

Susan laughed. "Yes and no, a shrink's favorite response. Could any woman *not* be attracted to him? But if he ever looked my way I'd run in the opposite direction—with regret, but I'd definitely run."

"Why?" Jessica was feeling rather the same, although she knew the urge to run wasn't as strong as it should be.

"Because there's just too darned much of him. In every way. I think I'd be afraid of losing myself somehow."

Jessica gave Susan an abbreviated version of her encounter with him. "He was really obnoxious, but I just couldn't seem to stay angry with him."

Susan frowned. "That doesn't sound like him. From what Sherri, my friend who dated him, said, he's not the kind who comes on strong like that. In fact, her complaint was just the opposite. She said once that he was *too* much of a gentleman."

"What do you know about him—as a cop, I mean? I've heard some things."

"Everyone seems to think he walks on water. The press loves him, and he always seems to be involved in high-profile cases. I suppose it would be easy to think of him as being brutal, but I doubt that. When you're his size, you just don't need to use force that much, and anyway, he didn't strike me as the brutal type."

Jessica went home still thinking about Casey and about her reaction to him. What continued to trouble her most was the fleeting impression that he somehow belonged to her past, even though she couldn't place him. And then, too, there was that odd mixture of fear and warmth she'd felt when she first saw him.

There had always been a part of her past that remained a mystery to Jessica. Her "black hole," as she called it, was a place deep inside that she couldn't seem to reach, but that had surfaced over the years in the form of terrible nightmares.

Jessica's parents had died in an auto accident when she was just three years old, and she'd then gone to Philadelphia to live with her wealthy maternal grandparents. She'd long suspected that her "black hole" had something to do with that tragedy, although she had no memory of it. In recent years she'd stopped having the nightmares. She'd thought they were gone forever.

At least, until she awoke later that night, drenched in sweat, with echoes of shouts and screams reverberating through her head.

She sat there shivering, trying as always to remember something, anything. But the images that had terrorized her moved beyond her reach, retreating as they always did into that black hole. She never remembered anything except for the shouts and screams, but she was sure the nightmare was always the same.

Then later, as she was again trying to find her way back to sleep, she recalled those feelings she'd had when she met Casey. Could it be mere coincidence that the nightmares had started up again now? Surely it must be. How could Casey be connected to her past?

JESSICA FOUND a parking space, pulled in and surveyed the area known as the District. Somewhere in this worst of the city's slums a prostitute had been stabbed to death only days ago. The media was already speculating about a psychopathic serial killer.

The neighborhood she was in now was made up of small, seedy bars and convenience stores, dingy tenements and boarded-up buildings. Jessica made her way down the block to Patsy's, the bar where Joel Matthews had said he won the money the police had found on him.

Two days had passed since their encounter, and she'd heard nothing further from Casey. She'd called yesterday and left a message, but she suspected that it now rested in his wastebasket along with the earlier ones. Mac was out of town for a few days, so Jessica had discussed the situation with Millie Davis, who was acting chief in Mac's absence.

"Forget about Casey," Millie had advised her. "Despite what he might have said, he won't help you. To his way of thinking, Matthews is guilty. Whether he's guilty of this crime or some other crime in the past or future doesn't matter to him."

So Jessica had decided to pursue the matter on her own. She knew she had no hope of getting Patsy to testify on Joel's behalf, but she was hoping he might be willing to confirm the man's story. Then she just might be able to persuade the DA to look into the matter more closely.

She knew as well that Casey wasn't going to be happy with her if his arrest was challenged, but she was more concerned at this point about her client. He continued to come in every day and kept saying in his soft voice that he was afraid of going to jail, afraid of losing his precious freedom.

She walked through the open door into the dimly lit bar and was immediately assaulted by the stench of beer and cigarette smoke. When her eyes adjusted, she could see that there were only a few customers in the place. All of them turned to stare at her for a moment, then returned to their business. She walked up to the bar and asked to speak to Patsy.

"What business you got with him?" the bartender asked.

Jessica explained who she was, then told him about Joel.

"We don't take no bets in here," the man said.

As he spoke, another man got up from a stool halfway down the bar and walked toward her. He looked like an ex-boxer gone to seed.

"This is important," Jessica said to the bartender as the other man took a stool next to her. "I'm not going to ask him to testify. I just want to know if my client won money that day." Then she described Joel, since it occurred to her that it might well have been the bartender he'd dealt with.

The other man's meaty thigh brushed against her and she moved as far away as she could, which wasn't far enough, since she was standing between two bar stools that were bolted to the floor.

"You some kind of social worker?" he asked her.

"No, I'm an attorney." She glanced at him briefly, then turned back to the bartender. But he was walking away.

"I sure wouldn't mind having you defend *me*, honey. How about a beer?"

Jessica shook her head and turned to leave, but the man grabbed her arm.

"Please let me go," she said firmly, trying to pull her arm free. But he merely tightened his grip.

"You and me could have some fun, honey—and maybe I can help you. If you don't want a beer, how about some wine?"

"No, thank you. I would like to leave."

He had relaxed his grip slightly and she tried again to pull her arm free. But this time his other arm shot out to grab her around the waist. He began to pull her toward him and she lost her balance.

Fear shot through her, followed quickly by a blazing anger. She drew back and slapped his face with all her might. The blow caught him by surprise and he let her go. She took sev-

eral quick steps backward to regain her balance—and collided
with a solid wall of flesh.

Another arm encircled her waist firmly. Her fear escalated.
But before she twisted around to confront this latest threat, she
saw fear on the face of her first assailant, as well.

"I imagine the lady must have said no, Patsy. Maybe you
didn't hear her."

Jessica recognized the voice even before she turned to look
up into the pale eyes of T. S. Casimiricz. He relaxed his grip
slightly, sliding his hand down to curve it familiarly against her
hip as he grinned down at her.

"Jessie, honey, we've got to have a conversation one of these
nights about your reckless tendencies."

She hated the nickname Jessie and she was nearly as angry
over his broad suggestion of intimacy as she was with the other
man's behavior. But she prudently kept her silence—for now.

Casey turned them both around, his big hand still curved
against her hip. "I'll be back to see you later, Patsy. Right now
I've got other plans."

As soon as they were outside, she pulled away from him angrily. "You're no better than he was, Casey! Keep your hands
off me!"

He took her arm and began to propel her down the street as
he exchanged greetings with several passersby. Then he leaned
close to her.

"The difference between Patsy and me is that I'll ask. He'll
just take. Now, say 'thank you, Casey, for rescuing me.'"

"I would have gotten away without your help," she replied
icily.

"Maybe. And of course you wouldn't have been there in the
first place if I'd done as I promised."

That was exactly the point she'd intended to make next and
it irritated her that he'd beaten her to it. He gave her a decid-
edly smug grin.

"Don't you just hate it when someone steals your best line?"

She came to a halt. "My car's over there."

"I wondered who was dumb enough to leave a Mercedes
here. And I didn't know that being a P.D. paid so well these
days."

She walked to the curb. "Are you going to talk to him?"

"Well, I was. But I'm not in the habit of doing favors for ungrateful people, especially when they're P.D.'s."

She stopped and turned to face him squarely. "Listen, Casey, I truly believe that there's a halfway decent person hiding somewhere inside you. So why do you persist in trying to prove me wrong?"

He grinned. "I'm just naturally perverse. Come on. We'll take your car. Mine's safe here."

"Where are we taking my car?" She frowned in confusion.

"You're going to buy me lunch for saving your butt. I'll try not to eat enough to keep you from making the payments on your pretty little toy here."

Chapter Two

"Don't expect me to keep a straight face if you get stuck," Jessica said as she watched him attempt to fold himself into the passenger seat of her low sports model.

"Don't worry, I'm an expert. I've been suffering humiliations like this since I was a kid. Just don't make any quick stops or I'll have teeth marks in my kneecaps."

He crouched in her car like some large, dark beast, overfilling the cramped space—and overfilling her senses, as well. She started the car.

"You didn't have to be so obnoxious back there, you know."

"There was a purpose to my familiar behavior. If you choose to ignore my advice and come back down here again, it might save you some trouble. Turn right at the next corner."

"I was told that it was safe enough during the day," she protested.

"It couldn't have been Mac who told you that."

"No, it was Millie Davis. She said she'd never had any trouble down here."

"Millie Davis is tough as nails and ugly as a mud fence."

"She's very fond of you, too," Jessica replied dryly as she made the turn.

"Now turn left up here."

She did as told, turning onto a street that looked far worse than the one they'd just left. Boarded-up houses and buildings leaned toward each other for support. Only a few buildings appeared to be occupied by marginal businesses, and the sidewalks were deserted. He told her to stop, and she did so, then looked around. There weren't any restaurants in sight.

"Right over there," he said, pointing. "See those marks on the sidewalk?"

"Yes." She could vaguely make out what looked like yellow chalk markings.

"That's where Jewel, the prostitute, was killed."

She drove on. "You're not very subtle, are you?"

"Just making a point. Right at the light up ahead." He paused for a moment. "I knew her. I'd warned her a couple of times about working alone. I liked her. She had a kind of dignity."

Jessica glanced over at him, but he was looking out the window. His tone of voice surprised her. It was rather like discovering a flower growing out of a rock.

"Are you working on the case?" she asked.

"Sort of. I'll definitely be working on it when the next one happens."

"The next one? Then you agree with what the media is saying about a serial killer?"

"Yeah. They're probably right for once. We've got a real psycho out there, my least favorite kind. Give me a nice normal drug dealer anytime.

"Jewel had this long blond wig—the same color as your hair. She was really proud of it. This wacko ripped it off and tore it to shreds. That's not for publication, by the way."

"Why would he do that? Do you think he was mad because she wasn't a natural blonde?"

"Uh-huh. That's exactly what I think. It took some time and effort to rip it up like that, and he'd already taken enough time with her. That street's pretty deserted, but he was still taking a risk."

He turned to face her as she waited for a light. "What I'm saying is that sometimes these nuts are fixated on some physical type, and I think that might be the case here. Jewel was about your height and build, too. So be careful. And speaking of hair, you can lose that pigtail, by the way. I like your hair down."

"It isn't a pigtail, it's a French braid. And I'm so sorry that I didn't think to consult you about the style," she replied in a voice dripping with sarcasm.

He directed her to a restaurant on the edge of the District, a smallish Italian place.

"It's not much to look at, I'll admit, but they've got the best garbage pizza in town."

"Garbage pizza?" she echoed quizzically.

"Pizza with everything. You aren't one of those bean sprouts and tofu types, are you?" he asked suspiciously.

"No, I tried vegetarianism once, but it didn't take."

When they entered the tiny restaurant Casey was greeted warmly, while she was politely scrutinized. He didn't bother ordering for himself, but told them that she'd have a small pizza with everything but anchovies.

"How do you know I don't like anchovies?" she asked as they settled into a booth.

"You don't. I can see that you're a woman of taste. Besides, *I* don't like them, and I'll finish what you don't eat."

Jessica wondered if she'd ever before met a man who was so irritating and yet so undeniably attractive. Every moment she spent with him, she felt pulled in two directions at once. But she reminded herself that she needed his help.

"Casey, there's something I don't understand. If you know that Patsy's engaged in illegal gambling, why hasn't he been arrested?"

He leaned against the high back of the booth and gazed at her steadily. "Because he's more valuable to me out of jail than in. This way, he owes me."

"But will he tell you the truth?"

He nodded. "I don't like that hippie of yours. There's something about him. Why was he running when I caught him?"

"He says he was running to catch a bus."

"Well, at least he hasn't changed his story. And speaking of stories, what's yours, Jessica Aylesworth?"

"What do you mean?"

"Like all good cops, I suffer from terminal nosiness. You look like the type to be working in some big, prestigious firm, charging corporate crooks two hundred dollars an hour."

"I did do that for a while—and it was for more than two hundred dollars an hour. But I don't need the money and I wanted to put my skills to better use."

"How did you end up here?"

"How do you know I'm not from here?" she challenged.

"The accent's wrong. Eastern seaboard."

"I'm from Philadelphia, and I came out here because I wanted a change. I had a friend living here, so I chose to move here, too."

"And your friend is your boyfriend?"

She'd forgotten all about not correcting him earlier. "No, she's my oldest friend. Her name's Susan Heverly. She's a child psychologist."

"I've met her. So the boyfriend is someone you met here?"

She wished that he wasn't so persistent, and wondered if she should continue the charade; it might be safer. But she met his eyes and all thoughts of safety vanished.

"There's no boyfriend."

He grinned—not the lecherous smile she'd half expected, but a smile of pure pleasure that made her feel inordinately pleased, as well. Then, before he could pursue the topic any further, she asked him about himself.

"I grew up here. My dad was a cop who was killed in the line of duty when I was twelve. I went to State on a football scholarship and majored in football, women and drinking, pretty much in that order. Then I played pro ball for three years, until I finally decided to listen to that little voice that had been saying all along that I was going to be a cop."

Their pizza arrived. She stared at the huge pie that was set before him. Could he really eat all that?

"I'm afraid that I've never followed football," she admitted. "Were you a big star?"

"Yep. Big star. Big bucks, too. But it began to seem like a pretty silly business for a grown man to be in."

"I've often thought that myself," she remarked as she saw the first slice vanish. "But it must have been difficult to give up that kind of money."

"It would have been if I hadn't found another way to make it."

"As a cop?" she asked, frowning.

"You must be joking! No, I write crime novels—what are usually called police procedurals."

She nearly choked on her pizza. "You do? How many have you written?"

"Five. The last two have made it to the bestseller lists, and one of the networks is negotiating with my agent now for TV rights."

Jessica tried to contain her surprise. It began to dawn on her that there was even more to this man than she'd originally thought. It also occurred to her that they were alike in at least one way, and then he seemed to reach right into her thoughts.

"We're kind of alike that way, aren't we? I don't have to be a cop. I do it because that's what I want to do. And you don't have to be a P.D." He paused, then went on in a regretful tone. "But that's about all we have in common, isn't it? On balance it isn't much."

"No, it isn't," she agreed as she met his gaze and felt once again that powerfully sensual current that made liars of them both.

"On the other hand, there's always a case to be made for opposites attracting," he went on.

"I've always thought that phenomenon was greatly overrated," she lied.

"But you came to live out here for a change," he observed. Silver lights were dancing in his eyes.

"What are you trying to say, Casey?" she challenged. "I'm afraid that the subtlety of this conversation is lost on me."

"Well, we may not be off to a promising start, but I don't think we should give up yet, do you?"

"Give up what?"

"This prospective affair."

"Is this another of those times when you feel compelled to live up to your reputation?" she inquired archly, barely able to restrain herself from pointing out that according to Susan, that reputation was nonexistent. Which of course raised the question of why he was behaving this way toward *her*.

"Actually," he said, "I lied about that. I'm usually very well behaved. You just seem to bring out the worst in me. Why do you think that is?"

Jessica was saved from having to respond by the sudden appearance of the owner, who informed Casey that there was someone waiting out back to see him.

Casey excused himself and left. Jessica could actually feel her body begin to settle down again in his absence, as though an electric current had been switched off. What was it about him that affected her so powerfully? And his comment seemed to suggest that she had an equally potent effect on him.

Chemistry, she thought. All those pheromones flying around. Lust at first sight.

And while she had in fact moved out here to find a new and different life, she hadn't envisioned that life to include a cop. Cops and P.D.'s were like oil and water. They just didn't mix.

Besides, along with everything else, she was still troubled by the feeling that Casey touched something buried deep in her memory. Was that the real reason she was so drawn to him?

Over the years Jessica had thought about going out to Oregon to look into her past. It wasn't likely that the commune where she'd once lived still existed, although she'd read that a few of them had in fact survived and she knew from her birth certificate the area where it must have been.

She was still thinking about Casey's possible connection to her when he returned.

"Sorry for the interruption. That was one of my snitches. They know I come here regularly."

"I'm afraid I don't know exactly what you do," she said, grateful for the change in conversation. "Except for ignoring my phone calls, that is."

He chuckled. "I wasn't ignoring your phone calls, at least, not after I met you. I was just busy and hadn't found the time to see Patsy.

"I'm on permanent special duty, out of headquarters. Detective lieutenant grade. Basically, I operate a network of snitches who let me know when anything's happening. Most of them are involved in minor illegal business that I overlook as long as they provide information. It's called intelligence work." He gestured toward the rear of the restaurant.

"This one just found out about a stolen shipment of TVs and VCRs. They were hijacked from a van a couple of days ago, and they're about to be sold to some of the more disreputable local dealers. Or they *were* about to be sold. The sale is scheduled for tonight, so I'll have to round up a couple of guys and get out there."

"Will it be dangerous?"

"Probably not. I know this bunch. They'll whine and claim they're innocent, and before long they'll be in your office, seeking your services. We make the perfect team, don't we? I arrest them and you try to get them off."

"That's the system, Casey."

"I know that, but I don't have to like it. And I don't like that hippie creep of yours, either. I hope he's lying about the money."

She bristled. "Does that mean you'd lie to me?"

He fixed those ice blue eyes on her. "Never. That's no way to start a relationship. Now, if you were Millie Davis...."

"Why do the two of you dislike each other so much?"

"Let's just say that we have some philosophical differences. I'm a man and she's trying to be one."

"She's a feminist—and so am I."

"Yeah, but you're not noisy about it."

"How can you be so sure about that?" she challenged.

"Cop's intuition. Why are you so hung up on this hippie?"

"I'm *not* hung up on him. I just think there's a good chance he's innocent."

"Well, he sure as hell didn't act innocent when I grabbed him."

"He was probably scared half to death. If you grabbed me, I'd be scared, too."

He grinned. "As I recall, I did just that, several times, and you didn't act scared to me. In fact, one might go so far as to say that you—"

"Stop it, Casey! You know what I meant."

"Okay, but just stroke my ego, will you? You know how we men are. Don't I turn you on just a little bit?"

He had leaned over the table until his face was inches from hers. Silver lights danced in his eyes. Somehow she managed to resist the temptation to back away. Instead, she lifted her arm and looked at her watch.

"How time flies when you're having fun," she said with a smile. "I really have to get back to the office." She dug into her bag for a tip, then picked up the check and rose from her seat.

"It's unhealthy to keep your feelings bottled up inside, you know," he muttered as she started toward the cashier. "Ask your friend, the shrink."

"Maybe you have more in common with 'my hippie' than you think," she replied. "Isn't letting it all hang out part of the credo?"

"I get very suspicious when someone keeps changing the subject. It suggests that they have something to hide."

She drove him back to his car and extracted a promise that he would be in touch with her after he talked to Patsy. Then she returned to her office, thinking that Susan was definitely right: his image stayed with her long after he was gone.

FOR ONCE, JESSICA WAS glad for the lack of privacy in her office cubicle. Robert Collins was scary—the first client with whom she'd felt truly uneasy. He sat there, silent, dark and brooding, while she explained the charges against him. His dark eyes were fixed unwaveringly upon her, but she still had the impression that he wasn't listening, or at least, that he wasn't listening to *her*.

He was charged with theft, as well as a few lesser charges. According to the police report, he'd walked into a convenience store and picked out several items. Then he'd gone to the checkout at a time when the manager was removing cash from the register. He'd dumped the items on the counter, then snatched the money from the manager's hands and walked out of the store. The police had caught up with him only blocks away, and he still had the cash clutched in his hand.

She read the report to him, then asked him to tell her his side of the story. He said nothing and continued to give the impression of listening closely even after she'd stopped talking.

"Robert, you were caught with the money. Unless you have something different to tell me, I'd suggest that you plead guilty. The money was recovered and, unless you have a prior criminal record, you can almost certainly get off with probation."

Once more she waited in vain for him to reply. His gaze skittered around the office, then rested on her again. She asked if he had a prior criminal record, and after a long pause he shook his head.

"Do you want to plead guilty?" she asked, hoping that he'd agree and then leave. By now she had begun to suspect that he was mentally disturbed and badly in need of help.

"He called me names!" he said suddenly in a vehement tone. "He's one of them."

"Who called you names?" she asked, trying not to react to his barely controlled rage.

"The man at the store. He was laughing and talking about me. He's one of them."

"What do you mean, 'one of them'?"

He made an angry, slashing gesture with his hand. "People—like the people in the park. I only go there to watch the birds. I like birds."

"Robert," she said in a carefully reasonable tone, "isn't it possible that you were mistaken? Maybe they were just talking to each other. Maybe you misunderstood."

He glared at her. "They make fun of me. They hate me. They're the ones."

Jessica cast about desperately for some reply. There was no longer any doubt in her mind that he was disturbed, and she was wondering how she could go about having him evaluated by a psychiatrist. But before she could think of a way to proceed, he got up. She barely had time to remind him about his court appearance before he walked out of her office.

She sighed and picked up the police report and her notes, then went to find George. It would be easier to ask him about the laws regarding psychiatric evaluations and possible involuntary commitment than to check it out herself in their law library. She already knew that such laws were vaguely worded and often subject to the interpretation of individual courts.

But when she reached George's office she found that he had a visitor: Casey. The two men were laughing and talking and it was obvious that they got along well, which surprised her, given what Millie had said about Casey. If even half her complaints against Casey were true, George would never be so friendly with him.

Both men looked at her as she stopped in the office doorway, but it was Casey who caught and held her attention. She felt that supercharged current crackle along her nerve endings. The feeling was so powerful that she feared for a moment even George could sense it. There was certainly no doubt that Casey knew just what effect he had on her. His ice blue eyes narrowed slightly, both taunting and challenging her.

"Let me guess," George said dryly, breaking the electric silence. "You want to know about psychiatric evaluations and involuntary commitments."

"How did you know?" she asked in surprise.

"I saw him in the waiting room when I came in. He was holding a highly animated conversation with a lamp, and I happen to know that that particular lamp stopped talking long ago."

Jessica laughed. George gestured to Casey. "He's been complaining that you strong-armed him into helping you out with that hippie."

She shot Casey a glance, then turned back to George. "He's going to have a difficult time proving that one in court. On the other hand, I just might have a case for sexual harassment."

"Not true," Casey insisted self-righteously. "She threw herself at me—several times, as a matter of fact. *I'm* the one who's being harassed."

"Children, children, why don't you settle your differences somewhere else? I have to prepare my annual pitch to the budget director for more money, hopeless though it may be. I'll pull a couple of cases on involuntary commitment for you, Jessica."

"Well," she said as soon as they had returned to her office, "what did Patsy say?"

"You might try smiling at me and telling me how nice it is to see me again."

She laughed and rubbed the back of her neck. "I'm sorry. It's been a long, difficult day."

"Allow me," he said, taking her hands and drawing them away from her neck, then replacing them with his own.

He began to knead the taut muscles with strong, sure fingers while she stood there, so close to him that she could feel her own identity beginning to blur. What this man could do to her was truly scary.

"Better?" he murmured, his face scant inches from hers.

"Mmm," she said, not trusting her voice at the moment. Then she quickly backed away from him. "Thank you."

"You're welcome," he said softly, with amusement in his voice. His eyes swept over her. "I'll bet the rest of you is tense, too. I give a great massage and I work cheap."

She forced herself away from the images his words conjured up. "Patsy," she stated succinctly—or as succinctly as possible, given the huskiness in her voice.

"Right." His pale eyes gleamed with triumph. "Patsy says that Matthews *did* win some money the day before I snagged him. But I decided that it still doesn't change things."

She glared at him, hands planted on her hips. "Why doesn't that surprise me?"

He ignored her anger. "The fact that he won some money proves nothing. So I went to the hospital to talk to the victim again, and she's still certain that he's the one."

"I got her medical records, and she's practically blind," Jessica retorted.

"She also described what he was wearing at the time."

Jessica made a sound of disgust. "A white T-shirt and jeans. Now there's a distinctive outfit."

He shrugged. "I did what you wanted me to, Counselor. If you want to do your best to get him off so he can mug some other little old lady, that's—"

"Get out of here, Casey!"

"Yes, ma'am. But you ought to think about some way to relieve that stress."

WHEN HER PHONE RANG that evening Jessica was still angry with Casey for his attitude toward Joel Matthews. She was certain that he was prejudiced against Joel because he was a hippie. Still, as she picked up the receiver, she was hoping that it might be him. But what she got instead was silence on the line.

After saying hello several times and getting no response, she slammed down the phone and continued her mental litany against Casey while she dug through her law books. The volumes were still in crates because she had yet to do anything about bookshelves.

Casey was a typical cop, every bit as bad as Millie Davis had said. Maybe even worse. How could she let him turn her into a bowl of mush every time he set his eyes on her? She needed to find some way to separate that undeniable physical attraction from the truth about the man before she got herself into real trouble.

The phone rang again just after she'd gotten into bed, and it became immediately apparent that her little talk with herself hadn't done any good at all. She still picked up the receiver hoping it would be him. But once again she was met with silence.

Thoughts of Casey slid away, replaced by a feeling of uneasiness. She got up to check the windows and doors. Her apartment, a truly lucky find, was the entire first floor of a charming late-Victorian house, complete with twelve-foot ceilings, long windows bordered with stained glass, wonderful plaster moldings and beautifully maintained wood parquet floors.

But what she thought about now, in the silence of the night, was how vulnerable she was here. There was almost no exterior lighting, and tall bushes and shrubbery along both sides of the front door could hide a veritable army of would-be intruders. The locks weren't all that good, either.

"Don't be ridiculous!" she said aloud as she started back to her bedroom. She'd checked out the neighborhood and knew it was one of the safest in the city. But still, as she stood for a moment staring out into the dimly lit park just beyond the backyard, Jessica felt that same frustrating vulnerability that every woman feels when she lives alone.

She soothed herself with a promise to do something about the locks and inquire about the possibility of installing outdoor lights, then went back to bed.

SHE AWOKE JUST BEFORE dawn, drenched in sweat and trembling. The echoes of shouts and screams bounced around in her head. She pounded her pillows in frustration. Why was this happening again, now?

She sat up and practiced deep breathing to calm herself, then got out of bed to change her nightshirt. There *had* to be a reason for the return of the nightmares after so long a hiatus. Furthermore, it seemed the whole feel of the dreams was becoming more vivid.

Then she began to think again about settling this once and for all. It was time to go to Oregon and explore her forgotten past. If she had in fact been lied to, the truth must be there.

Unfortunately, it was too soon for her to ask for time off from work right now, but she decided that she would do it as soon as possible. Even if she learned nothing that contradicted the story she'd been told, it might still end the nightmares. They could be feeding off her uncertainties.

And she sure had a lot of uncertainties in her life these days. Not the least of which was T. S. Casimiricz.

"JESSIE, IT'S CASEY. Wanna go fishing on Saturday?"

She didn't immediately respond because she was too busy reacting—*over*reacting—to the sound of his voice coming out of the phone.

"Your enthusiasm is underwhelming. Okay, I'll sweeten the offer. Go fishing with me this weekend and I'll take you to the best restaurant in town next week. I'll even throw in a concert in the park if it's absolutely necessary."

She laughed. "If I still hold out, are you planning to offer a change of heart about Joel Matthews?"

"Nope. That's business and this is pleasure. I trust you can separate the two."

Would that she could! "I don't like the name Jessie."

"Oh? Well, I don't like Jessica much myself. Suppose I call you Jessie and you call yourself Jessica, then?"

"I love your idea of a compromise, Casey. All right, I'll go fishing if I don't have to bait a hook."

"Now, wait a minute! If you're going to turn out to be one of those cutesy squealing types, I take back the invitation. I thought you were made of sterner stuff than that."

"I am, but I still don't like worms."

"As it happens, we're going fly-fishing. How do you feel about flies?"

"I thought fly-fishing meant using fake flies."

"Aha! The woman's not a novice, after all. I've gotta get back to my writing now. I left my hero running across a rooftop with the bad guys in hot pursuit. Either he gets rescued by a helicopter or he jumps to the next roof. I hate jumping roofs myself. I'll pick you up at seven Saturday morning."

Jessica stood there listening to the dial tone. Now she'd done it: she'd agreed to spend a whole day with him. But how could she have refused? The man was about as resistible as a nuclear attack.

She put down the receiver and dug through her shopping bag until she found the book *Body, Can You Spare a Dime?* by T. S. Casimiricz. She told herself that she hadn't really intended to buy it. She'd almost succeeded in pushing him out of her mind. But there was the book, prominently displayed in the window. And now here was the man himself, back in her life just at the moment when she'd decided to write him off as a foolish fancy.

A short time later she was propped up in bed with his book, the echoes of his voice still bouncing around in her head.

The reviews on the back cover were quite impressive, using words like *realistic, intelligent* and *insightful.* There was a photo of him inside the back cover. The background was a blurred winter scene. He wore a sheepskin jacket, and his thick black hair was windblown. His wide mouth was curved in that familiar half smile. The photo was in black and white, but it failed to lessen the impact of those ice blue eyes.

Jessica stared at it for a long time as little curls of warmth unfolded themselves inside her. Maybe it was time to stop trying to analyze her feelings about him and simply accept them.

She started to read, expecting to find clues to the man rather than to actually enjoy the story. But it was well past her usual bedtime when she finally forced herself to put down the book. She was surprised—no, perhaps shocked was the more appropriate word.

He was a very good storyteller. His insights into his characters and their motivations were almost worthy of a psychologist, and he had a true gift for conveying the essence of a scene in a few words. His sense of humor was also very much in evidence.

Jessica thought again about Susan's statement that there was entirely "too much of him." She understood that even better now. There was indeed something very daunting about a man who could walk the worst streets of the city, then go home to write with wit and style and even tenderness.

She *did* feel rather overwhelmed, but she still liked the way he made her feel—wonderfully, gloriously alive, as though electricity were surging through her veins. It was a wholly new feeling for her, what she'd unconsciously sought when she'd decided to escape her stagnant life in Philadelphia.

She got out of bed to go to the bathroom, then walked around the apartment, checking the windows and doors. She'd had strong new locks installed on the doors yesterday. She'd also spoken to her landlord about adding some bright exterior lighting, but he'd told her that there were restrictive covenants in the deed prohibiting such lights. The property owners were determined to preserve the character of the charming old neighborhood.

She returned to her bedroom, then peeked out through the drapes into the darkness of the yard and the small park beyond the hedges. There hadn't been any more phone calls, but she still hadn't quite let go of that uneasiness.

Then she drew in a breath sharply. Was there someone out there, back at the rear of the yard where tall privet hedges were planted against the fence that separated the yard from the park? Certainly something had moved, but it was windy, and it could have been nothing more than the light from the park, casting the shadows of tree branches into the yard.

She waited for several minutes, keeping her eyes glued to the spot, but she saw nothing more and finally decided there was nothing to see.

HE'D BEEN HANGING AROUND the plaza for a couple of hours, just watching people. For a time he sat on the rim of the big fountain. Then he wandered over to the outdoor café and had some coffee. After that he went into the park and sat on one bench, then moved to another. Now he was sitting on the wide steps of City Court, leaning against the granite wall just below a big planter filled with red geraniums.

Anyone watching him would have seen immediately how agitated he was, but the area was filled with hundreds of people rushing from one city building to the other, so no one paid him any attention.

He'd been like this for days now, ever since he'd found her. The sheer ecstasy of it was singing through his veins. After all this time he'd found the Perfect One. He'd felt it in the very first minute. But he knew he had to be careful, very careful. He had to watch her, get to know her, before he made his move. This time he wanted it to come out right.

But he was having trouble containing himself, and the feeling was far worse than in the past. Maybe he'd have to find another one, or even a couple of other ones, just to take the edge off while he laid his plans for her.

Yes, he liked that idea. He hated them all now, even more than he had before. They'd all been poor imitations of the real thing, and he was even more sharply aware of that now that he'd found her. They deserved to die.

He began to feel better, more justified, when he suddenly saw her.

She was walking across the plaza from the annex to the courthouse itself. The sunlight flowed over her long, honey blond hair. She walked in long, confident strides, her chin tilted upward and thrust slightly forward in a manner that brought bittersweet memories flooding into his mind.

He saw others cast glances her way, and he wanted to shout to them all that they couldn't have her. She belonged to *him*. And this time, there was no one else to claim her.

When she disappeared into the courthouse he felt deflated, diminished. But he knew how to make himself feel powerful again. And he knew he'd have her. It was only a matter of time.

JESSICA SORTED THROUGH her mail, her thoughts already on her day with Casey tomorrow. A few bills, a lot of junk mail and one letter with no return address, bearing a local postmark. Mildly curious, she slit it open.

"YOU ARE THE ONE." She stared at it in disbelief. The four words had been cut from a newspaper and glued to a single sheet of typing paper. For one brief moment she almost laughed. Any devotee of mysteries like herself was familiar with this technique. It was the standard way to send threats, and for that reason she couldn't at first take it seriously.

But then she knew she should. There'd been those phone calls and that person she might or might not have seen out back. She studied the envelope. Her name and address were hand printed in block letters, the careful kind of letters a child might make, or the writing of someone who wanted to be sure that his handwriting was carefully disguised.

She set the letter down with the rest of her mail and went to prepare her dinner, thinking about who could possibly be responsible. The first name that came to mind was Robert Collins, her mentally disturbed client. He'd been in to see her again today, still rambling on in his disjointed fashion about those who were "out to get him." He hadn't been overtly hostile toward her, but she couldn't begin to guess his thoughts.

Although he'd given no indication whatsoever that he'd understood when she'd tried to talk to him about his upcoming trial, it was likely that he *did* know, on some level, that he was in serious trouble. And given his state of mind, it seemed possible that he might blame her for that.

After he'd once again departed abruptly, she'd received a phone call from the DA's office. They were willing to let a commitment hearing be held before, and possibly in lieu of, a trial on the criminal charges. The hearing had been set for next week, and Jessica had little doubt that Robert would be committed. She'd reminded him several times about the hearing, but without telling him its purpose.

She thought about those words in the letter. *You are the one.* That could have meant he was convinced *she* was now the one "out to get him."

She put in a call to Susan, who wasn't home. And by the time Susan returned the call, Jessica had convinced herself that Robert was responsible for the letter and probably the calls, as well. She told Susan about him.

"Classic paranoia," Susan said when Jessica had finished describing his behavior. "But if he's as bad as you say, it seems to me that he'd be too disorganized to have sent the letter, and probably to have made the calls, too."

"What do you mean?" Jessica asked.

"From your description, his thought processes are very disorderly, and cutting out those letters, gluing them onto paper and then getting your address would require a certain level of organization. It might not sound like much to you, but for someone in that condition, it is.

"I could maybe see him calling you if you were in the directory, but you're not yet. So he'd have to get your number from information. That's another step. And, come to think of it, he'd have to find a way to get your address, as well.

"The point is that someone like you're describing might be able to go from A to B, but he's unlikely to be able to go from B to C, and so forth. Has he ever been violent?"

"No, not that I know of, and he's been through the system before. He was arrested once for making threats, but he never actually attacked anyone.

"I just don't see who else it could be. Most of the other clients I have at the moment are in jail awaiting trial because they couldn't make bail, or because, if they're juveniles, they've been made wards of the court."

"What about your hippie?"

"No, it couldn't be him. If you met him, you'd agree. Maybe I've just made Robert sound worse than he is. I haven't had much experience with the mentally ill. Anyway, his commitment hearing is next week and I'm confident that he'll be put away."

They talked for a while longer about other things. Jessica told her about her fishing date with Casey and Susan laughed, saying that she'd been thinking about the two of them together.

"I can see you two as a couple, actually. You're very strong and sure of yourself, which is just the type of woman he needs. I know how important a good sense of humor is to you, and he certainly has that. The more I think about it, the more I'm convinced that Casey might finally have met his match."

Jessica just laughed and denied any serious interest in Casey, but those denials sounded hollow even to her. After they'd hung up, she wondered if she should have told Susan about the resumption of her nightmares.

Susan knew she'd had them when they were children, and she'd once told Jessica that they could somehow be tied in to the deaths of her parents. But she'd also pointed out that bad dreams didn't necessarily mean that Jessica had been lied to about anything. The nightmares could well be the product of a child's mind that had magnified some incident from before her parents' deaths. It was very common for children to blame themselves when something happened to a parent.

But why had they returned after all this time? If she was really the strong person Susan believed her to be, wouldn't she have gotten over that trauma long ago?

She turned her attention back to the letter and began to crumple it to toss it away. Then she smoothed it out again. Perhaps she'd better save it. Other attorneys in her office had been harassed by clients; it seemed to come with the job. They didn't overreact to it, and neither would she. She knew that Mac already had some doubts about whether or not she was tough enough for this kind of work.

Chapter Three

Jessica turned to Casey with a grin. "When you said you had a cabin, you really meant it. I've never seen a real log cabin before."

"I built it myself. It came as a kit. Tab A into slot B—that sort of thing. A grown-up version of Lincoln Logs."

"It's wonderful!" she exclaimed as she got out of his Wagoneer and stood there admiring the structure.

Casey smiled at her enthusiasm. He was, in truth, inordinately proud of the place, even though he generally came up here alone. And on those rare occasions when he did bring someone along, it had always been a male friend for a weekend of fishing.

She was staring at the tall stone chimney. "Surely you must have had some help."

"Nope. Did it all myself. It became a sort of challenge."

She helped him unload the things he'd brought along: a big cooler and several bags of groceries. "This is a lot of food for one day," she commented as they started toward the cabin.

"Well, actually, I thought we might stay over if we can stand each other's company that long." They'd spent most of the hour-and-a-half trip arguing about the law and the criminal justice system.

He was busy unlocking the door as he spoke, but he still sensed a sudden tension in her. "There are two bedrooms," he added.

A slight flush crept through her fair skin, but he hid his smile as he bent to pick up the cooler again. Obviously she trusted him enough to come up here with him, but there were clearly limits to that trust, as well.

Casey had surprised himself by deciding to bring her up here. Then he'd been even more surprised when she'd accepted. Not that there wasn't a whole lot of mutual attraction, but there was an almost equal amount of wariness—especially on her part. Every time he was with her, he envisioned this big sign over her head that read Keep Your Distance.

While he went off to start the generator that supplied the cabin's power, Jessica explored the place. She was rather surprised to find it comfortably furnished, since she'd expected something on the order of Salvation Army castoffs. She also liked the fact that instead of putting up interior walls he'd simply lacquered the logs. And she saw that there were indeed two bedrooms, the larger of which was nearly wall-to-wall bed.

Thoughts that had nothing whatsoever to do with fishing crept into her head as she stared at it, and she turned quickly from the bedroom doorway, only to see him coming down the hallway toward her. He was shrugging out of his jacket, and beneath it was a shoulder holster with a gun.

He stopped when he saw her staring at the gun. "I'm a cop, Jessie, and cops carry guns. I'm getting rid of it now."

She was embarrassed at her overreaction. "I'm sorry, but it's just that I've never even known anyone who owned a gun."

"Consider yourself lucky, then. I know too damned many of them." He walked past her into the bedroom and removed the holster.

"Have you ever shot anyone?" she asked.

He rolled his eyes. "Everyone's favorite cop question. Do you know that the vast majority of police officers get through their entire careers without ever firing a shot, except on the practice range?

"Yes, I wounded two men and killed another. The one I killed was charging me with a very big knife. He was our last serial killer here. I shot him at point-blank range. I had his blood and other bits of him all over me. Do you want to hear any more?"

She shook her head, chastened. "I'm sorry."

"Nothing to be sorry about. Maybe I'm a little sensitive about it. You know how men are—we don't like to talk about our feelings. And it may be bothering me more now because we've probably got another psychopath on our hands."

"But it's been nearly two weeks and there haven't been any more murders," she observed.

"These guys have cycles. The last one started out killing one a month. He specialized in little girls. It turned out that he had a little sister who got all the attention, while he took all the abuse. He probably started his career by killing her, although that was ruled an accident."

She shuddered. "We *did* say that we weren't going to talk business anymore today."

"Right. Let me get the fishing gear and we'll start with some lessons in the fine art of fly casting."

He brought the gear and they went down to the dock, where a rowboat was tied up and covered by a tarp. It was a fairly large boat, but she still looked at it skeptically, wondering about its stability with someone his size in it.

"How big is the lake?" she asked. It was impossible to tell because his cabin was located on a bend, and on both sides the water curved away out of sight.

"A lot bigger than it looks from here," he replied. "And it's actually a series of lakes, connected by wetlands. Later on it's great for swimming, but the water's still too cold now."

She glanced back at the rowboat again, hoping she wasn't going to discover just how cold it was. She was a strong swimmer, but ever since one of her cousins had overturned their boat when she was a child she'd had a fear of small boats.

"The boat would safely hold four people my size," he said as he bent to pick up one of the rods.

"Are you a mind reader, too?" she asked in astonishment.

"No, I'm just very observant." He straightened and stared at her. "Does my size bother you?"

She shook her head quickly, but his question seemed to echo inside her, way down in that black hole. Could that be it? Did he remind her of someone—someone from her past who was as big as he was? For a brief moment she was certain that was it. But then she realized that he was still watching her closely.

"I was always tall myself," she told him. "I reached the height I am now when I was only thirteen, so I towered over other kids my age. It wasn't much fun. At that age girls like to feel very feminine, and it was hard for me to feel that way when every boy I knew was at least a head shorter than I was."

"By the time *I* was thirteen, I was already nearly six feet. And if girls like to feel feminine, boys like to fight. The problem I had was that no one would fight me."

She smiled. "But I'll bet the girls liked you a lot."

He chuckled. "I never had any trouble in that department, except that most of them were too little. Little people make me nervous. I'm always afraid I'll accidentally step on them or something.

"When I was about thirteen or so and starting to get interested in girls, Mom sat me down and gave me the standard lecture, then pointed out that because of my size, I had to be extra careful not to intimidate them. That little talk taught me to pay attention to *their* feelings, and not just to my raging hormones. It's a shame that all boys don't get that lecture. I realized that when I worked for a time with the sex crimes squad and had to deal with rape victims."

Jessica recalled what Susan had told her about her friend's experience with him and her complaint that he'd been too much of a gentleman. But she couldn't resist needling him a bit.

"With all due respect to your mother, Casey, the lecture didn't work. You were pretty darned intimidating when I met you."

He laughed and nodded. "Yeah, but I could tell right away that you could take it and dish it right back. Besides, I *did* apologize, and I *didn't* attack you...."

She laughed, too, then pointed to the fishing rod. "Back to the subject at hand."

"Yes, ma'am." He picked up the rod. "Now watch my arm, not the rod."

He demonstrated several times and then she tried it, and nearly snagged his shirt. "Darn! Talk about a big one that got away!"

"Maybe some hands-on instruction would work better," he said, moving to stand right behind her, then putting his hand over hers as she held the rod.

Somehow she managed to get it right, but it wasn't easy. She felt surrounded by him as his big, hard body pressed close to hers. His breath tickled her ear as he issued instructions and criticism and praise. She didn't even try to fight the waves of erotic heat that rippled through her body. It was hard enough to keep her legs from turning to jelly, and the fact that neither of them would acknowledge what was really happening added yet another dimension to an already overpowering sensuality.

When he finally decided that she'd gotten it right and stepped away to let her try it on her own, she felt as though she might just melt and run down between the planks of the dock. But she did as told and earned his praise.

He rowed out to his favorite spot and they began casting. Before they returned to the dock, they had caught four fish. He returned three to the water, but the fourth—a fourteen-inch bass—was *her* catch. He, of course, attributed it to beginner's luck.

Back at the cabin they ate lunch on the screened porch. "You're a good fishing companion," he remarked. "Most women couldn't keep quiet that long."

"I don't know whether to thank you or condemn you for your male chauvinism."

"But it's true," he protested. "Most women talk all the time."

"And it's also true that most men don't talk *enough*—about their feelings, for example."

"Good point," he conceded with a smile. "Under the circumstances, it's remarkable that we've managed to put up with each other well enough to keep the species going."

He leaned back in his chair and finished off his beer. "My problem is that I spend most of my time pretty much in the exclusive company of other men. There aren't that many women on the force to begin with, and even fewer have made it to detective yet. You're the first woman I've brought up here, by the way."

She was surprised and didn't bother to hide it. "Why?"

"Why no other women, or why you?" he asked as he gazed steadily at her.

"Both."

He looked out at the lake, frowning. "I don't know. I generally come up here alone. That's what I built the place for. But when I decided to come up this weekend, I just got to thinking that it might be nice to bring you along."

Jessica recognized a compliment when she heard one, however casual it might be. "I'm glad you did. I've decided that I was right all along—you're not nearly as bad as I thought you were when I met you."

He chuckled. "Just keep that to yourself, will you? I'd hate to have my carefully cultivated reputation ruined."

Their eyes met and held in a silence that was suddenly no longer comfortable. Both of them could easily read beneath the words to a mutual acknowledgment of something more than casual interest.

Then he got up and went to dispose of the remains of their lunch, while she sat there thinking about the day—and perhaps the night, as well—that stretched before them, fraught with dangerous, seductive possibilities.

When Casey returned, he suggested that they go for a walk in the woods along the edge of the lake. They passed several other widely scattered cabins, then came to a spot where a huge flat rock jutted out over the water. He took her hand and helped her up onto it and they sat down side by side.

She told him that she'd just finished reading one of his books. "It's very good. I'd never read that kind of story before."

"Most of the readership is male, but my editor says that more women are beginning to read them and I should think about putting some romance into them."

"That could be difficult, given the type of protagonist you've created."

"Why? I think he's a pretty nice guy."

"Oh, he is, but he's not exactly charismatic." Unlike the author, she added silently.

"Hmph! Well, maybe I'll have to kill him off and start over."

"And it probably doesn't help that he hates violence and gets queasy at the sight of blood, either. Romance heroes are supposed to be strong, macho types."

He shook his head. "So that's been my problem, has it? And here I thought it was just my obnoxious personality."

She stared at him. "Are you saying that *you* get queasy at the sight of blood?"

He nodded. "Like I said, I've never had to do much fighting. And I hate the sight of blood, especially my own."

"But you still became a cop."

"Uh-huh. Cops are supposed to prevent violence, or at least prevent violent types from being out there."

"But you played football and that's certainly violent."

"Football is carefully controlled violence. I can handle that. As you probably heard, I operate on fear—the fear of everyone else that I'm going to *become* violent. It works."

"So you're a fake?"

He nodded and grinned at her. "I'm a real pussycat."

"I'm not sure I believe all this, Casey."

"See? That's how well it works."

She laughed. He just might be telling the truth. Then she remembered something she'd intended to ask him before. "What do your initials stand for?"

"I'm not sure I know you well enough yet to answer that question."

"I promise not to laugh," she said with mock solemnity.

"Okay. They stand for Tadeucz Seamus. Tadeucz is a Polish name. My father, obviously, was Polish. Seamus is Irish—my mother's side. They knew they wouldn't be having any more children, so they each dumped a family name on me."

She laughed, despite her promise. "A lot of good it did them, since you ended up being Casey."

"Not to them. Dad always called me Tadeucz and Mom still calls me Seamus. It's a wonder I didn't end up with a split personality."

She wasn't so sure that he hadn't as she thought about the many parts of him that she had yet to reconcile. She asked him if his mother still lived here, and he told her that after she'd retired from teaching she'd moved back to Ireland. Then he asked about her family.

Casey listened as she described the grandparents who'd raised her. He had the picture now: old money and blue blood. He'd guessed that, in any event. She had that look about her, and it wasn't just the clothes and the Mercedes and the expensive furnishings he'd glimpsed when he'd picked her up this morning.

"I'm afraid my grandmother thinks that despite her best efforts with me, my bad blood must have surfaced."

"What bad blood's that? You mean your father?"

She nodded with a smile. "My parents were flower children of the sixties. They lived in a commune. I did, too, for my first three years, but I don't remember any of it."

"Flower children?" he said in mock horror even as his mind registered something in her tone that disturbed him. And now he was beginning to understand her interest in that hippie client.

"I'm afraid so." She smiled. "I was fifteen before I could drag the truth about them out of my grandmother, and I still know next to nothing about my father."

She went on to describe what little she did know and told him how she'd often thought about going out to Oregon to see her birthplace. And as she talked, Casey identified what he'd heard before: fear. He filed the information away for future consideration. Now didn't seem to be the time to pursue it, but he was nearly certain that she was holding something back.

He told himself that it was just the normal curiosity of a cop, but he wasn't very good at self-deception. A little voice was already beginning to whisper in his ear that this one was a keeper.

THEY RETURNED to the cabin and then went fishing again. This time he caught three sizable bass, while she caught one. Later they sat on the edge of the dock and talked away the remainder of the afternoon. A couple of times Casey tried to steer the conversation back to her parents, but she always deflected it, and he didn't push it, despite his curiosity.

Then they prepared dinner together. He cleaned and grilled the fish while she put together a pasta salad. When he saw the quantity she was preparing, he announced that it looked like enough for him, but if she wanted some for herself, she'd better make more.

"The rule of thumb for feeding me is to multiply what you eat by two."

They ate dinner on the screened porch as the sun dipped behind the hills on the far side of the lake, leaving a brilliant glow in the sky that was reflected on the still water. An orchestra of crickets began to tune up in the woods.

After dinner they made coffee to have with the strawberry cheesecake he'd brought along. The evening quickly began to grow cool. She hadn't brought a jacket or sweater, but Casey thoughtfully provided a thick Aran cardigan his mother had knitted for him. It fit her more like a coat and she snuggled gratefully into its warmth.

They continued their careful exploration of each other, with both of them silently agreeing that they had little in common—except, of course, for a mutual desire that continued to vibrate just beneath the surface of their conversation.

He glanced at his watch. "If you want to go back to the city, we should leave soon."

"Do you want to go back?" she asked, caught between not wanting their time together to end and an uneasiness about spending the night here with him.

"No, I want to stay here and spend the night ravishing your lovely body. Or, failing that, we could take the boat out for a while."

She gave him a look of disgust even as the soft heat of anticipation swept through her. "You blew it, Casey! You almost got through an entire day without making one suggestive remark. But because I know you must be very contrite about it, I'll stay and we can go out in the boat. That is, if it's safe to go out at night."

"It's safer than my bed," he replied, obviously not at all repentant. "And I'm only saying aloud what we've both been thinking."

She rolled her eyes and got up. "Let's go." Since he was right, she definitely did not want to pursue this discussion.

By the time he had rowed out to the middle of the lake, the nearly full moon had risen above the dark line of the hills and was laying down a shimmering path across the water. A light breeze carried with it the scent of pine. Jessica leaned back to stare up at the starry heavens.

She knew that she'd never felt before the way she was feeling now. She thought about other men she'd dated over the years and found that they all blurred together: investment bankers, lawyers, stockbrokers. She'd known most of them all her life and had felt comfortable with them—but she hadn't wanted them.

Everything about Casey excited her. Before she met him, no one could have convinced her that she could feel this way about a man. It was scary.

She was just starting to think again about that strange feeling she'd had when she'd seen him for the first time, but her thoughts were cut off abruptly by his urgent whisper.

"Look!" he said, pointing toward the shore.

She sat up and peered in the direction he indicated, but saw nothing. He dropped the oars and moved to her, dropping an arm across her shoulders and pointing again.

"On the bank, near that overhanging tree."

"Oh!"

"He's a big one. I've seen him before."

"Do bears swim?" she asked fearfully.

"They can, but don't worry. When he sees us, he'll take off. Black bears aren't dangerous."

And just as he spoke, the bear raised its huge head and stared in their direction, then lumbered off into the woods. They continued to sit there for a moment, his arm still draped across her shoulder, their heads close together. The silence and the tension grew and she began to cast about mentally for some remark to defuse the mood. But he dropped his arm and returned to his place at the oars.

He rowed to the far end of the lake, where they startled a small herd of deer that had come down to the water's edge to drink. Casey remarked about the large set of antlers on the one buck among them.

"Do you hunt?" she asked, hoping that he didn't.

"Only two-legged critters," he replied. "And I'm not crazy about hunting some of them, either."

Then she saw a shooting star, the first one she'd ever seen. It was gone so quickly that she didn't have time to tell him, and so kept it as her secret, then remembered that she should make a wish. She looked at Casey's strong profile as he turned to stare toward the shore and wished that this man could really be all that she thought he was. She just couldn't trust her feelings at this point.

By the time they finally returned to shore, Jessica was stifling yawns. He said he was glad that she found his company so interesting and she laughed.

"It isn't your company. I'm not used to getting up so early on weekends. I've really enjoyed this day."

"Does that mean I won't have to take you to the ballet in order to persuade you to see me again?"

"The ballet? Do you have tickets for the performance next weekend?" she asked excitedly.

"Uh-oh. Something tells me it's time to dust off the tux."

"I wanted to go, but it was sold out by the time I came here."

"It's always sold out well in advance. It's an annual charity thing for the homeless shelters. I always buy tickets, but I never go."

"Then I'll buy the tickets from you."

He shook his head. "I'm not giving you tickets to take some other guy. We'll go, and I'll try not to snore too loudly."

"I feel honored that you'd make such a sacrifice for me, Casey," she said with a smile.

"I'm glad you appreciate that," he said as he tied the boat to the dock and then reached down to help her out. "I wouldn't do this for just any woman, you know."

She started to step up onto the dock and he circled her waist to lift her from the boat. Then they both stood there. Her racing pulse punctuated the long moment as she looked up at him. The night had suddenly become very still; it seemed to her that even the crickets were holding their breaths.

Her lips parted involuntarily and his gaze immediately focused on that slight movement. She felt a sudden tensing of the muscles in his arm that was still wrapped around her waist, but he didn't move. Their eyes met, a silent message passed between them and she lifted her hand to curve it around his neck.

His mouth touched hers softly, tentatively, and his warmth surrounded her as she felt herself flow against him. His great gentleness had a unique sensuality that sent a liquid warmth through her veins. She arched to him with a low sound that was close to a purr. In response he groaned and cupped her head with one big hand as he began a slow, thorough exploration of her mouth.

Jessica was lost in an all-encompassing awareness of him: his taste, his scent, the gentle hands that began to roam slowly over her body, the unyielding hardness of his maleness against her female softness.

And through it all, as their kiss deepened and their tongues intertwined in a delicate, erotic dance, she could feel both the growing urgency of his need and his careful control. It was that control she felt most keenly, the certainty that it was she who would set the pace and the limits.

He lifted his mouth from hers slowly and pressed warm lips against her ear. "I want you, Jessie. Oh, God, how I want you!"

His urgency called to her own, and for one fleeting moment she wanted to respond to that need, to tell him that her own desire matched it. She teetered on the edge, both ready and not ready. But then she stiffened. How could she explain to him what she didn't understand herself?

Then he took the decision from her by releasing her. "I can wait," he said huskily. "I didn't intend to get carried away like that."

"You weren't the only one who got carried away," she admitted shakily.

"We have time," he said, lifting her hand to press his lips to her palm. "As much time as you need."

He continued to hold her hand as they walked back up the hill to the cabin. Jessica's thoughts were tangled. He wasn't demanding an explanation, but surely he must want one. What was he thinking? And what if wanting him wasn't enough?

He offered her a T-shirt to sleep in and she waited in the doorway of his bedroom while he dug one out of the dresser drawer. His big bed beckoned. Her lips still bore the imprint of his. Her body still registered his touch. Then he handed her the T-shirt, and she stretched up on tiptoe and kissed his cheek.

"Thank you. Good night, Casey." And she knew that he understood she was thanking him for far more than the T-shirt.

CASEY STRETCHED OUT on his bed, knowing that sleep wasn't going to come quickly this night. His mind was tormented by her: her warmth, her soft curves, the huskiness in her voice.

Over the years Casey had become very adept at reading the subtle signals women sent to indicate their desire and willingness. He knew she wanted him, but he also knew that something was wrong. It could simply be that she didn't feel she knew him well enough yet, but his instincts told him it was more than that.

She was afraid of something, and he didn't think it was him. He recalled the fear he'd sensed in her when she'd talked about her parents. For all her sophistication and poise, there was a strange vulnerability to her.

He began to wonder if the real reason she'd left Philadelphia might have been a love affair gone bad. Maybe he'd just better back off for a while, even though it was going to be damn difficult.

THE CRY SHATTERED her sleep and brought her upright in bed even before she was fully awake. Then the strangeness of her surroundings terrified her still more, until she remembered where she was.

She took several deep breaths, willing herself to calmness as she hoped she hadn't awakened him. Her cry had seemed loud to her, but perhaps it hadn't been.

Even as she struggled to rid herself of the aftereffects of the nightmare, she became aware of a difference this time. It seemed that more of the nightmare might have followed her into wakefulness.

Suddenly there was a sharp rap on the door, and before she could respond, it opened.

"Jessie, are you all right?"

He stood there filling the doorway—a huge, dark silhouette backlit by the hallway light. She caught her breath sharply. For one brief moment something that seemed to have come from the nightmare spilled over into her consciousness with an eerie sense of déjà vu.

"Jessie?" He moved cautiously into the room, his voice soft. The nightmare receded as she focused on him.

He had put on his jeans, but he was bare chested and his dark hair was sleep tousled. Even in the shaky aftermath of the nightmare, she felt the memory of that body holding hers brush over her. The bone-deep chill that invariably followed the nightmare abated, driven deep into her by a voluptuous heat.

"Nightmares?" he asked as he switched on the bedside lamp and sat on the edge of the bed. His weight sent her tumbling against him. He took her hands in his and she felt the contrast between her icy fingers and his strong warmth.

She nodded, swallowing to moisten her dry throat. "They're nothing new," she said bitterly. "I've been having them all my life."

"The same one?"

She nodded again, but distractedly as she began to think again about the difference this time.

"Before, I could never remember anything about it except for the shouts and screams." She frowned as her mind snagged on a memory. "That table," she murmured. "Why was it so big? Everything seemed so big."

"What table?" he asked gently.

Her gaze focused on him as though she had just become aware of his presence. Casey saw the sheen of perspiration on her face, and saw, too, how his T-shirt clung damply to her breasts, outlining the darker nipples. He forced himself to concentrate on her face as she answered him hesitantly.

"It was clearer this time than it's ever been before. But I still couldn't see any people, even though I heard shouts and screams like I always do. But that table, and the chairs and counter...." Her voice trailed off for a moment, and when she spoke again, her tone was both wondering and fearful.

"They were so big—the way a child would see them."

She stopped again, then seemed to gather together the threads of her self-control. "I'm sorry I woke you. I'm surprised that you didn't come running in here with a gun."

Her attempt to make light of it told him that she didn't want to talk any more about it, but he persisted. He released one of her hands and ran his fingers along her sweat-slick cheek. "It must have been one hell of a nightmare."

She wiped her face with a hand and still trembled slightly. "Yes. That always happens."

"And this has been going on all your life?"

She sighed. "For as long as I can remember. I've always suspected that it had something to do with my parents' deaths."

"You said they died in an auto accident, right? Were you with them at the time?"

"No, or at least, my grandmother said I wasn't."

"You've talked to her about these nightmares?"

"She knows about them because she's the one who always came to comfort me afterward. But she always dismissed the possibility that they could have resulted from my parents' deaths. My grandmother is very good at dismissing anything unpleasant." She grimaced and shrugged.

"Anyway, the nightmares happened less and less often as I grew up, and until recently, I thought they'd gone away forever."

She stared off into space for a moment. "For years I thought about going to Oregon, to see if there's something my grandparents didn't tell me, and to see if there was any way I could find my father's family. Gran has always claimed to know nothing about him. I don't know where the commune was, but I know where I was born, and I thought I could start there."

"Why didn't you go?" he asked curiously. It seemed strange to him that she hadn't. Surely she must want to know something about her father. Or had her grandmother brainwashed her on the subject?

"I...don't know," she said after a moment. "There's always been this little voice inside me telling me that maybe I didn't want to know. I know it sounds crazy, but it seemed easier to just forget about it, especially after the nightmares stopped."

She gave him a small, slightly ashamed smile. "Maybe it's just that I like thinking of him as a long-haired flower child like the ones I've seen in pictures. I never even had a picture of him."

"Jessie," he said, taking her hands again, "maybe this isn't any of my business and maybe it's just my cop's nosiness, but it seems to me that you *should* try to find out about him. That uncertainty could be what's causing your nightmares.

"I'll come with you, if you like. I may be able to help. People tend to get very talkative around cops."

She stared at him in silence for a moment and he could see the fear in her eyes. But then she smiled. "Would you really come with me? I think maybe one of the reasons I haven't gone is that I didn't want to go alone."

Casey found that statement interesting, since it seemed to suggest that there'd never been anyone she felt close enough to to ask.

"Give me a week or so to get some things wrapped up, and we'll go. In the meantime, maybe you should talk to your grandmother again. If she knows you're serious about going out there, she might be more willing to talk."

She nodded, and he leaned over to kiss her on the cheek. "Good. Now why don't you go take a shower? I'll get you another T-shirt."

She looked down at herself and seemed to realize for the first time that his T-shirt was clinging to her like a second skin. She made a move to cover herself, and he chuckled and stood.

"Have I made up for my lack of self-control earlier?"

THE SHOWER FELT GOOD, and as she began to dry herself, Jessica realized that she felt amazingly good herself—far better than she'd ever felt after one of her nightmares. The difference this time, she knew, had to be Casey.

Then she remembered that moment when he'd stood silhouetted in the doorway. Something about that scene had felt so incredibly familiar—familiar and yet also different. A fragment of memory suggested that the doorway should have been closer, that there should have been something—or someone— in between. She tried to grasp the image in vain.

CASEY'S INSTINCTS WERE telling him loud and clear that Jessie was in deep trouble. He didn't know a whole lot about dreams, but it sure seemed to him that if she'd been having this one all her life, there was something hidden in there that needed to be brought into the light of day.

He was glad that she'd accepted his offer of help and he was determined not to let her back down. That old male protective instinct was asserting itself. He had to admit, it wasn't a bad feeling, however much she might resent a man protecting her.

Something big is happening here, he told himself. Jessie was rapidly becoming far more than just a very desirable woman to him. She had become very real, and very precious.

He was still mulling over that unsettling thought when he heard the bathroom door open. He poured some brandy into the hot chocolate he'd prepared, and when he saw her walk into the kitchen, he had to stifle a powerful urge to pick her up and carry her off to his bed.

Strangely, though, making love to her wasn't the uppermost thought in his mind at the moment. He just wanted to hold her, to keep her nightmares at bay. Instead, he handed her the mug of hot chocolate.

"I put a little brandy in it. That should help you sleep."

She murmured her thanks and took a seat at the small kitchen table. He sat across from her and did his level best to ignore the fact that they were sitting here in this isolated spot in the middle of the night and she was wearing his T-shirt. He wanted to ask her more about the nightmares, but that would have to wait.

"YOU SAID THAT your nightmares stopped until recently. Do you have any idea why you're having them again?"

The question caught Jessica by surprise. They'd both slept in late, and after eating breakfast in the kitchen, were now seated on the dock with their second cups of coffee. He hadn't mentioned last night until now.

She was quiet for a moment as she considered whether or not she should tell him. What would he think? If it sounded crazy to her, it wasn't likely to sound any more sane to him. But she trusted him, and she discovered that she wanted to tell him.

"They started again right after I met you."

He turned to her and raised both brows in surprise, but said nothing, obviously waiting for her to continue.

"That day I met you... It's really hard to put it into words, but at first I was really frightened, and then I felt ... safe, protected. I know how weird that sounds." She paused, thinking about last night.

"Then, when you were standing in my bedroom doorway last night, I had this sense of déjà vu—except that certain things were wrong."

"Wrong?" he prompted when she paused again.

"It was as if the scene was right, but certain things were wrong about it. You were too far away, and there should have been things in between us. Shapes, shadows of people, something. I don't know what."

He sat there in silence for a time, long enough to make her wonder if she'd been wrong to tell him about it. She didn't really know him very well, after all—even if she felt as though she did.

"I must be reminding you of someone from that time, someone you don't remember, except subconsciously. And it must have been someone important to you, like your father, maybe."

Jessica stared at him in shock, wondering why that had never occurred to her. She'd long ago made up an idyllic image of her father, but if Casey's theory was right, that would certainly account for the safe, warm feelings she'd had—but what about the fear? She said as much to him.

"You told me that your grandmother claimed she didn't know anything about him," he said, reaching over to take her hand. "Maybe she was trying to protect you from the truth about him rather than the truth about the accident."

She saw immediately where this was leading and felt a chill. "You mean that he might have been ... abusive." Her blood turned to ice water as she recalled Susan's having told her how children can repress the memory of abuse until something years later brings it to the fore.

"Maybe," Casey admitted. "But it seems to me that if that was the case and I remind you of him, you'd still feel afraid of me. And it doesn't explain the other feelings." He heaved a sigh.

"Hell, I don't know. I took a few psych courses and all they did was convince me that we don't know very damned much about how we work. In fact, as far as I'm concerned, the whole field of psychology can be summed up in one sentence—nobody knows how any one person is going to think or act at any given point in time. And just to make matters worse, in this case we're dealing with the mind of a three-year-old."

Jessica smiled in spite of her grim thoughts. Susan would enjoy hearing Casey's Law of Human Behavior. She might even agree with it. But his mention of a three-year-old brought back to her that part of the nightmare she'd remembered. It must have reminded him of that, too.

"You said you remembered seeing things the way a little kid would see them. That never happened before?"

"No, all I ever remembered before were the shouts and screams."

He continued to hold her hand, resting it against his thigh and kneading it gently as he stared out at the lake. She thought he might not even be aware of what he was doing, and that somehow made the gesture seem more intimate.

"Well, we're going to get to the bottom of this," he said, then turned suddenly to face her again.

"You can tell me to back off if I'm shoving my way into your life too much."

She smiled. "You're not. I'm glad you're willing to go to Oregon with me."

His gaze moved slowly over her face, then came to rest on her mouth. After a long, heart-stopping moment, he leaned toward her and kissed her—a warm, soft touch of lips to lips, lingering but not demanding.

"Strange things are happening here, Jessica Aylesworth," he murmured. "We seem to be getting awfully tangled up in each other. It could be dangerous, you know."

THEY WERE ABOUT a half hour out of the city when he reached for the mike that hung beside his police-issue radio. "Against my better judgment, I guess I'd better check in."

He identified himself and immediately a raspy male voice came out of the speaker. "Where the hell have you been, Casey? The chief's looking for you. There's been another one."

Casey swore. "Tell him I'll be there in about forty-five minutes. Was it another hooker?"

"Negative. I'll tell the chief."

"So you were right," she said after he had replaced the mike. He nodded. "I'd be happier if I was wrong."

"And the chief will want you to work on it?"

"Yeah, he'll put me in charge. I'm the department's poster boy. He'll tell the press that he's put me on it and they'll expect an arrest yesterday. Dammit, I *hate* psychos!"

Chapter Four

The doorbell rang at a few minutes past midnight. Jessica was in bed, reading the second of Casey's novels. She tensed at the sound, then quickly relaxed again. Intruders weren't in the habit of ringing doorbells. Pleasure flowed over her at the possibility that it might be Casey.

She got out of bed and put on a robe, still slightly wary. When she'd come home after her weekend with Casey she'd discovered three calls on her machine—and no messages. Each time the caller had stayed on the line for a few seconds, then hung up. She still suspected that it was Robert Collins, but Susan's doubts had planted some small seeds of doubt in her mind, as well.

The front door was solid, but there were long, narrow, stained-glass panes on either side. She peeked through them, then opened the door to Casey.

He ran his eyes over her attire. "Sorry. I saw a light on and thought you were still up."

"It's on a timer," she explained. "And I wasn't asleep. I was reading one of your novels."

"I was on my way home, but I just got this urge to hear a soft voice and see something pleasant."

She smiled, pleased at his rather offhand way of saying that he'd missed her after only eight hours. "Would you like a drink?"

"Bourbon, if you have it."

She let him fix the drink for himself and they settled down on the sofa.

"I saw you on TV earlier," she told him. "It sounds as though you know quite a lot about serial killers."

"Far more than I want to. You could call it on-the-job training. I was in charge the last time, too."

"The reporter said that this victim was definitely not a prostitute, even though the police had believed that it might be someone out to get them."

Casey nodded. "A couple of years ago we had a guy who killed two hookers and almost killed a third. He was one sick weirdo, but he wasn't really a serial killer. He was into rough sex and got carried away. Of course, the victims weren't any less dead for that, and they didn't deserve to die any more than this woman did. But the public tends to view the death of a hooker with less outrage than they do the death of a schoolteacher. So now we have outrage, not to mention panic. Did they show her picture on TV?"

"Yes." She knew what was coming.

"Your height, your build, your hair color—just like Jewel."

"Casey, there must be hundreds, even thousands, of women here who fit that description."

"Maybe so. But you're the one I know and care about. Come here and let me hold you. I promise to behave. I'm too tired to do anything else."

She slid across the sofa and settled into the curve of his arm, wondering how it was that at times like this she felt as though they were longtime lovers and not two people who'd met only two weeks ago.

He looked around her living room. "I don't like the setup here. It's too dark outside and you've got all those ground-level windows. Why don't you move in with me until we get this guy? I've got plenty of room."

She was tempted, since she'd become all too aware of her vulnerability here. But things between them were already moving too fast, and if they were living together . . . She shook her head.

"I've had good locks put on the doors and I always lock the windows at night or anytime I'm not home. Besides, my upstairs neighbors are usually home. And anyway, they said on TV that there was no sign of a break-in."

"No, it looks as though she let him in. Her roommate said she was like that."

"Well, I'm not. Do you think you'll catch him soon?"

"Not unless he does something really dumb or we get very lucky. With most murders you develop some leads pretty quickly. There's a standard list of suspects—family members, ex-husbands or ex-lovers. And those who knew the victim are often a big help with names or motives. But none of that works with serial killers."

"But they *do* get caught."

"Yeah, they do, but look how many some of them have killed before that. They usually get caught because they start to come apart and get careless. That's what happened with the last one here. The FBI keeps good records on serial killers. I'm going to get in touch with them in the morning to see if this one might be a traveler. That happens sometimes."

He hugged her close. "I enjoyed this weekend. You're good company."

"Thank you. So are you."

"Well, I'm probably not going to be again until we catch this guy. But we'll still go to the ballet and we'll go out to Oregon as soon as this is over. In the meantime, why don't you try getting some information out of Grandma? If you make it clear to her that you're definitely going there, she might talk."

"You don't know my grandmother, but I'll try."

He drained his glass and got up, drawing her to her feet as well and then circling her with his arms.

"You're getting to be a habit, Jessie. Something just doesn't feel right when you're not around."

She tilted her head back and smiled up at him. "I think the addiction might be mutual."

He raised a hand to stroke her hair. "Always the cautious one. Lots of mights and maybes."

Then he lowered his face to hers and touched her lips, moving softly against them and teasing her tongue briefly before letting her go.

"Do you have anything on under that robe?" he asked huskily.

"Yes."

"Too bad. I wanted a nice fantasy to take to bed with me."

He gave her another quick kiss and was gone, pausing only to remind her again to be careful.

THREE DAYS LATER Jessica was eager to see Casey again, even though the setting left quite a lot to be desired. They'd been communicating via their answering machines, but in a few minutes they'd be face-to-face in a courtroom.

Jessica slanted a glance at Joel Matthews, who sat beside her at the defense table. He'd met her at her office a short time ago and she was both surprised and worried about the change in him. He was very nervous, which was certainly understandable, but he also seemed to be just barely suppressing a great anger.

At least he was dressed appropriately for his court appearance. She'd tried to stress to him how important it was for him to make a good impression on the judge, and he'd apparently taken her advice to heart. He was wearing an inexpensive but neat suit with a white shirt and dark tie, and he'd pulled his hair back into a ponytail.

All in all, she thought he looked quite presentable and not at all like a mugger of little old ladies. Her only concern now was that if she was right about his anger, he could have some problems during the prosecutor's questioning.

She'd told him candidly that she didn't think she could get the charges dismissed, explaining that the standards for an indictment were far lower than those required in the trial to come.

She also said that she was fairly certain that if he was indicted, she could prevent his bail from being raised. It would help if he had a job or a long history in the city, but he'd brought along a list of places where he was seeking work. Given the overcrowding at city jail, she doubted that the judge would increase his bail.

"Will that cop be here—Casey?" Joel asked suddenly.

"Yes, the arresting officer has to be present," she replied, grateful that Joel couldn't know about her relationship with him. She wondered if she should tell him about it if he was indicted. She'd have to ask George for his advice.

"He's out to get me," Joel muttered, and she saw him clench his fist briefly.

"Why do you say that?" she asked, thinking of what Casey had said about him.

"Because he *is*."

"He was just doing his job, Joel. Besides, right now he's busy trying to catch that serial killer."

Then she saw Joel looking past her. His eyes narrowed and for one brief moment he looked like a very different—and dangerous—person. She turned and saw Casey standing at the prosecutor's table. Their eyes met, and for a moment she was spun back to that first time she'd seen him. It hadn't occurred to her before, but it was Joel who had brought them together. She rather doubted, however, that he'd be pleased to hear that.

We would have met in any event, she thought. Joel just made it happen sooner.

The hearing began with the usual preliminaries. The assistant DA called Casey as her first witness. Detective Lieutenant T. S. Casimiricz wore a beautifully tailored light gray suit, crisp white shirt and a conservatively patterned silk tie. He looked and sounded very impressive, and Jessica thought that the assistant DA was doing everything but drooling over him. By the time it was her turn to question him, Jessica was wishing that she'd handed over this case to someone else.

Casey's pale eyes remained on Joel until she was standing before him. Then he shifted his attention to her. Not a muscle moved in his rugged face, but she hoped that she was the only one who saw the sudden light in his eyes.

"Detective Casimiricz," she began, using her best lawyer's voice and wondering if anyone else could hear that slightly husky tone, "when you stopped Mr. Matthews, as you just described, did he tell you why he was running?"

"He said he was hurrying to catch a bus."

"Isn't it possible that he was doing just that? People often run to catch buses."

"They do, but not when the bus they were supposedly running to catch had just gone past them."

Jessica stared at him, fighting her anger. He hadn't told her that. She knew perfectly well that he saw her anger, but his poker face remained.

"Are you saying that you saw the bus go past?"

"Yes, only a few seconds before I stopped him."

She thought fast, which wasn't easy, given her urge to smack him. "Are you able to say how frequently the buses stop at that particular intersection?"

"I don't know the exact schedule, but most of them in that area run at half-hour intervals."

"I see. Thank you. And now, Detective, I'd like to go over the situation regarding the money you found on Mr. Matthews."

But he was as noncommittal as he'd been earlier. The sum of money came close to matching the amount the victim claimed to have been carrying, including the denominations of the bills. Jessica was both angry and frustrated, and she had made a mistake. She asked Casey a question she had not yet asked Joel.

"Detective, could you tell me where you found this money? Was it in his wallet?"

"No, it was in the pocket of his jeans." He paused, then added, "There were only a few dollars in his wallet."

"Thank you, Detective. That will be all." Jessica turned away from him quickly now as angry with herself as with him. She'd given him a chance to make an even stronger case against Joel.

Next came the victim herself, just released from the hospital the day before. She was obviously frail and walking with a cane. It was a difficult situation for Jessica, who didn't want to risk alienating the judge by being too hard on the woman.

After the woman had told her story to the assistant DA, insisting that Joel was indeed the man who had assaulted her, Jessica rose to begin her questioning. Out of the corner of her eye she could see Casey at the back of the nearly empty courtroom, standing next to the bailiff. She had been hoping that he'd be gone.

She framed her questions very carefully, trying to ask tough questions in a gentle manner. The woman admitted to having poor eyesight and also admitted that she'd just barely glimpsed her assailant. But Joel had walked past her and there was no one else in sight at the time. It was nearly dusk and she was returning from visiting a friend down the street. Joel, she said, had just come out of a convenience store, then walked past her. According to her, she was then struck from behind no more than a second or two later.

Jessica could not shake the woman's testimony, although she thought she might be able to do so at the trial. The evidence was circumstantial at best.

The only other witness was a man who hadn't actually seen the assault, but had heard the victim cry out and had run from his shop to see Joel running away down the street. It was his shout that had caught Casey's attention.

She asked him if anyone else was nearby when he came out of his shop, and he stated that several kids were hanging around in front of a building nearby. But he couldn't recall what they'd been wearing and didn't know who they were. He did admit, however, that they had vanished as soon as he yelled.

Joel proved to be an excellent witness in his own defense. He was polite and soft-spoken, and his earlier nervousness and anger seemed to have vanished. He claimed that he hadn't seen the bus go by, saying that it must have passed before he came out of the store.

He also explained why the money was in his pocket instead of his wallet. He'd started to leave his rooming house, then decided at the last minute that it would be safer to carry it with him than leave it there. The room locks weren't very good and the landlady was known to be careless about collecting keys when tenants left. So he'd stuffed the bills into the pocket of his jeans and then decided to leave them there so no one would see the cash if he opened his wallet in a bar.

As Jessica had guessed, he was bound over for trial. The judge wasn't happy about Joel not having a job, but seemed to accept that he was seriously looking for one. Bail remained the same.

Jessica and Joel left the courthouse together. She told him that she felt confident about their prospects at the trial and explained how she would be able to sow doubts in the minds of the jurors.

When they emerged from the courthouse Jessica saw Casey standing on the wide steps just a short distance away, talking to the district attorney and another man. He turned in her direction briefly, then quickly turned away again, presumably because Joel was with her. Since she was in no mood to talk to him now, she was glad for Joel's presence. The way she was feeling toward Casey at this point, she might have found herself facing assault charges.

"He thinks he's a big man," Joel muttered as they walked on.

"He *is* a big man, Joel," she said with a laugh intended to defuse his anger. "But he's not our problem. He just gave the facts as he saw them, and you did a wonderful job of explaining them."

Joel said nothing, and a few minutes later they parted company after she reminded him to stay in touch. Then a thought suddenly occurred to her and she turned back and called out to him.

"Joel, I just had a thought. I know you're looking for fulltime work, but would you be interested in doing some work for me in the meantime?"

"Sure," he said eagerly. "What do you need?"

She explained how she needed bookshelves for her new apartment. "I have a lot of books and I'd like to line two walls with shelves."

"When do you want me to start?"

"Why don't you come by tomorrow about seven in the evening and we can decide what should be done."

"Sure, anytime."

She took out a card and wrote down her home address and phone number. Then she hurried back to her office to prepare for Robert Collins's hearing, which was scheduled for later in the day. She was glad she'd thought about giving the work to Joel. His eagerness indicated that he must have needed the money, and she very much wanted to get her apartment in order.

ROBERT COLLINS DID NOT show up for his hearing. The judge issued a warrant for his arrest, but Jessica knew that finding him wouldn't exactly be a high-priority matter with the over-worked police. She considered telling the judge about the phone calls and the letter, but in the end decided against it. She had no real evidence to link them to Robert, and as a newcomer in the P.D.'s office, she hadn't yet established the credibility that would make anyone take her suspicions seriously.

But she was very worried about Robert. He was mentally ill and needed help. Susan's descriptions of the tangled thought processes of people in his situation had made a powerful impression on her. It seemed to her that Robert must be living constantly with the kind of terror that she herself experienced in her nightmares.

So it was with some difficulty that she managed to put Robert Collins from her mind and turn instead to a review of the next day's cases. She was halfway through the stack of folders on her desk when she looked up to see Casey standing in the doorway of her cubicle.

"Go away, Casey. I'm in no mood to deal with you now."

He ignored her and walked into the small space, filling it far too completely. Her anger with him and with herself mixed explosively with the memory of his kisses.

"You can throw something at me if that will make you feel any better."

"Don't tempt me! If I had anything here big enough, I would!"

He planted his hands on her desk and leaned toward her. "Remember what I said about keeping business and pleasure separate. You were very good in court, by the way."

"Good?" she exploded. "Don't you dare patronize me! I was a *disaster!* A second-year law student would have known better than to ask a question that hadn't already been answered by her client." She glared at him. "That was a rotten trick, Casey. You didn't tell me about the bus."

"You didn't ask. I did what you asked me to do. And anyway, your hippie did a good job of explaining himself, even though I know damned well he was lying."

"You can believe what you want, but can you prove it?" she challenged. "You got him indicted, but I'm going to get him acquitted."

"That's the spirit. You're already shaping up to be a great P.D."

"This is not going to work, Casey."

"What isn't going to work?"

"Us."

"Remember that I have tickets for a ballet that you want to see. And that's the best way for you to get back at me. Not only will I have to put on a tux, but I'll also have to sit through two hours of total boredom."

She got up and stuffed the remaining folders into her briefcase. "I'm too exhausted to argue with you anymore."

"How would you feel about a nice relaxing swim, followed by a steak dinner?"

She folded her arms across her chest and tilted her head, regarding him curiously. "If I told you to get out of my life and stay out, would you do it?"

"No. I'd just assume that you had a bad day."

She laughed. "Why does your answer not surprise me? Where can we swim?"

"At a nice private club. I'll pick you up in an hour."

"Where is this club?"

"Just outside town. You'll like it."

She sighed. "It *does* sound wonderful. Swimming is about the best way I know to relax, but I haven't gotten around to checking out clubs yet."

"Swimming is the *second* best way to relax—but I'm trying to remember that I'm a gentleman."

BY THE TIME CASEY ARRIVED to pick her up, Jessica's anger with him was a fading memory. She knew he was right, they had to keep their professional and personal lives separate. And she knew, too, that she had allowed herself to become too emotionally involved in Joel Matthews's case. In fact, even though she badly wanted to have those bookcases, she was beginning to regret that she'd hired him.

They took the freeway out of the city, then exited into a suburban area. A short time later they were driving through a pleasant neighborhood of large homes set on multiacre lots, many of them just barely visible beyond thick fringes of trees.

Then Casey came to a stop at a gated driveway. He punched out a code on a steel box mounted at the edge of the driveway and the gate lifted. Jessica saw no sign announcing a club. Even the mailbox bore only the street number. She was about to question him when she saw ahead of them a large, handsome house constructed of old brick and cedar shakes. He touched a remote device on his dashboard and the one garage door rolled up. At the same time a huge German shepherd came running across the lawn toward them.

"Just how private is this club?" she asked dryly.

"As private as it gets—a membership of one, with occasional guests."

They got out of the car. The dog greeted him, then turned its attention to her. German shepherds had never been her favorite breed, and this one was the biggest she'd ever seen. He was also very dark, which gave him an even more menacing appearance.

"Friend, Adolf, friend!" Casey said sharply as the dog continued to stare at her.

Then the animal walked over to her, sniffed the hand she held out rather hesitantly and sat down. He lifted one of his big paws and she crouched down and took it in her hand.

"I'm pleased to meet you, Adolf, although I can't help wishing you were a poodle."

She straightened again and looked out at the large property. "Does he run loose all the time?" That seemed rather dangerous to her.

"The whole property is fenced," Casey told her. "And don't worry about him. He's well trained. The two of us graduated at the top of our class."

The house was as handsome inside as out: lots of windows, earth tones, comfortable modern furnishings and many plants. She was impressed and told him so.

"So this is the house that Kincaid built." He was the protagonist in Casey's novels.

"No, pro football built this house, thanks to a smart agent who convinced a dumb kid that he should invest his money instead of blowing it all on wine, women and other dubious investments."

He gestured to a small set of stairs. "The guest wing is up there. You can change there and I'll meet you out back."

Jessica changed into her "serious" swimsuit, a black one-piece with a racing back, then found her way to the sliding doors that opened onto a wide stone terrace. He was already there, dropping some towels onto a big padded chaise longue.

She paused in the doorway, staring at him. He wore snug-fitting black trunks that displayed his big, hard body to its greatest effect. And it certainly had an effect on her! She was certain that she'd never before known a man who was so incredibly, uncompromisingly male. She literally tingled with an awareness of him. Then Adolf spotted her and began to wag his tail, and Casey turned as she stepped out onto the terrace.

"That'll do," he said, running his eyes over her with deliberate slowness. "Of course, I was hoping for a string bikini."

"I thought we were going to a club," she reminded him.

"I'll bet you don't even own a string bikini," he challenged.

"Well, I own a bikini for sunbathing, but. . . ." She gestured to the long, narrow pool beyond the terrace. "What a perfect lap pool."

"I had it built extra long so I could at least swim a few yards before bumping into the other end."

There were no steps and no shallow end. He dived into the pool first, sending up a wave of water that covered her before she followed him. She'd thought it would be impossible to relax with him in the pool, but she was wrong. The water temperature was perfect, neither too cold nor too warm.

They both gave every appearance of ignoring each other as they swam back and forth, moving at different speeds that had them regularly passing each other. But if there was never a moment when she wasn't aware of his presence, she also felt comfortable. It was very strange how she could be so excited, so intensely aware of him, and yet so completely relaxed at the same time, and she was reminded once again of that warm feeling of trust she'd felt when she met him. Was it Casey himself, or a memory?

He was still swimming when she finally hauled herself out of the pool, gasping for breath and thinking that she'd certainly

let herself get out of shape these past few months. It was definitely time to find a club to join.

"Ready for a drink?" he asked as he levered himself out of
the pool a few minutes later.

"That would be nice. Gin and tonic?" she asked, tossing
aside the towel after drying herself, then sinking onto the chaise
longue. Be casual about this, she counseled herself. Don't let
him know that the mere sight of his nearly naked body has any
effect on you. No effect at all. Her toes weren't curling. Her
blood wasn't racing hotly through her veins. Not cool, always-
in-control Jessica Aylesworth.

When he returned with the drinks she asked him about local
clubs. "I really need to find one. I'm out of shape."

"I'll forgo the obvious response to that," he said dryly as he
handed her her drink, then sat on the edge of the chaise. "But
don't worry about finding a club. I'll give you the code for the
gate and a house key and you can come here anytime you
want."

He looked at her levelly. "That was my subtle way of letting
you know that there's no one else in my life, in case you haven't
already guessed. But I still wish you'd move in here until we
catch this nut. I thought that maybe bringing you here would
help persuade you. You can have that whole wing to yourself."

Jessica wasn't too concerned about the killer. But she *did*
begin to think again about Robert Collins. She was tempted to
tell Casey about the calls and letter in the hope that he could
persuade the police to search for him. But that meant entan-
gling their professional and personal lives again, and she was
resolved not to do that.

Besides, moving in with Casey just wasn't a good idea. No
matter what he said about her having space to herself, she
wouldn't. He probably didn't even realize just how overpowering he could be. Susan had certainly been right; it would be
all too easy to lose herself around him.

"I can't persuade you, can I?" he asked, breaking into her
thoughts.

She shook her head. "Thanks for the offer of the pool. I'd
like that. But I think you're overreacting, and I also think

you're not giving me any credit. I'm not a naive country bumpkin, Casey. I grew up in a city and went to law school in another city. And I've lived alone for a long time. I know how to take care of myself.''

She did. But saying it to him sounded somehow inane. She wondered if, despite what she'd told him, his size really *did* bother her. His size and that aura of invincible maleness.

"Yeah, maybe I am overreacting," he admitted after a moment. "But at least promise me that you'll be even more careful until this is over. And if anything unusual happens, no matter how insignificant, tell me right away. We don't have any proof that this guy stalked his victims before he killed them, but he could have."

She was somewhat surprised that he'd given up so quickly. It made her wonder if he, too, might be belatedly thinking about the ramifications of them living under the same roof. Several times before, she'd thought he seemed uncertain about what was happening between them, maybe even a bit frightened, difficult as it was for her to believe that anything could frighten him.

They finished their drinks as the terrace fell into shadows. Then, just as Casey got up to start the gas grill, a big orange cat came strolling across the yard, rubbed itself against Adolf, then went to Casey, who bent to pet it.

"This is Howard. Adolf brought him home one night not long after my other cat died."

"Why Howard?" she asked as the cat came over to inspect her.

"He reminds me of someone I used to play football with."

The cat had a broad face with markings that gave him a menacing appearance. But he quickly submitted to her strokes and began purring loudly.

Jessica was both surprised and touched by Casey's domesticity. She wondered if she'd ever get over the contrasts she found in him: the tough cop exterior and the gentleness beneath.

She helped him prepare dinner, which they ate on the terrace as dusk fell. She marveled at how comfortable she could feel with him, how he seemed always to have been a part of her life. Was it only because he reminded her of someone from her unknown past? She knew that she had to answer that question—soon.

After they had cleaned up they returned to the terrace. Casey drew her down beside him on the chaise longue, curving his arm around her. Adolf flopped down near them and Howard climbed onto Casey's lap, glaring at her in an obvious statement of possession. He'd turned on the stereo, and soft jazz poured from the outside speakers.

She sighed happily. "This is exactly what I needed. Thank you for bringing me here."

He kissed her brow. "You're too hard on yourself, you know."

She couldn't very well dispute that, since it was true. "And you're not?" she challenged instead.

"Nope. I've learned to cut myself some slack. I took off the shining armor and sent the white charger back to the stable." He heaved a sigh.

"Of course, I do have a tendency to bring them back again when something like this happens. Speaking of which, I'll have to leave soon and get down to the District to see if anyone's picked up any information."

"Do you think they might have?"

He shook his head. "It isn't likely. This guy could appear to be perfectly normal until you dig below the surface. And people like him don't usually let anyone get beneath the surface."

They went inside and she asked him where he did his writing. So he took her down to the lower level, where a large room had been set up as a workroom. A big blackboard on one wall was covered with names and bits of information in neat columns with arrows going every which way.

"That's the book I'm working on now," he told her as she examined it. "It's loosely based on a case I worked a couple of years ago."

She wandered around the room, looking at various plaques and trophies from his athletic career, as well as several that honored him for community service.

Then she saw his framed college diploma and frowned. "I thought you told me that you majored in football, drinking and women.'' The diploma said he'd graduated with honors in pre-law.

"In between I managed to get some studying done. As a matter of fact, your law school said they'd take me. But at twenty-one, when you're faced with a choice between being a starving law student and being a big-bucks player in the pros...." He shrugged.

Then the phone rang. He listened, said little, then hung up in disgust and turned to her. "The lab reports and crime scene reports are all in. Nothing, except that the medical examiner confirmed what we already knew. It was most likely the same killer with the same weapon."

"What hours do you work?" she asked curiously.

"I have my own schedule. I keep it that way so no one knows when I'll be around. It's not a nine-to-five job."

Something in his tone told her that he was issuing a warning—letting her know that his job could be a problem for them.

"I know that," she told him. "Aren't cops supposed to have a very high divorce rate for that reason?"

He nodded, his eyes locked on hers. "That's the one reason I haven't gotten married. There's enough Catholic left in me that I don't believe in divorce."

JOEL MATTHEWS SHOWED UP on time the next evening and Jessica discussed the project with him. She'd been uncertain about which two walls of the small room she wanted to use for books. The layout of the room was such that the wall with a window would have been one of her choices, but she'd thought that might pose too much of a problem. Joel, however, said he could easily build around the window, then suggested she might even want a rolling ladder, so that he could build the shelves clear to the ceiling. Considering the number of books she had, Jessica thought that was an excellent idea.

"Where can I buy something like that?" she asked.

"You don't have to buy it. I'll build it, too. It just means putting a track along the edges of the shelves, and I can make it out of oak, just like the bookcases themselves."

She knew she was probably going to too much expense for a rented apartment, but decided to do it, anyway. Her landlord had said that he might want to sell the property in a year or so when he retired, and she thought she might just buy it herself.

She told Joel that his plans were fine and wrote him out a check to cover half the price he quoted, which certainly sounded reasonable.

"When can you start?" she asked, eager to see the project completed and her books in their proper place.

"I can start Saturday morning if that's okay with you."

"Fine. I'll see you then. Will you be able to work in the evenings?" She felt rather bad about not letting him come during the day, but that was risky. She trusted him, but she didn't really know him that well.

"I'll have to," he said. "I got a job today."

"Oh, Joel, that's wonderful! Is it a carpenter job?"

He nodded. "It's only going to last about a month, though. I'll be doing the finish work on a new house."

"But it's a start. If they like your work, maybe there'll be more."

They were back in her living room and she saw his gaze go to a small portrait of her sitting on a table. The picture had been taken when she was five, and she'd always liked it.

He picked it up and stared at it, then set it down again without comment. A few moments later, as he was about to leave, he asked her if she'd grown up here.

"No, I grew up in Philadelphia," she said, rather surprised by the question. "I just moved here recently."

He nodded. "See you Saturday, then."

She stood there watching as he drove away in his battered truck. What a strange man he could be, she thought. He always left her with the feeling that strong emotions were brewing just beneath his surface calm.

Then she thought about his dislike of Casey and Casey's similar feelings toward him. She'd better see that they didn't meet while Joel was working for her; otherwise, she might be left with half-completed bookshelves.

Chapter Five

They walked across the plaza that connected the parking garage to the new civic center, surrounded by other well-dressed ballet goers. Jessica stole a sidelong glance at Casey. "Devastating" was the only word that came to mind. His beautifully tailored tux was set off by a pale blue shirt that was a perfect match for his eyes.

She'd shopped for a new gown, but had finally settled on one she'd had for several years. After all, no one here would have seen it. It was a gloriously feminine concoction of dusky rose silk crepe that draped her body beautifully and left one shoulder bare. With it, she wore long, delicate gold earrings, and to ward off the evening chill she carried a silk-and-cashmere shawl in shades of rose and pink and cream.

Casey had been very appreciative of both her dress and the fact that she'd let her hair down instead of piling it up as she usually did for formal occasions.

When they reached the starkly modern center Jessica saw several TV cameras set up and a small band of photographers swarming around the crowd. Given the fact that most of the city's society set and other notables would be here, she was surprised when several photographers converged on them and one of the cameras swung in their direction, as well.

"Hey, Casey, are you going to give us the lady's name?" one of the photographers shouted as he clicked away.

Casey ignored him and all but dragged her through the crowd toward the entrance.

"Casey, slow down! I can't keep up with you in these heels," she protested. "I don't care if they know who I am."

He said nothing until they were in the vast, two-story lobby. "*I* care. I should have sneaked us in a side entrance."

He looked so grim that she frowned at him in confusion. He bent to give her a quick kiss.

"Sorry. I'm probably just being paranoid again, but I don't like the idea of seeing your picture in the paper with me while I'm working this case."

"Oh!" She hadn't thought about that and didn't want to now, either.

But she soon forgot all about it as he introduced her to various people, many of whom professed great shock at seeing him there. Several teasing comments were made about her apparent influence over him.

Then they were shown to their seats, which turned out to be a private box, one of about a dozen along the sides of the mezzanine level.

"These are wonderful seats!" she exclaimed happily.

"Yeah. No one will notice if I fall asleep."

"*I'll* notice, and I'll poke you in the ribs. A little culture never hurt anyone, Casey."

"What? You mean football and hockey aren't cultural events? Or how about the bowling and softball tournaments I play in every year?"

She threw him a disgusted look. "Have you ever been inside a museum or art gallery, or gone to a concert?"

"Sure. We had a homicide in one of the city's best galleries a couple of years ago. And when I was in uniform, I worked some of the concerts in the park."

She rolled her eyes. "I give up. Just don't start to snore."

He leaned close to her. "If you weren't so damned good at resisting my charms, you'd know by now that I don't snore."

She merely laughed and turned toward the stage as the lights began to dim. Casey made himself as comfortable as possible and watched her instead of the stage.

The soft lighting at the back of the box cast a glow over her hair and her bare shoulder, leaving the graceful curve of her neck and her classic profile in shadows. After seeing her either in tailored business suits or jeans, he thoroughly enjoyed her elegant, feminine dress this night. She looked good enough to eat, and he was ready to start nibbling right now.

He'd forgotten that the tickets he bought each year and then gave away were for a box, and he began to wish that he hadn't been so generous. At least if they were down there in the midst of the crowd he'd be better able to keep his thoughts from straying. The intimacy of the private box was all too tempting. On the other hand, though, if they were down there, he'd be crammed into a seat even more uncomfortable than this chair that was clearly designed for midgets.

He read the program, which insisted in overblown language that there was actually a story unfolding down on the stage, then ignored the performance and continued to watch her instead.

Was there anything about her that he *didn't* like? If there was, he hadn't discovered it yet. In fact, he was uncomfortably aware of the fact that he might be trying too hard to find fault with her, because if he didn't...

He left that unsettling thought unfinished and thought instead about her nightmares. It seemed likely to him that her grandparents had lied to her, or at least had kept something from her. And whatever it was was locked up inside her, struggling to get out.

It also seemed likely that he was unintentionally triggering these nightmares, and that was all the more reason they needed to find the truth. It could be rough on her, he knew. But he'd be there for her and they'd get through it all right.

Of more immediate concern to him was her refusal to stay with him until they caught the killer. He supposed that the chances of that wacko turning to the society pages and seeing their picture were probably negligible, but he was still annoyed with himself for not having thought about it.

Casey knew that serial killers often became fixated on the one who was hunting them. When he'd caught the last one, they'd found a whole stack of newspaper clippings and videotapes the guy had kept. He'd even taped to his wall a photo of Casey at one of the scenes.

And now this one was preying on women who looked like Jessie.

He continued to stare at her as she sat there, transfixed by the action on the stage. He followed her gaze briefly and decided that one of those guys might have had a pretty good career in the NFL as a pass catcher. He had great moves and he sure as hell could jump.

She turned toward him and he opened his eyes wide as though he'd just awakened. She smiled and turned away again.

You don't know it yet, Jessica Aylesworth, he thought, and maybe I'm not ready to admit it myself, but we're on our way to something big. It was just damned inconvenient that her nightmares and the serial killer seemed to have gotten in their way.

JESSICA WAS THOROUGHLY enjoying the ballet, but there was scarcely a moment when she wasn't also aware of the man next to her—possibly because every time she glanced his way, she found him watching her. After a while she leaned toward him.

"If all you wanted to do was stare at me, you didn't have to buy these tickets, you know."

He made a move to get up. "Okay, let's go. It must be about over, anyway."

"I'm sorry to have to tell you this, but it isn't even intermission time yet."

She turned back to the performance, but she heard him move his chair closer, then felt him drape his arm across the back of her chair.

"Casey!" she warned.

"What?" His breath tickled her ear as he leaned closer.

"Behave! People down there can see us."

"Do you see any of them looking up here? Most of them are asleep, anyway, especially the men. Ballet is the torture women designed to get back at men for watching football."

She laughed softly. "You should have given that line to the reporter outside."

His fingertips brushed against her ear as he lifted one of her dangling earrings. "They're pretty."

"Thank you." She kept her eyes on the stage, trying her best to ignore him.

But it seemed that he was bent on distracting her. His lips and tongue touched the rim of her ear, then moved to the curve of her neck. His arm slid between her and the back of the chair, then slipped around her waist, drawing her closer as he continued to nibble lightly at her neck and shoulder.

The effect was devastating. The orchestra music rose and fell in a haunting melody. Hundreds of people were only a short distance away and yet the box gave her a spurious sense of privacy. She continued to try to ignore him, but the soft heat of desire was stealing through her, rippling sensuously along her nerve endings and giving rise to that unique ache deep inside her.

"You smell good," he whispered, his lips now tracing the outline of her collarbone.

"Why don't you just go to sleep?" she whispered back in a very husky voice.

"It's a lot more fun to torment you."

Then, finally, it was intermission. The lights came on and he stood quickly. "Come on. I'm going to need a drink to get through the rest of this. And the supper afterward had better be good."

"Coming here with you is like bringing a five-year-old," she muttered as they left the box.

He gave her a smug look. "I thought I was just adding an extra dimension to your pleasure."

They made their way back down to the vast lobby, where bars had been set up at either end. Crowds were already milling about, but Casey made his way through them easily. There were distinct advantages to being his size, she noted as people moved out of their way. In no time at all he'd gotten drinks for them.

"Susan is here somewhere," she told Casey. They both scanned the crowd but couldn't find her, and after he'd exchanged greetings with still more people, he grabbed her hand and led her away.

"Where are we going?" she asked as he started off into a deserted hallway.

"Anywhere the reporters aren't," he replied, pulling her along after him.

Then he stopped at an intersecting hallway. "You wait here and let me know if anyone's coming."

"Why?" she asked, but he was already moving down the short, dark corridor.

She held both their drinks as she saw him reach into his breast pocket and remove his wallet, then extract a card. He slid it between a door and its frame, and in a few seconds opened the door and motioned for her to come.

"What are you doing?" she asked as he led her into a stairwell. "That door was locked."

"They should have better locks," he said as he started up the stairway, still holding on to her hand.

"You're a cop, for God's sake, and you're breaking the law."

"I'm not breaking it, just bending it a little."

He pushed open the door at the top of the stairwell and they stepped out onto the roof.

The civic center was built atop a slight rise, so the view of the city was spectacular. In the distance she could see the courthouse and the annex where she worked, as well as police headquarters and all of the downtown area. She placed the drinks on the ledge of the building.

She hadn't brought her shawl with her and she shivered as the cool breeze swept over her. But then he came up behind her and circled her with his arms, drawing her back into his sheltering warmth. She turned within that small circle and pressed against him, lifting her face to meet his.

There was a fierce hunger to their kisses, even though he was, as always, gentle. Jessica could feel the leash of his self-control become taut, close to the breaking point. And along that dangerous edge her passion grew, spreading molten fire through her throbbing body.

Her fears were melting away beneath this erotic onslaught. There no longer seemed to be any reason to hold back. He slid the gown from her shoulder until it slipped below her breasts, revealing a lacy demibra that barely contained their fullness.

And then his hands and lips were on her, forcing her breasts out from their confinement, freeing them to be explored by his lips and tongue. She arched her body to him and a low moan rose from within her as he surrounded a dusky tip with his mouth.

"Casey, we have to stop!" she gasped as a final awareness of where they were surfaced briefly from the ocean of sensations that was swelling around her. Her feet were no longer touching the gravel surface of the roof, and she knew that her legs wouldn't have supported her in any event. She had become a creature of liquid fire.

"I know," he murmured. "We will."

But he didn't, not for countless moments. The cool wind played over her heated flesh as he continued the torment, his lips, teeth and tongue roving over her.

Then he lifted her onto a low concrete wall that surrounded some sort of equipment and backed off a few steps to run his hand shakily through his hair. She shivered, both from the cool air and the burning intensity of his stare. He moved to her quickly surrounding her again with his warmth.

"You'd better understand something right now, Jessica Aylesworth," he said in a husky voice. "When it starts, it isn't going to stop."

She was nodding even before she managed to murmur yes. She knew what he meant. Somehow she'd understood that from the beginning.

He tugged her bra back into place, his fingers rough and warm against her skin, then pulled up the bodice of her dress as well before giving her one last, soft, lingering kiss.

THEY FOUND SUSAN and her date Todd after the performance, while they were on their way to the dining room where a sumptuous buffet had been set up. The two couples shared a table, although they were interrupted regularly by people stopping to talk to Casey. He knew everyone, it seemed.

"Are you holding out on me?" Susan asked at one point, leaning close to her.

"What do you mean?" Jessica asked, even though she knew perfectly well.

"You have a look on your face that I've never seen before," Susan said pointedly. "And the looks he's been giving you are definitely X-rated."

"You're the one who said we make a good couple." Jessica smiled.

"Yes, but I didn't expect to be so right so soon. What happened to your famous restraint?"

Then, when she saw that she wasn't going to get an answer to that, she asked about Robert Collins.

Jessica glanced quickly toward Casey, but he was deep in conversation with the mayor and a state senator. So she explained the situation to Susan and Todd, who was now also listening. He was a psychologist as well, and he and Susan exchanged looks of disgust.

"I feel sorry for him if the police find him," Todd said.

"Why?" Jessica asked.

With a quick glance at Casey, who still had his back to them, Todd leaned closer. "Cops don't generally deal very well with the mentally ill. A lot of it is just ignorance on their part, but they also hate the temporary insanity defense, and probably for good reason. It's overused."

"If they pick him up," Susan said, "he's going to end up in jail, which is the worst possible place for him at this point, because it will feed right into his delusions."

Then they all quickly changed the subject as Casey turned to them, apologizing for the interruption. After that the conversation became more general, but Jessica continued to mull over what Todd and Susan had said. If only Robert would come into the office again. That way she might be able to guarantee that he received psychiatric help.

Then, just as they were finishing their dessert, Casey's beeper went off. Since both Susan and Todd carried them as well, there was a moment of amusing confusion before it was sorted out. Casey glanced at the pager, then swore as he got up to find a phone. A few minutes later he was back, his expression grim.

"Has there been another murder?" Jessica asked.

"An attempt. They caught the guy. They seem to think he might be the serial killer, but I have my doubts. I've got to go down there."

"We'll see that Jessica gets home," Todd offered. Casey thanked him and then tipped up her chin to kiss her softly.

"This isn't what I had in mind for the rest of the night," he murmured in her ear. "But maybe we both need a cooling-off period."

Jessica watched him making his way through the crowd. She didn't know whether to be relieved or regretful, and decided that she was a bit of both.

HE WAS WATCHING TV. He liked to catch the news, to see what they were saying about him. But there wasn't anything to-night, so he was about to click past it and try another channel when he saw him: Casey the cop, all decked out in fancy duds. The announcer was saying something about an annual charity thing at the civic center.

There was a woman with him. He didn't get a good look at her because there were others between her and the camera, but he caught a quick glimpse of long blond hair, and then the camera moved on.

He wondered who she was: a wife or girlfriend? His mind began to twist around a thought. She'd looked tall, too—even beside the Incredible Hulk.

There might be some pictures in the paper. Maybe he could find out who she was that way. Yeah, it was definitely worth checking out.

He went out early the next morning and got both papers, then tore them apart until he found the society sections. The pictures were on the front pages of both sections.

At first he was too stunned to think as he stared at Her, standing there smiling with her hand on Casey's arm. But then the rage built quickly and explosively as he tasted her betrayal. He tore the paper to shreds.

Then finally, as the rage went back deep inside him, he sud-denly remembered something his mother used to say to him. *The fruit never falls far from the tree.* Something like that.

They would pay—*both* of them.

"I'LL BE LEAVING NOW."

Jessica snapped awake to find Joel standing in the entrance

to the living room. She stifled a yawn and rubbed the back of her neck. "Fine. Will you be here tomorrow evening?"

He nodded. "A couple of evenings should do it."

She got up and saw him to the door. "Thanks, Joel. I'll see you then."

After he'd gone she stood there for a moment, still groggy from her unintentional nap. She'd intended to offer Joel dinner, but she'd fallen asleep instead.

She went back into the living room and gathered up the papers that had slid to the floor when she'd fallen asleep. Now she'd have to spend part of the evening going over her new cases. She was tired because she'd stayed up reading after Todd and Susan had brought her home, and then she'd been awakened by the nightmare.

There hadn't been anything new; it was that same child's-eye view and the same shouts and screams. But she had the inexplicable sense that things were coming ever closer to the surface.

She went into the kitchen, then flipped on the TV before taking some spaghetti sauce from the freezer. The local news was on.

"Police refuse to confirm if the man who attacked a twenty-nine-year-old stockbroker in her home last night is the same man responsible for two other killings. The victim, Sherri Thompson, was stabbed twice and is reported in guarded condition at City Hospital."

A picture of the victim appeared on the screen. She was a blonde, although her hair was both shorter and lighter than Jessica's. Jessica thought it strange that the police weren't sure about the attacker's identity, but she recalled that Casey had expressed doubts before he left her.

She hoped he would prove to be the one—at least partly for selfish reasons. If the serial killer had been caught, then she and Casey could go to Oregon. It was certainly not a journey she was looking forward to, but she had decided that the truth, no matter how terrible, could scarcely be worse than her nightmares and her fears.

Casey called a few moments later, sounding as tired as she herself felt. He told her that he was about to take a break and get some dinner and asked her to join him. She countered with a suggestion that he come over for spaghetti, an invitation that he quickly accepted.

When she greeted him at the door a short time later, she could see the tiredness in his eyes. "Didn't you get any sleep last night?" she asked after he kissed her.

He shook his head. "I'm getting too old for this."

"I just saw the news. They said that you don't know yet if he's the serial killer."

"*I* know he isn't, but the higher-ups are still deluding themselves."

"Why are you so sure he isn't the one?" she asked as he followed her to the kitchen.

"She walked in on him while he was burglarizing her home, and he's got two priors. Besides, the medical examiner doesn't think the knife he was carrying could cause the types of wounds found on the other victims."

"That sounds pretty convincing to me," she said, disappointed. "Does he have alibis for the times of the other murders?"

"He says he does for one of them, but we haven't been able to confirm it yet. It's pretty thin, anyway. He was out on bail on a breaking and entering. The hearing was last week and he was bound over. He isn't one of your clients, is he?"

She shook her head. "No, I heard his name earlier, and it didn't ring a bell."

Casey reached into his pocket and withdrew a mug shot. She stared at it. "Oh, I remember him. He's Millie's client. Our offices are next to each other and he wandered into my office by mistake a couple of weeks ago. I remember him because of that scar."

She didn't add that she also remembered him because of the way he'd looked at her and what he'd said about wanting *her* to be his lawyer.

Casey went off to the bathroom to wash up. When he returned to the kitchen a few minutes later he remarked that her new bookshelves looked good.

"Yes, Joel's doing a great job," she replied—then could have bitten her tongue.

"Joel? You mean the hippie?"

"Uh, yes. He's a talented carpenter. He just got a job, too, but he's been working on the bookcases in the evenings and this weekend."

"Jessie! Dammit, I—"

"We're both too tired to be arguing about him now," she interrupted. "And anyway, he hasn't tried to mug me or make off with the family silver yet."

"Why are *you* so tired?" he asked, apparently giving up on the subject of Joel Matthews.

"I stayed up late reading one of your books, and then I had the nightmare again."

He slid his arms around her from behind and kissed the top of her head. "Anything different this time?"

She shook her head.

"We'll get to the bottom of it, honey. I promise. We'll go out there just as soon as I catch this fruitcake."

His beeper went off when they were halfway through dinner, and he made his call from the kitchen phone. After he had hung up, he gave her a sheepish look.

"Sorry about the language. Cop talk."

"I've heard it before," she said, amused at his obvious embarrassment. "In fact, some of my clients are teaching me a whole new language. What was that all about?"

He sank heavily into his chair. "Oh, nothing. Just a drug turf war. One of my snitches has turned up with a hole in his chest. But I didn't like him much, anyway."

"Casey!"

"Okay, okay, so maybe he didn't deserve to get shot, but he isn't exactly a candidate for sainthood, and he'll probably pull through."

They finished their dinner and she asked him if he had to go back to work.

"Yeah. I was thinking about going home and grabbing a few hours' sleep, but it's probably not worth it."

"Why don't you take a nap here?"

He allowed as how that wasn't a half-bad idea, and she knew he must be really tired when he didn't even hint that she should join him. She told him to use her bed, since it was larger than the one in the guest room, then promised to wake him in three hours.

THREE HOURS LATER Jessica stuffed the files back in her briefcase and walked back to her bedroom. She opened the door quietly. He was lying facedown on her bed, having taken the time only to remove his jacket, holster and shoes.

She walked in and bent over him to kiss the corner of his mouth. He sighed and his eyelids fluttered briefly. She waited a moment, then kissed him again. This time he rolled over, and before she could move away he'd tumbled her into the bed with him.

"Didn't anyone ever tell you to let sleeping cops lie?" he muttered thickly as he pinned her beneath him.

"I'll try to remember that next time." She smiled.

"You have a nice smile," he said, kissing the tilted corners of her mouth. "In fact, you have a lot of nice things."

He trailed his mouth down across her neck into the V of her open shirt, dipping his tongue into the soft crevice between her breasts.

"Casey, you have to go to work, remember?" she said breathlessly.

"Uh-huh." He unbuttoned another button and buried his face in the soft pillows of her breasts for a moment, then heaved a noisy sigh.

"A cop's work is never done."

"My, but you're full of witticisms tonight," she said with a laugh.

He gave her another kiss, then reluctantly hauled himself up from the bed. "When is Matthews going to be finished?"

"Will you stop worrying about him? He'll be finished in a few days."

"You didn't give him a key, did you?"

"No, of course not. He only comes when I'm here."

"I don't like him."

"You've said that before. Would you like some coffee before you go?"

He put on his shoes, then strapped on the holster. "Yeah. That might keep me going for another couple of hours."

"What do you have to do now?"

"I'm trying to track down some people who can confirm Johnson's alibi, and also see what else I can turn up about him."

His beeper went off again just as she was pouring the coffee. "What now?" she asked after he'd made the call.

"My snitch is out of surgery and refuses to talk to anyone but me. So I'm off to the hospital first. I hate hospitals."

"They're a whole lot safer than the streets of the District," she observed.

"The first time I was ever in a hospital was when Dad died. That's why I hate them."

She wrapped her arms around him and pressed against his chest, taking care to avoid the gun. "I'm sorry. Be careful."

"Don't worry, I will be. I've got plans, lady." He gave her a quick, hard kiss and was gone.

Later, as she lay in the bed he'd vacated, Jessica turned her face into the pillow and caught a faint scent of him. For the first time, she began to worry about him. It was so easy to believe he was indestructible—but she knew he wasn't.

And after she'd gone to sleep, the nightmare came again.

THE ENVELOPE LAY ON TOP of the small pile of mail that had been dropped through the slot. Jessica set down her briefcase and bent to stare at it, unwilling as yet to touch it. There was a city postmark and no return address. Her name and address were printed in the same careful block letters.

A chill swept through her as she finally picked it up, then carefully slit it open with the antique letter opener she kept on the foyer table. It was exactly like the previous letter: a single sheet of typing paper with letters cut from a newspaper and glued to the page. "JESSICA + CASEY ="

She started to crumple the paper, then stopped and instead carried it with her as she went into the living room and sat down. For the first time she began to wonder seriously if she'd been wrong. What if it *wasn't* Robert Collins?

She stared at the enigmatic message. What did it mean? She thought about the other one. *You are the one.* Did it mean that the sender had some sort of obsession with her and was angry about her relationship with Casey? But how could he know about that?

She shivered as she imagined someone stalking her, perhaps hiding outside her house and seeing Casey. She recalled that night when she thought she'd seen someone out there.

Jessica knew that she could no longer afford to ignore this. The only question in her mind now was what she should do about it. She left the letter on a table and went back to her bedroom to change as she considered her options.

Her gaze fell on the photo she'd clipped from the newspaper. It was a rather good picture of both Casey and her, with their names in the caption beneath it. Somehow the photographer had found out who she was.

And then she realized that this was how Robert could have found out about them. The picture had appeared two days ago, just the right amount of time for him, or anyone else, to have sent the message.

She knew she should talk to Casey about this, especially now that he had been brought into it. But she was still reluctant to do so for several reasons. First of all, she knew he'd insist that she move in with him until the matter was resolved, and secondly, he would then see to it that the police began a serious search for Robert Collins. He'd probably drag Joel in for questioning, as well.

She weighed the consequences of various courses of action as she ate dinner, then decided that she'd try to find Robert herself. If she confronted him, she was convinced that she could find out if he'd sent the letters. She was a lawyer, after all, and getting the truth out of people was a part of her job.

And if she succeeded in finding him, she could surely persuade him of her concern for him and see to it that he got some help. As things stood now, if the police found him, he'd be put in jail, and as Susan and Todd had said, that would be the worst possible place for him.

JOEL SHOWED UP a short time later to finish the bookcases. She spent an hour preparing for court the next day, then joined him in her new library.

"Will I be in your way if I start to unpack some of my books?" she asked. "I can hardly wait to set up my library again."

He shook his head. "No problem. I'll be finished in another half hour, but you'd better wait a couple of days before you put books on this section, just to make sure the finish is dry."

She smiled happily as she looked at the handsome bookcases. "You've done a great job, Joel. And the way you put them together is perfect." He'd done it completely without nails, using dowels so that each bookcase could be disassembled easily.

"How's your job coming?" she asked as she began to arrange the books.

"Okay. They like my work."

"You said you did some folksinging, too. Are you going to look for work here?"

"Maybe, but people around here seem to go in more for country."

They talked about folk music as they worked. She told him about her parents. "They died when I was three."

"Yeah? What happened to them?"

"They were killed in an auto accident. Then I went to live with my grandparents in Philadelphia. Did you ever live in a commune?"

"Sure, a couple of them. Where'd they live?"

"In Oregon, some place not far from Eugene."

"I was in Oregon once, but not in a commune. The problem with communes was that they usually wanted you to make a commitment, you know what I mean? And I just wasn't into that."

He finished his work and she offered him something to eat. So they sat in her kitchen and talked about the sixties for several hours. By the time he finally left, Jessica was feeling closer to her parents than she'd ever felt before. Joel had made that time come alive as no article or book she'd read had ever done.

She insisted that he take a check now for the balance she owed him, and he promised to get the ladder to her within the next week. She stood in the doorway and watched him drive away, feeling very grateful to him for having given her a glimpse into her parents' world.

By WORKING VERY HARD all the next day she managed to get away from the office an hour early, taking home with her the work she needed to complete for the following morning. It was time to start searching for Robert Collins.

She found the address he'd given, a large, shabby house on the edge of the District, on a street where half the buildings were either in the process of being torn down or were boarded up and abandoned.

There was a row of mailboxes just inside the front door, but she didn't find his name listed. That probably meant nothing, though, since several boxes had no name on them. She was about to start knocking on doors when an obese, unkempt woman appeared in the hallway next to the staircase.

"You lookin' for someone?" the woman asked in a querulous tone. Alcohol fumes wafted in Jessica's direction as she spoke.

"Yes. I'm looking for Robert Collins. Does he live here?"

"Not anymore he don't," the woman said belligerently. "I got no time for fruitcakes like him."

"When did he leave?"

She shrugged. "Couple days ago, right before the cops come lookin' for him."

Jessica was rather surprised that they'd acted so quickly. "Did he leave a forwarding address?"

The woman shook her head. "I didn't ask for none. All I cared about was gettin' him out of here. He was botherin' my other tenants."

Jessica considered it highly likely that her other tenants weren't much better, but refrained from pointing that out to the woman. "Do you have any idea where I might find him? It's rather important."

"You a social worker or somethin'? 'Cause that's sure what he needs. He oughtta be put away before he hurts somebody."

"No, I'm a lawyer. But I *do* want to help him. Are you saying that he was threatening people here?"

"Yeah. Like I told the cops, he gave us all the creeps. He was always goin' up to someone and pointing to them, sticking his finger right in their faces and sayin' they were 'one of them.' ''

"But you have no idea where he might have gone?"

The woman shook her head. It was clear that she didn't care, either.

Jessica suddenly remembered what Robert had said about a park and liking to watch the birds. "Is there a park around here anywhere?"

"Griffin Park's just a couple of blocks, but I'd be careful goin' in there, if I was you. Nothin' but druggies."

She got directions from the woman and drove to the park, although when she saw it she decided that "park" was a rather glorified description. And she didn't see a bird anywhere, not even a pigeon. No doubt they had too much sense to come to a place like this. From where she sat in her car she could see the entire park. There were only a few struggling trees and a lot of asphalt and some battered concrete-and-wood benches, most of them with slats missing. The only people there were some kids shooting baskets through a netless rim.

So she went home, feeling frustrated but not yet ready to give up. She believed that Robert had been telling her the truth about liking to watch birds, so he must have gone to another park. The only question was which one.

She got out her map of the city and began to check for other parks in that general area. Henderson Park wasn't all that far away. She recalled having seen it as she was driving by. It was fairly large and full of trees.

She turned over the map and found a brief description of the city's attractions on the other side. Henderson Park was mentioned—and so was the fact that it boasted an aviary.

"That's it!" she exclaimed happily. She'd been thinking of wild birds, but now she was sure that he must have been referring to the aviary.

THE NEXT DAY, when her eleven-o'clock appointment failed to show up, Jessica set out for Henderson Park. The park was something of a dividing line between the District and a recently gentrified neighborhood that bordered the downtown area.

She found the aviary without difficulty. It wasn't large, but it was very attractive, designed to look like a gigantic Victorian bird cage. Many people were walking along its perimeters, staring at the colorful, chattering birds. But Robert wasn't there.

She knew she couldn't continue to come here every day unless she could be certain that she had the right place. After looking over the crowds, she walked over to two women with babies in strollers, who were seated on a nearby bench.

"Excuse me," she said when she reached them. "Do you come here often? I'm trying to find someone and I think he might come here."

"We're here almost every day," one woman told her, then asked who she was looking for.

Jessica described Robert and the two women exchanged glances, then nodded.

"He hasn't been here for the past few days, thank heavens. Are you a psychologist?"

Jessica smiled. The question proved that they'd seen him, all right. She explained that she was his attorney and was trying to find him so she could get some help for him.

"He certainly needs it," one woman said, shaking her head. "Most of the time he's harmless enough. He just walks around mumbling to himself and picking up newspapers that people leave behind. But a couple of times he's started to shout and point fingers at people. The police have chased him out several times, but he always comes back."

Jessica didn't miss the reference to newspapers. "What does he do with the newspapers he collects?"

"As far as I know, he takes them with him. I've never seen him read them."

Jessica gave them each her card and asked them to call her if they saw him in the park again. They assured her that they would. There was a pay phone not far away.

BUT TWO DAYS PASSED and Jessica heard nothing from the women. She stopped by the park both days, but without success. She hadn't seen Casey, but he'd called several times, and with each call she felt guiltier and guiltier for not telling him about the calls and letters.

That evening she was returning after dark from a shopping trip, and had just started to turn into her driveway when she saw someone emerge from the bushes on the far side of the house and take off down the street.

Deciding that she was safe enough in her car, Jessica backed out again and started to follow him, searching the yards of neighboring houses as she drove along slowly. But she saw no one. All the houses had trees and large shrubs, and of course there was the park behind them. The fence was fairly high, but anyone with minimal athletic ability could get over it.

She drove back home, parking her car this time on the street, which was closer to her door than the garage in the rear, and better lit, as well. She hadn't been really frightened before, but it caught up with her now.

Could it have been Robert Collins? She tried to recall the quick glimpse she'd gotten of the shadowy figure. He had seemed to be about Robert's height and build, she thought, but then, so were thousands of other men.

After sitting there for a few moments, peering out into the darkness, she opened the car door, key already in hand, and made a dash for her front door, leaving her packages in the car.

Then she called the couple who lived upstairs and told them about the prowler. They hadn't seen or heard anything, and they both came down to go out to the car with her and then walk her back to the house after she'd put the car into the garage. Jessica then called the police and reported the incident.

The two officers who showed up about a half hour later checked outside and through the neighborhood, but found nothing. She hadn't expected them to, and wouldn't have bothered to call them if her neighbors hadn't insisted. They all agreed that it was time to insist upon better exterior lighting.

Jessica spent the rest of the evening peeking out through the drapes, and when Casey called she was greatly tempted to ask if she could stay at his house. But then she'd have to explain it all, and she wasn't yet ready to do that.

One more day, she told herself. She'd make one more attempt to find Robert Collins at the park, and if that failed, she'd tell Casey everything.

THE NEXT MORNING, as she listened to the radio news on her way to work, Jessica learned that there'd been a mass escape from city jail early the previous evening. One of the escapees was the man who'd been arrested for the recent knife attack, Millie's client. Casey still hadn't confirmed his alibi for the times of the killings, but he remained convinced that the man wasn't the serial killer.

Jessica thought about the way he'd looked at her that day, and then thought about the prowler last night. The escape had happened just after dinner, the result of an old and overcrowded facility and what appeared to have been some lax security procedures. So he'd been out long enough to have found his way to her home, but only if he'd already known where she lived.

But what about the letters? He could have written the first one, but she realized now that he couldn't have sent the second one because he would have already been in jail, and both incoming and outgoing mail would be read first.

I'm getting paranoid, she told herself disgustedly. If this keeps up, I'll soon be as bad as poor Robert.

She *had* to find Robert Collins soon, and if she couldn't, she had to tell Casey.

Chapter Six

It was well past the normal lunch hour by the time Jessica was able to get to the park the next day. Robert Collins wasn't at the aviary, so she began to stroll around the park, wondering just what she could say to him if she did succeed in finding him. She had the two letters with her, but she couldn't see herself waving them in front of his nose and demanding that he own up to them. She'd learned enough from Susan to know that she had to avoid doing or saying anything that might seem threatening to him. That would only drive him farther into the tangled darkness of irrationality.

She knew that she was out of her depth here. And she knew, too, that she was doing just what Mac had lectured her against doing: becoming emotionally involved with her clients. But there was enough of a parallel between Robert's waking nightmares and her own dark dreams to call forth a deep sympathy for the man. And she just could not help seeing those calls and letters—and perhaps his visit to her home—as a cry for help.

She stayed in the park for nearly an hour, finally buying a hot dog and soda from a vendor and sitting on a bench that gave her a clear view of the aviary. But Robert Collins did not appear.

She returned to her car, knowing that the limits she'd set for herself had run out. There was no other way she could think of to find him. She knew that he had done construction work in the past, but a call to union headquarters had proved fruitless, and in any event, it was highly unlikely that he could find work anywhere, given his present condition.

She drove reluctantly back to the city center. She didn't yet rate a parking space in the small lot behind the courthouse, so she drove to the city garage, then started across Center Park to the plaza.

Her footsteps dragged. Now that she knew she had to tell Casey, she was finding it very difficult, impossible, really, to justify not having told him before.

She knew exactly what the problem was. She didn't want to lean on Casey, to become dependent upon him. From the beginning she had always been conscious of the need to establish her independence from him, rather than to let herself be overwhelmed by his powerful presence. And it did no good at all to tell herself that he was a cop, after all, and this was a criminal matter. Already she had unwittingly drawn him into the dark secret of her nightmares, and she thought that she was even beginning to regret that.

When she emerged from the park she was directly across from police headquarters and she saw Casey jogging up the steps into the building. Reluctant but determined, she followed him.

By the time Jessica entered police headquarters, Casey was nowhere to be seen. She identified herself to the officer at the desk and said that she had to see him and knew he'd just come in.

"Yeah, he did," the veteran cop said. "He's probably down in his office by now. You remember the way?"

"I think so."

He gave her directions and she made her way through the noisy maze of offices and squad rooms, wondering if it could really have been less than a month since she'd come here to meet him for the first time. It seemed to her now that there couldn't have been a time in her life when she hadn't known him.

He was leaning far back in his old swivel chair, his feet propped up on his desk as he listened to messages replaying on his answering machine. Then suddenly he turned her way.

Neither of them spoke for a moment as their eyes met and held and tension gathered its invisible threads. But the tension was different this time, a tension born of shared memories and unspoken promises.

"Déjà vu all over again," he said, smiling and dropping his feet to the floor. "Have a seat."

He gestured to the broken chair and they both laughed. But perhaps he detected the slightly false note in her laughter, because he sobered quickly and stared hard at her.

"What's wrong?" he asked sharply, getting up and motioning her into his chair. As before, he perched on the edge of his desk, but this time his closeness felt comforting.

She told him the whole story. To his credit, he didn't show any anger over her failure to tell him before. It made her wonder if perhaps he understood her better than she understood herself, a thought that did little for her peace of mind at the moment.

"Susan and Todd have some doubts that Robert could have sent the letters," she finished. "But I think it's him. It must be."

"I doubt it," he stated succinctly. "The picture you're drawing is of someone too mentally disorganized to have carried it off."

She looked at him in surprise. "How do you know that?"

He shrugged. "I took some courses in abnormal psych a couple of years ago. Cops deal with just about every abnormality there is."

"But I don't see who else it could be," she protested, then put up a hand to ward off his next words. "Look, I know you're obsessed with the serial killer right now, but it isn't him."

"How do you know? Have you decided that you're invulnerable?" He looked up from the letters she'd given him.

"No, of course not. But the papers said there was no evidence that he had contacted his victims first."

"That's true, but it's also true that they often do just that. It's part of their mind games, to make themselves feel powerful."

He frowned as he stared at the two letters. "Sometimes these guys have an ideal in mind. She could be someone he once wanted who rejected him, or maybe even someone who reminds him of his mother. That other serial killer I told you about went after little girls with dark, curly hair because that's what his sister had. And it could be that you come very close to that ideal.

"Then add to that the fact that he sees you with a cop who's out to get him. So now he's got two reasons to go after you."

She listened but didn't really hear him, because she didn't believe that the serial killer could have targeted *her*. "Casey, I didn't come here to talk about your serial killer. I came because I want to find Robert Collins and see that he gets some help."

"Okay, who's the judge and when was the hearing?"

She told him and he picked up the phone. While he talked to various people, she tried to consider the possibility that she could be the target of a serial killer. But it just seemed too bizarre. The killer seemed unreal, while Robert Collins was very real indeed.

"Okay, it's done. You were right. No one has spent much time looking for him. But we will now. Lieutenant Harris will be getting in touch with you this afternoon to get any information you have. And Lieutenant Casimiricz will be at your house at seven o'clock this evening. Be packed and waiting."

She smiled. "Am I being taken into protective custody?"

"Definitely. And don't try to give me any grief about it."

"I won't, but I still don't think it's a good idea."

"Jessie, dammit, haven't I proved that I'm not going to pressure you into sleeping with me?"

She stared at him, rather surprised at the seriousness of his tone. It made her wonder for a moment if he somehow knew *all* her secrets. She got up from the chair and kissed his cheek.

"I know that and I appreciate it." Then she glanced at her watch. "I have to go back to the office."

He surprised her again by not taking her into his arms. It certainly wasn't out of a lack of interest. She had only to look into his eyes to see that.

He walked her back to the front desk. As they passed through the squad room, Jessica heard someone begin to whistle "Here Comes the Bride." Casey either didn't hear it or chose to ignore it, but as she hurried across the plaza to her office, that taunt stayed with her.

Casey put up with the good-natured teasing for a couple of minutes, then retreated to his basement office. He'd been getting a lot of grief ever since that damned picture had appeared in the paper. Someone had cut it out and posted it on the bulletin board by the coffee machine, with a note beneath it saying that a collection was being taken up for a wedding present.

He'd laughed it off with his usual pungent remarks about marriage, but this time his words had a slightly hollow sound to them. He just hadn't seen himself as the marrying kind. He'd thought his life was pretty good as it was. Now he wondered. It seemed like something had been sneaking up on him ever since Jessica Aylesworth had walked into his life.

He felt as if he was picking his way across an emotional minefield, expecting the whole thing to blow up in his face at any minute. He congratulated himself on having avoided that explosion when she'd told him about the phone calls and letters and that prowler.

He forced his thoughts to the issue at hand. He hoped they could find Collins quickly, and he sure as hell hoped that Jessie was right about his being the one who was harassing her. He realized with some chagrin that he couldn't trust his own instincts in this.

SHE AWOKE WITH the familiar shouts and screams echoing through her head, and the equally familiar clamminess brought on by her sweating. Through the pounding of her heart she listened for the sound of his footsteps. But all was silent in the big house. Perhaps she hadn't really screamed this time. Or if she had, it hadn't been loud enough to awaken him on the far side of the house.

This could not go on. The nightmares were coming nearly every night now, depriving her of her sleep and leaving her emotionally drained and tired.

It was a long time before she got back to sleep, but by the time she did, she'd reached a decision.

"Casey, my grandmother's been taken to the hospital and I'm going home for a few days. I don't think it's serious, but I need to be there."

Jessica held her breath, hoping he wasn't going to question her too closely or ask for her grandmother's phone number. She'd decided that lying to him over the phone would be much easier than lying to him in person.

"I'll certainly be back by Monday," she went on. "I have several trials next week."

"I'm sorry about your grandmother, honey," he said, "but it's probably not a bad idea for you to disappear for a while."

They hung up and she breathed a sigh of relief. He'd seemed distracted and she'd heard voices in the background. No doubt he was glad to have her out of the way for a while.

She had decided that whatever truth awaited her in Oregon, it just could not be worse than her nightmares or her waking fears that were undoubtedly feeding those nightmares. And she was more and more convinced that this was something she had to do herself. It was enough to know that she would have Casey waiting here for her when she returned.

She went to Mac's office and gave him the same story she'd given Casey, because it was easier to lie than to explain the whole tangled story. Then she went home to pack, taking with her as much work as she could. She even stopped to buy a laptop so she could tap into the legal data bank.

Just before she left for the airport she called Susan and told her the truth, asking her not to let Casey know. Fortunately, Susan was between clients and couldn't demand too many details, but Jessica promised to call her later from Oregon.

She wished that she'd been able to reach Joel, but she didn't have a number for him. He hadn't yet contacted her about the ladder, but he might well do so in her absence. She'd have to check her machine by remote. Maybe he'd leave a number then.

An hour later she was on her way to a journey back in time.

IT WAS NEARLY MIDNIGHT when Jessica finally reached the town of Hollowell. Finding a motel wasn't likely to be a problem. Both of them had Vacancy signs. So instead of checking in, she followed the signs to the local hospital.

She drove slowly through the nearly empty parking lot, staring at her birthplace. It was an old brick building, three stories high, with a newer wing that had almost certainly been added since her birth.

It felt weird to think that she had come into being in this place. She tried to imagine her parents there, but found that she could no longer imagine her father. The image she'd created years ago had vanished.

She drove back to the better of the two motels and woke up a napping desk clerk whose look suggested that no normal person would show up at a motel at this hour of the night, which was probably true in this isolated community.

JESSICA AWOKE the next morning, surprised that she'd slept the night through. Somehow she'd thought that the nightmares might be even worse here, and the fact that she hadn't had one seemed more ominous than reassuring.

She got out of bed and looked at the list she'd drawn up on the flight. Then, after showering and dressing, she got down to the first order of business. Fortunately, her grandmother was at home.

"I'm in Oregon, Gran," she said after exchanging greetings. "I arrived late last night and I've already seen the hospital where I was born."

A long silence greeted her announcement. Then her grandmother sighed heavily. "I just don't understand why you'd go there, dear."

"I need some answers, Gran. My nightmares have come back."

"I'm sorry to hear that, Jessica, but those nightmares have nothing to do with the accident."

Jessica resisted the temptation to call her a liar, which wasn't easy. At times like this, Jessica had to bite her tongue and try to remind herself that her grandmother undoubtedly had her best interests at heart.

"Gran, I can understand that you might have wanted to . . . protect me, but I'm not a child anymore, and I need to know the truth."

"I told you everything I know years ago, Jessica."

No, you didn't, Jessica screamed silently, even though she wanted very much to believe her.

She wasn't really disappointed, since she'd expected nothing from her grandmother. She wasn't about to admit that she'd been lying all these years unless she was confronted with irrefutable facts—facts that Jessica intended to have before this day was over.

After breakfast her first stop was the hospital again. No address had been given for her parents on the birth certificate itself, but she was hoping that the hospital could provide one. Unfortunately, they couldn't.

"We just don't keep patient records that far back," the woman explained. "Especially when there's been no recent patient activity. We keep them longer now that we're computerized, but we didn't have computers then."

The woman appeared to be about Jessica's age, so it didn't seem likely that she'd know about any communes in the area that long ago. But she asked, anyway.

The woman frowned. "I remember that there were several in the area back then, but they're all gone, except for one. They raise organic vegetables now. It's a nice place."

Jessica got directions and thanked the woman, then headed toward her next stop: the town's newspaper. But once again her search was frustrated. There had once been a local daily newspaper, but it had folded more than ten years earlier and the current weekly had none of their records.

The small-town library was right next door and she decided to try there, in the tentative hope that they might have old newspapers on file; but they didn't. The librarian told her that they always destroyed the newspapers as soon as they began to deteriorate.

She got back into her car and drove the few blocks to the local police station, wondering how good they were at keeping records. She really hadn't expected to have such a difficult time resurrecting the past.

The middle-aged woman at the desk listened to her story and shook her head. "I don't think we'd keep auto accident records that long, but the chief was on the force back then. Let me see if he has time to speak with you."

While the woman called him, Jessica wandered over to the big window that overlooked the downtown from its slightly elevated site. What a sad little town, she thought. She wasn't sure what she'd expected her birthplace to be, but she knew she hadn't anticipated this. Perhaps it had been different then.

Beyond the town, however, dark, fir-covered mountains rose to an impressive height. Timber, she guessed, must be the mainstay of the local economy. She'd seen the hideous scars of clear-cutting on her way here, and recalled several sawmills, as well.

"I'm sorry," the woman said, drawing her out of her reverie. "The chief won't be able to see you today. He's really tied up."

Jessica did her best to contain her disappointment. "Could I make an appointment to see him tomorrow, then?"

"No, he doesn't make appointments, but you could try dropping by about this time."

She returned to her rental car, wondering what progress Casey would have made by now. He couldn't have conjured up records that no longer existed, but she was willing to bet that the chief would have found the time to see him today.

Thoughts of Casey brought a sharp pang of loneliness to her. She felt so very far away from him, and so irrationally uncertain that he would be there when she returned. But of course he would be. It was just that she was uncertain about everything right now.

She got out the directions to the commune that the woman at the hospital had given her, hoping against hope that the one remaining commune would be the one where she'd once lived.

She found it without difficulty, aided by several attractive signs that pointed the way to Nature Garden Farm. It was a lovely spot, nestled in a small valley about five miles from town. The entrance was marked by a large, colorful sign and two huge wooden tubs filled with bright marigolds.

She drove up the long driveway, moving very slowly as chickens scattered every which way. No doubt these were the "free-range" egg producers announced on the sign.

No one was in sight as she parked and got out of the car. There was a big old white frame farmhouse and numerous other buildings, all of them freshly painted and in good repair.

She looked around, waiting in vain for some feeling of familiarity. By the time a young woman came out of the barn, she was preparing herself for yet another disappointment. Surely if this place had once been her home, she would feel it.

The woman appeared to be slightly younger than Jessica herself. She wore faded jeans and a T-shirt emblazoned with the farm's logo, and she had a healthy glow about her that Jessica thought must be a very good advertisement for the farm's products. Her name was Stacey.

After introducing herself, Jessica explained the purpose of her visit. "I was told in town that there used to be several communes in the area, but that this is the only one left. So I came here hoping that this might be the one." She shrugged ruefully. "But nothing looks familiar to me."

Stacey smiled. "This isn't really a commune anymore, although the locals keep thinking it is. My husband and I own it, together with his brother and wife. We moved down here from Portland about four years ago. I was about to take a break. Would you like some ice tea?"

Jessica thanked her and they were soon settled on the front porch with tall glasses of delicious sun tea. She asked how they were doing with their business.

"We're doing fairly well. We don't sell much locally. Our big market is in Eugene. We've been selling through a store there, but we're thinking about opening up our own place." Stacey leaned back in the big old rocker and propped her feet on the porch railing.

"This *was* a commune back in the sixties and early seventies, but I don't really know anything about its history. The place had been empty for nearly seven years when we bought it. You probably noticed that this isn't exactly a booming real estate market."

Jessica laughed. "It's beautiful country, though."

"Oh, it is. The land is gorgeous. The problem is what's been done to it. People around here seem to use the woods for one of two purposes. Either they cut down the trees or they dump old cars and refrigerators in it."

"It's the same in a lot of rural areas," Jessica said, thinking about some parts of Pennsylvania.

"I know there were a couple of other communes around here. My sister-in-law was born here and she told me about them. One of them isn't far—just down the road a piece, as we say in these parts. Carole should be back any minute. She just went into town. Maybe she can help you. It must be really strange not to know anything about the first part of your life."

"It is," Jessica assured her. "Especially since I think my grandmother might be lying to me."

"Really?"

Jessica nodded and then told her about the nightmares that had finally driven her to come out here. Stacey shivered.

"That's really weird. I don't blame you for wanting to find out the truth."

At that moment a dusty Volvo wagon came up the driveway, and Jessica was introduced to a woman who appeared to be in her early twenties.

"Stacey told me that you grew up around here," Jessica said hopefully.

"Well, I was born here, but we moved away when I was only four," Carole told her. "That was nineteen years ago."

Jessica repeated her story, including the nightmare. Carole frowned and stared off into the distance for a while. Then she shrugged.

"I don't know. For a minute there, I started to remember something—something I heard about, I think. But it was so long ago. It's really just a vague memory about one of the communes—that something happened there. It's just down the road."

"I told her about that one," Stacey put in. "And now that you mention it, I think you told me once that something had happened there, but you didn't remember what it was."

"You know who you really should talk to?" Carole said. "Ed Waters. He's the police chief and I'm pretty sure he would have been on the force back then. He's lived here all his life."

Jessica told them that she'd stopped to see him and planned to go back. "But you think it was something connected with the commune itself?" she asked, thinking about her nightmare and that briefly glimpsed scene in what must have been a kitchen.

"I don't know. Memory is such a funny thing for a kid that age. I can show you the place, if you like. It's been empty for years and it's in really bad shape. But maybe seeing it will bring back some memories for you."

So the three of them piled into Carole's station wagon. Fifteen minutes and two turns later, they were driving up a deeply rutted, weed-choked lane with thick forests on both sides. Then they emerged into open fields. Ahead of them lay ramshackle, weathered gray buildings, some of them almost completely collapsed. Carole pulled to a stop in front of a tumbledown barn and they all got out.

Jessica stared at the place, trying to envision it before time and neglect had destroyed it. What was memory and what was a wish for a memory? For a moment it seemed vaguely familiar, but she couldn't be sure. She walked across the weedy gravel to a big old farmhouse that had partially caved in where a long-dead tree had fallen on it. She saw that the rear of the house was largely intact, although some windows were broken.

The back door was locked, so she went up to a window, stepping carefully around shards of glass. "I'd like to get inside," she told her companions. "Is there something we can use to break out the rest of this glass?"

They looked around and finally found a three-foot length of wood that might have been part of a porch railing. Jessica used it to poke out the rest of the glass, then hoisted herself up and over the windowsill. The other two followed.

"This must have been the dining room," she said, staring at the faded and water-spotted wallpaper and warped wainscoting.

She turned toward the doorway that led into the kitchen. The floorboards creaked and sagged beneath her feet and Stacey remarked that they'd be lucky if the floor didn't cave in. But

Jessica barely heard her. Her heart was thudding noisily in her chest as she moved toward the kitchen, with her nightmare replaying itself in her head.

But it was just an old kitchen, stripped of its appliances and furnishings. There were old-fashioned wooden cabinets that had once been painted white, and counters covered with an ugly yellow laminated plastic that had held up considerably better than the paint. The filthy floor was a garish yellow-and-white linoleum that was unevenly worn.

She stood there in the doorway and closed her eyes for a moment, trying to recapture that brief image from her nightmare. Then she opened her eyes again and shuddered.

The counters and cabinets seemed much like her nightmare, but the yellow counter was wrong. She walked over to examine it more closely. Surely it couldn't be twenty-five years old. Beneath the heavy layer of dirt it seemed to be in very good condition.

"Do you know when this place was last occupied?" she asked, turning to her two companions, who were watching her curiously.

Carole shook her head. "No one's lived here since we moved here, but I'm sure it's been empty much longer than that."

Jessica backed off to the doorway again and considered the space between it and the counters, the logical place to put a large kitchen table like the one she'd glimpsed in her nightmare.

It seemed to her, as she stood there staring at the room, that if this was where she'd spent those first few years, something should feel familiar to her, if only vaguely. And if something terrible had happened, wasn't it even more likely that she'd feel something? Or had she repressed the memory too completely?

With that possibility nagging at her, she went through the other doorway that led from the kitchen into a hallway. The hallway ran straight to the front door, but the ceiling had collapsed halfway along its length, leaving a gaping hole above and a pile of debris on the floor.

Just before the spot where the hallway became impassable, a door dangled loosely on its one remaining hinge. Without quite knowing why she was doing it, Jessica found herself moving toward the closet. It was big and deep and shadowy, running beneath the staircase. She stared at it and suddenly felt a chill so deep that it seemed to freeze her very bones. For one brief moment the screams from her nightmare seemed to be echoing in the old house.

A terrible, wrenching fear took hold of her, tightening its icy grip until she thought she wouldn't be able to breathe. She stumbled backward as her mind seemed to be on the verge of forcing a waking nightmare on her.

"Jessica?"

She whirled around to see Stacey and Carole standing there, their faces grave with concern. She swallowed hard and managed a smile.

"Sorry. I...I don't know what came over me. I'm fine now."

She wasn't, and she knew they suspected as much. But they were kind enough not to push her for information as they all made their way back out through the broken window.

JESSICA AWOKE TO FIND that she'd slept away the remainder of the afternoon and the early part of the evening. She was hungry and also still suffering from the lingering effects of the headache that had forced her to lie down. She rarely had headaches, but this one had come on swiftly after she'd left the old house.

She got up, showered and dressed, then walked out to the motel office to inquire about dinner. The motel had only a small coffee shop that served breakfast and lunch. The clerk directed her to a place only a few blocks away and she decided to walk.

Only after she had forced herself to eat the unappealing "home-style" food and walked back to the motel did she allow herself to think about those moments in the old house.

Had she overreacted out of a desperate need to find something of her past there? That question hammered at her as she relived the scene. That closet. Why had it produced that incredible fear when the kitchen hadn't? It was a kitchen that she remembered from her nightmare.

Through her mind ran all the stories she'd ever heard of parents locking their children in closets, mixing painfully with Casey's suggestion that her father might have been abusive.

Dear God, she thought. What if I'm about to remember abuse that I've repressed all these years? She knew that happened. And wouldn't that explain why her grandmother had lied to her?

In those moments, in her lonely motel room, Jessica felt as though she was teetering on the brink of a bottomless, dark pit that would surely swallow her if she so much as looked into it. So instead, she reached for the one strong certainty in her life now: Casey.

Suddenly she wanted desperately to talk to him. But when she dialed his home number, all she got was his machine. She hung up without leaving a message and considered trying to reach him through the dispatcher. But she'd almost certainly have to leave a number and wait for his return call, and there was a chance he would then realize that she wasn't in Philadelphia. So she called his home number again and left a short message saying that she would call back the next day. Even his brief impersonal message felt soothing to her now.

Alone, frightened, frustrated in her search for the truth and yet terrified of discovering that truth, Jessica wished that she hadn't been so impulsive, that she'd waited instead until Casey could come here with her. She *needed* Casey.

But that acknowledgment, too, was unsettling. Both her grandparents, her grandfather in particular, had always stressed the importance of self-reliance, of being her own person and making her own decisions. Only after she had grown up did she come to realize that they had probably done this because they believed that her mother had fallen under the influence of her father—an influence that they, of course, considered to be bad. Apparently they had determined not to make the same "mistake" twice.

She didn't want to need Casey, but she was too honest to lie to herself. She wanted him here, wanted that great strength of his, that rock-solid steadiness.

She finally fell asleep, half determined to leave the next day and wait until Casey could accompany her.

Morning didn't exactly bring a lessening of her fears, but it did bring a renewed determination to see this through. So she returned to the police station, only to be told again that the chief wasn't available. The woman at the desk, who'd been quite friendly before, seemed far less so this day. She said she didn't know when the chief might be available. He was so busy, after all.

Jessica walked around town, bought another of Casey's novels in a small bookstore, staring for a long time at his picture inside the back cover, then returned to the police station. This time she noticed a black-and-white patrol car that had Chief stenciled on the side. So he was definitely there.

But the woman still insisted that he had no time to see her and was unlikely to have any time later. This time Jessica noticed that she seemed nervous and refused to meet Jessica's eyes as she spoke. So Jessica left again, now beginning to suspect that the chief might be deliberately avoiding her. But why?

The answer came to her as she found herself, without conscious intent, on the road that led to the old commune. Her grandmother. Gran knew she was here, and if she was determined to keep the truth from her, she might well have called the chief.

So now you've become a conspiracy theorist, she told herself disgustedly. She was going to end up like poor Robert Collins if this kept up.

But there was no denying that the woman at the desk had seemed nervous. And how could a police chief in a dinky little town like this be so busy that he couldn't spare a few minutes to talk to her? She hadn't seen any evidence of a crime wave.

When she reached the old commune she spent nearly an hour walking around the tumbledown buildings before she found the courage to enter the house again. Once again she stood in the kitchen and superimposed that brief image from her nightmare onto the scene before her.

Then, without consciously intending to do so, she sank to her knees in the kitchen doorway, staring at the grimy counters and cabinets from the perspective of a three-year-old. A chill swept over her, prickling her skin and elevating her heartbeat. Those shouts and screams echoed horribly through her mind. But nothing more happened.

She got slowly to her feet, then just as slowly began to walk toward the hallway, fighting a powerful and totally irrational urge to run in that direction.

The deep, dark closet yawned before her. It didn't produce quite the same reaction this time, perhaps because she had anticipated it, or possibly because she was already caught in the cold, relentless grip of fear when she saw it. She hesitated, then stepped into it. But the fear closed in on her, seeming to leak out of the very walls, and she backed out quickly.

As she stumbled back into the hallway, a sudden image of Casey came to her and then was gone just as quickly. She stood there, frowning in confusion. Was her mind reaching out to him in the midst of her fear, or was there more to it than that? She'd nearly forgotten his as-yet-unknown role in all this, even though it was he who had triggered the return of the nightmares and forced her to come here.

She was back in the kitchen, still thinking about Casey, when she heard a male voice calling from outside.

"Hello. Anyone around?"

Jessica stepped into the dining room just in time to see a uniformed police officer put his head through the broken window. It occurred to her that she might be charged with trespassing, although maybe if she was arrested, she would get to see the chief.

"Are you thinking of buying this place?" the young officer asked her from the window. "It doesn't look safe enough to be walking around in there."

She could have lied, but she chose to tell the truth instead. "I think I lived here once, when it was a commune."

"No kidding," he said, gallantly helping her back out through the window. "I heard it was once a commune, but that was a long time ago. You must have been just a little kid."

"I was only three when I left," she acknowledged. "Did you ever hear anything about the place?"

"It's been empty for, oh, at least ten years, maybe longer. Before that, there was this big family living out here—real poor, on welfare, I guess. The county took the kids away for neglect and the parents disappeared not long after that." He frowned. "Seems I can remember the chief saying something once about this place being bad luck."

"But he didn't say why?" she asked.

He shook his head. "No, not that I can recall."

"How did you happen to come up here?" she asked as they started back to their cars. She knew that he couldn't have seen her car from the road. Could the chief have someone following her?

"I spotted your car." He gestured to a hill off to their left. "I was coming down off the ridge. There's a good view of the place from up there, not that there's much to see. I suppose you're trespassing, but I'm not about to run you in. It's dangerous, though. Those floors look like they could cave in at any time."

She promised him that she wouldn't go inside again and he left. After he'd gone, she looked at the hill he'd indicated. She could just barely see the road winding its way around it and over the top. Suddenly she had an urge to see the place from up there as he had, so she got into her car and drove along the narrow, twisting road, climbing steadily through a thick pine forest that blocked her view of the valley below.

Then, just before the road reached the crest of the hill, there was a turnoff at a spot where the hill fell away so sharply that the trees no longer blocked the view. She pulled in to it and got out of the car, her gaze already on the old commune far below her.

All the way up she'd been telling herself that she simply wanted to verify the officer's story. But now that she was here, she wasn't so sure.

Something felt eerily familiar about this spot, and this time she was almost certain that she was reaching for a memory that was just beyond her grasp. But if it *was* a memory, the feelings associated with it were far different from what she'd experienced down there. She felt happy, and for one brief instant could almost hear laughter in the pine-scented air. Then, instead of pine, she smelled lemonade.

She sniffed, but it was gone, as though an errant breeze had brought it to her from somewhere, then snatched it away again.

She'd always loved lemonade—the fresh-squeezed kind, not the store-bought variety. It was her favorite drink as a child, and remained a favorite still.

Was it a memory? She thought about how she'd read somewhere that the sense of smell is the longest lasting of all the senses. And she thought about how the first taste of lemonade every summer produced this strange longing in her. She'd always assumed that it was just because she associated it with the childhood she remembered, but what if it went back even farther than that? What if she had come up here with her parents?

It made sense, she thought. If this was the commune where they had lived, then surely they would have come up here. The view was lovely and the breeze would be refreshing on a hot summer's day. It was indeed a perfect spot for a picnic.

Jessica stayed there for a long time, staring down at the narrow valley and willing the ramshackle place to show itself as it had once been. At one point the image of sunflowers came to her, their huge yellow-and-black heads nodding in the breeze. She wondered if there might be some down there, but decided she wouldn't be able to tell them from the weeds growing all over the place. It was too early for them to be blooming now.

But she thought—felt—that they had indeed once bloomed in profusion down there, standing much higher than the head of a small girl.

Chapter Seven

Casey frowned as he listened to the message on his machine. It was Jessica's friend Susan, and she was worried about Jessie, who had apparently gone to Oregon instead of to Philadelphia. He felt a brief anger at her for lying to him, which was quickly replaced by growing concern.

But it didn't really surprise him that she'd decided to go out there on her own instead of waiting for him. He knew that the return of her nightmares was really gnawing at her, especially since she seemed to think that his appearance in her life had somehow triggered them.

He called Susan, who repeated the story, including the fact that Jessie had asked her not to tell him.

"Maybe I'm overreacting," Susan said. "But I just keep thinking that if she finds out something—something bad, that is—she shouldn't be dealing with it alone. She's a really strong person, but even the strongest people have their breaking points. She promised to call me, but I haven't heard from her and I don't know how to reach her."

"I'll find her," Casey promised after Susan had given him the name of the town. A few minutes later he was talking to the police chief of Hollowell, Oregon, certain that Jessie would have gone there in her quest. He introduced himself, then inquired if Jessica had contacted him.

There was a brief silence on the line, and then the chief asked what his interest was.

"It's, uh, personal, Chief. She means a lot to me. In fact, I'd promised her I'd travel out there with her, but she decided to go on her own. We've got a serial killer on the loose here and I couldn't get away."

"She's here, all right, but I promised her grandmother I'd try to keep the truth from her."

Casey felt a chill. "What truth is that?"

By the time the chief had finished his story, that chill had settled in deep. In fact, Casey was so stunned that he didn't say anything, causing the chief to ask if he was still there.

"I'm here. Listen, Chief, she needs to hear the truth, despite what her grandmother thinks. But I don't want her to face it alone. So what I'd like you to do is to go on avoiding her until I can get there. I'll call you as soon as I make flight arrangements."

After gaining the chief's cooperation, Casey hung up and sat there thinking about what Jessie had told him about her nightmare. There could no longer be any doubt that it wasn't just an ordinary nightmare, but a mercifully edited version of the truth. However, he still couldn't see where his appearance in her life could have had anything to do with it. A piece was missing somewhere.

He knew he was going to catch hell from his own chief for taking off now. There'd been another killing last night, and the mayor and the press were screaming for results.

Casey's career was very important to him. In fact, until this moment he would have said that nothing was more important. But now something was: Jessie.

JESSICA WENT BACK to her car, which she'd parked this time in a municipal lot across the street from the police station. Once again, the chief had been "unavailable," so now she intended to stake out the station and catch him when he came out. His car was parked at the front of the station lot, so she'd have no problem seeing him when he left.

Her need to know the truth had become all-consuming, and she had by now accepted the fact that she'd been lied to all these years. Whether the lie concerned her parents' deaths or something that had happened prior to that, she didn't know, but she was very sure that *something* had been kept from her.

Dread was a tight knot in her stomach as she sat there waiting for the appearance of the man who must surely hold the key to her past. Could it possibly be worse than the horrible scenarios that her mind was now tormenting her with? She doubted that very seriously.

Her thoughts began to drift to Casey. She hadn't called him again because she was afraid that if she actually reached him, she would be unable to continue with her lie, and he didn't need an hysterical female to add to the problems he already had. She decided now that she wouldn't tell him the truth until the killer had been caught and they had some time for themselves.

But how she wished he was here now. She no longer resented her need for him. Did that mean she was in love with him? How could she possibly be in love with a man she'd known for such a short time?

Then an awful thought struck her. What if Casey *was* reminding her of her father, and her father had indeed been abusive? How would that affect her feelings toward him?

She had no further time for reflection, because in the next moment she saw a man in uniform walking across the lot to the chief's car. She gasped. Her eyes saw the chief, but her mind was seeing Casey in a sort of split screen in her head.

The chief was every bit as big as Casey: the same height and the same broad, powerful build. His hair was mostly gray, but still bore traces of black. And allowing for the difference in their ages, his rugged features also reminded her of Casey.

She was so stunned by this revelation that she was still sitting there when he pulled out of the lot. Then she belatedly started her car and tried to follow him. But the exit from the parking lot was onto a side street, and by the time she had maneuvered back onto the main street, his car had vanished.

She drove slowly back to the motel, her mind spinning. There could no longer be any doubt that the chief had played an important role in that forgotten part of her life. Seeing his likeness in Casey had obviously triggered her nightmares.

But what did it all mean? She thought about that strange dual reaction she'd had to Casey when she'd met him: fear followed by warmth and a sense of trust.

She also began to wonder if she might have been wrong about her grandmother having had a hand in his refusal to see her. Was it possible that he was refusing for reasons of his own? What if his role hadn't been benign? Which should she believe, the fear or the trust? As Casey had remarked, the perceptions of a three-year-old can't always be fathomed—or trusted.

By the time she reached the motel Jessica was in the throes of a different kind of fear. What if the chief had something to hide, and her arrival here threatened that secret? Was she in danger?

With this new fear added to her other fears, Jessica walked down the hallway in a daze, opened the door to her room—and screamed.

A huge, dark figure detached itself from the shadows and moved quickly toward her. The chief! Even as the scream left her mouth, she was backing out of the doorway. Then she turned and fled down the hallway. She was halfway down the stairs to the parking lot when she heard him call her name.

"Jessie! It's Casey!"

She slowed down, but didn't stop. Adrenaline was pumping through her veins. Her pulse was pounding in her ears. And she simply could not believe either the words or the familiar voice.

But she paused at the bottom of the stairs, and then she saw him running toward her. She sagged against the railing, but she still didn't truly believe that it was Casey until she was caught within the strong, secure circle of his arms.

"I'm sorry," he murmured against her ear. "I didn't mean to scare you like that."

Jessica just held on to him, saying nothing as she finally accepted the reality of him. And the moment she accepted that, she frowned in confusion. How could he be here? She'd told him she was in Philadelphia.

He saw the question in her eyes before she asked it. "Susan called me. She was worried because she hadn't heard from you.

I took the room next to yours and there's a connecting door with a lousy lock."

"I'm glad you're here," she said, wrapping her arms around him. "Casey, something really strange is going on. The police chief won't see me. He says—"

"He's waiting to see us now," Casey said.

"He is? But...."

Casey took her arm and led her to his rental car. "He wouldn't see you at first because your grandmother called and asked him not to. Then, after I talked to him, he was just waiting for me to get here."

He stopped beside the car and bent to kiss her softly. "Let him explain, Jessie. It's better if you hear it firsthand."

They drove into town in silence. Casey glanced over at her and wondered if the truth would really be any worse than the torment she'd been living with. He could see the results of that in her rigid posture and in the dark circles under her eyes that told of sleepless nights. When he stopped at a light he reached out and squeezed her hand; it felt icy.

His second phone conversation with Chief Waters was troubling him as much as the first one, maybe even more. He was still having trouble believing that the chief could be right, but if he was, then it wasn't over for Jessie yet.

"Did you catch the killer yet?" she asked suddenly, startling him.

"No," he said grimly. "And he got another one two nights ago."

"Another tall blonde?"

Casey nodded, then turned onto a residential street. Several houses down he saw the chief's car parked in a driveway. He pulled in behind it and got out. She didn't move, so he went around to her side and opened the door, then reached in to take her arm.

"Jessie, honey, I'm—"

"What did he tell you?" she demanded, still refusing to get out of the car. "Casey, he could be lying. I've seen him and he's the reason I—" She stopped abruptly as she stared at the house.

Casey turned and saw the man approaching them. Then he turned back to her and smiled. "That answers a couple of questions. He's not lying, Jessie. Give him a chance to explain."

Jessica finally got out of the car. She still didn't trust the chief, but she trusted Casey, and that was enough for now. She watched as the two men shook hands. Up close they still seemed remarkably alike. The chief could have been Casey's father, and when he turned to her, she saw both warmth and sadness in his eyes.

"You were a pretty little girl, Jessica, and you've grown into a beautiful woman," the chief said as they shook hands. "Even prettier than your mother, I think."

She managed to murmur a thank-you as he led them into the house.

"There's a screened porch out back," the chief said. "We'll go out there." Then he called out, "Martha, they're here!"

A small, gray-haired woman appeared in the hallway that led to the kitchen. Her pleasant face broke into a beautiful smile when she saw Jessica, and she put out both hands to her.

"Dear little Jessica. I've thought about you so often over the years. CeeCee has mentioned you, too."

"CeeCee?" Jessica echoed. There was something vaguely familiar about this woman, and Jessica had a sudden, brief image of a little girl with fiery red hair.

"Our daughter," the chief told her. "She's a year older than you. She's living in Seattle now."

"Did she have red hair?" Jessica asked.

Mrs. Waters laughed. "Yes, and she still does. Unfortunately, I don't. So you remember?"

"A little, but I still don't understand." She was looking around the house, wondering if it, too, should be familiar. The chief apparently guessed the direction of her thoughts.

"We weren't living here then."

Mrs. Waters had turned her attention to Casey and was staring at him with unabashed interest. The chief saw her and laughed.

"He kind of caught me by surprise, too." He chuckled.

"It's amazing," Mrs. Waters said. "You could be father and son. I've always heard that everyone has a double somewhere, but I never believed it until now."

The chief turned to Jessica, his expression curious. "Did he seem familiar to you? I understand you met just recently."

Jessica nodded. "Yes, he did, but I didn't understand why until I saw you earlier when you left the station."

He led them out to the big screened porch and Mrs. Waters joined them a moment later, carrying a tray with a pitcher of ice tea and glasses. A small silence descended upon the group after the drinks had been poured, and then Casey spoke to the chief.

"I haven't told her anything, except that I called you."

Chief Waters nodded, then turned to Jessica. "Casey told me that you've been having nightmares. What do you remember?"

"Nothing, really. I've had the same nightmare for as long as I can remember, but all I could ever recall afterward were shouts and . . . screams." She had started off strongly enough, but by the time she finished, her voice was beginning to tremble. She felt as though she was now leaning far out over that abyss, staring into the black hole. She pushed on, struggling to keep her voice neutral.

"The nightmares stopped years ago, but then they started up again right after I met Casey."

She went on to describe what she'd felt at that first meeting. She still didn't know what role the chief had played in her past, but she was now certain that she trusted him.

Chief Waters nodded solemnly, then asked if she remembered anything else.

So she described what she recalled from her more recent dreams: a child's-eye view of a kitchen, perhaps the kitchen in an old house she'd visited that had once been a commune.

"That's the place," the chief confirmed. "Scott told me that he'd found you out there." He explained to Casey that Scott was one of his men.

Then Jessica remembered the closet at the house and told the chief about that. Once again he nodded solemnly, then leaned forward, cradling his glass between his knees.

"I'd like to tell you about something I remember from a couple of months before it happened. It might help.

"I was a rookie patrolman then, and one day in early June I was driving along the road near the commune. It was one of those really perfect days. There were wildflowers blooming in the fields and along the sides of the road. I came around a curve and saw you and your mother in a field, picking bouquets. You were wearing identical dresses, those long things." He shot a glance at his wife. "What were they called, Martha?"

"Granny dresses," she replied.

"Right. Long dresses with flowers all over them. I'd seen you both before in town dressed like that. But I never forgot seeing you that day, standing in a field of flowers.

"Your mother waved and I stopped and got out of the car. We talked for a couple of minutes, and then you handed me the little bouquet you had picked. You were both so happy."

He smiled at her. "I just wanted you to hear that first."

In the small silence that followed, Jessica found herself imagining the scene. She knew it wasn't truly a memory, but it felt like one, so she clung to it as that abyss beckoned.

"Two months later, August 12, I was out on patrol in that same area. The dispatcher called and said he'd just gotten a call from a woman who was hysterical and he couldn't make any sense out of what she said, except that she was calling from Freedom. That was the name of the commune.

"When I arrived, a woman I'd seen a few times before was sitting in the driveway rocking back and forth and crying. She was hysterical and she had some blood on her, so it took me a few minutes to figure out that the blood wasn't hers. I ran inside the house and found them in the kitchen. There was so damned much blood. I'd never seen that much blood before."

He paused and shook his head, seemingly oblivious to his audience at this point. Jessica sat there, now engulfed in that blackness. But she still felt Casey's arm around her shoulders and his big, hard body next to hers.

"M-my parents," she said in a dull tone.

"Yes. I recognized them right away. They were both beyond help, but I thought immediately about you. I remembered your name, so I called it a couple of times, and then I ran back outside to radio for help.

"After that I managed to calm the woman enough to ask where you were. She said you'd been there with your parents. Later I found out that the rest of the people had gone to a concert in Eugene. Your folks had stayed behind because your mother wasn't feeling well. The woman who found you had just returned from a visit with her family.

"The hardest thing I ever had to do was to go back inside that house. I was sure I was going to find you in there, dead like them. But I searched the house and there was no sign of you. By that time the chief and the others had arrived.

"Then I remembered all the times I played hide-and-seek with CeeCee, and how kids like to hide under beds and in closets, and I started to search for you again. I found you in that big closet, curled up behind all the clothes. You had blood on your dress, but it wasn't yours."

Jessica drew in a sharp breath and the chief stopped. The memory flashed through her mind and was gone: the dark closet, the door opening, someone big standing there, her view of him partially obscured by the clothes. And this time she knew it was a true memory and that it explained that sense of déjà vu she'd had the night Casey had come to her room at his cabin after she had screamed. She turned to Casey.

"That night at your cabin, when you came to my room after I woke up from the nightmare...."

She suddenly couldn't finish, but he nodded his understanding. The darkness was swarming over her again, but she tried to concentrate on the chief's words as he resumed his story.

"I took you to the hospital right away, and by the time I carried you into the emergency room you were holding on to me as tight as you could and wouldn't let go. We had to pry you loose so the doctor could check you. After we were sure you were unhurt, the county children's services people were called. But I talked them into letting me take you home, and you stayed with us until your grandparents came for you three days later. They were in Europe at the time.

"By then you were doing better, but you wouldn't talk about it. The chief brought in a psychologist to question you, but he said it was shock-induced amnesia, and you might never remember what happened.

"And in the end, we got enough information from the others at the commune to be pretty sure what had happened. We all decided that it would be best not to question you anymore. Not remembering seemed to be the best thing for you.

"I kept in touch with your grandmother for a while, and she said you were doing fine. She never mentioned any nightmares until she called me a couple of days ago. She wanted me to keep up the lie that your parents had died in an auto accident, and I promised her I'd do that. But then, when I talked to Casey, I realized that you needed to know the truth."

Jessica nodded. Her brain wasn't really working very well, but she realized that the chief hadn't yet told her who'd killed her parents and why he'd done such a thing. She wondered if she really wanted to know. It should matter if he'd been brought to justice, and she knew that at some point she would want to know that, but right now she wasn't sure how much more she could take. She felt almost numb—a blessed numbness at the moment, even though she knew it wouldn't last.

"Did you catch the killer?" she asked, the words coming out despite her uncertainty.

The chief shook his head. "We were pretty sure we knew who did it, but we never found him. His name was Anthony Bensen. According to the people at the commune, he'd shown up there about two months before it happened. They took him in, but apparently he caused trouble right from the beginning because he got obsessed with your mother. Most of them thought he was at least half-crazy, so they threw him out. They thought he'd left the area, but someone in town saw him on the morning of the day your parents were killed.

"They figured he came back to try to persuade your mother to leave your father, because that's what he'd been trying to do before they threw him out. And when she wouldn't do it, he killed them both."

The chief picked up a manila folder from a nearby table. "I brought the whole file home with me. There's a picture of him in it, but it's not a very good one."

He opened the file and withdrew a photo, then handed it across to her. Casey leaned over to look at it, too.

The photo showed a group of people gathered around a long picnic table. Jessica's gaze went automatically to the woman in the very center of the group shot: her mother. And then she found herself staring for the first time at a picture of her father. He was sitting next to her mother, his arm around her as they both laughed into the camera's eye. And his other arm was around Jessica herself, a grinning toddler seated on his lap.

He was tall and lean with long, slightly curly dark brown hair and dark, deep-set eyes, and his resemblance to the father she'd imagined all these years was so striking that she realized she must have subconsciously remembered him, after all.

Tears came to her eyes amidst a rush of love and warmth and sadness. He was younger in that picture than she herself was now, forever frozen in time. The chief and Casey were talking, but she paid them no attention as she continued to stare at that happy tableau and at the man she now knew must have been locked in her memory all these years.

"My father," she said softly as the tears started to flow.

Casey drew her closer. "That's right. I'd forgotten that you said you'd never seen a picture of him."

"I didn't realize that," the chief said, gallantly handing her his handkerchief and at the same time taking back the picture for a moment to examine it.

"It's a good picture of him. He was an artist, you know, and a good one. He used to set up sometimes in town and do sketches of kids. We still have the one he did of CeeCee, don't we, Martha?"

She nodded and got up. "Let me get it."

"He was real good with kids—one of those people who just naturally know how to act with them." The chief smiled. "Lots of people make fun of hippies nowadays, and it's true that a lot of them were drugged-out crazies, but when I think about them I always think of your folks—gentle, idealistic, good people.

"Your father had real talent, Jessica. As I recall, he sold most of his paintings through some place in Eugene."

Martha returned with a large charcoal sketch of a curly-haired little girl. "CeeCee was just three when he did it, and we always thought it was better than the studio portrait we had done about that time.''

Jessica took it from her. It *was* good. She wanted very much to keep it, but she knew she couldn't ask. It was obvious that they, too, loved it, since they'd kept it all these years. She handed it back to Martha.

"Do you remember the name of the gallery that sold his paintings?''

They both shook their heads. "But his parents must have that information," the chief told her.

"I never met them," Jessica admitted sadly. "Gran claimed she didn't know anything about them.''

The chief made a disgusted sound. "Jessica, you'll have to pardon me for saying this, but as the kids say now, your grandmother is a real piece of work. She had their names and address because I gave them to her. They didn't show up until after your grandparents had left with you. They'd been back east somewhere visiting family, and it took quite a while to track them down. They lived somewhere in Nebraska. The information will be in the file.''

"And I don't doubt that Gran still has it," Jessica said bitterly. "For all I know, they tried to get in touch with me and she kept them away.''

"Well, they weren't rich like your grandparents. They had a farm and were just plain folks. I'm sure they must have tried to get in touch with you because they were very concerned about you.''

"Jessie," Casey said, taking the picture from the chief, "look at this again.''

She turned to him, frowning, and then remembered the reason the chief had shown it to her in the first place. Casey pointed to a man at the edge of the picture. His face was somewhat blurred, as though he'd moved just as the shutter clicked.

"Does he look at all familiar to you?''

She shook her head, assuming that he thought she might now remember more of that terrible scene in the kitchen. Fearing that she might in fact begin to remember, she had to force herself to study her parents' killer. Anthony Bensen had dark hair nearly to his shoulders and a full beard besides. He was half-turned away from the camera. He could have been anybody—except that he was the man who'd killed her parents.

The chief drew from the file a large piece of sketch paper, unfolded it and passed it to them. "This sketch was done by someone from the commune after the murders, but there was a lot of disagreement about how accurate it was. Unfortunately, we didn't have computer artists in those days."

Both Casey and Jessica stared at it, and then Casey handed it back to the chief. "I haven't told her yet about your theory."

Jessica stared from one to the other of them. "What theory?"

It was Casey who answered her. "The chief has followed a series of killings over the years where the victims were all tall blondes. The first two happened in Portland only a month or so after your parents were killed, and the guy was never caught. But the Portland police had a witness who thought he'd seen the guy, and the description fits Anthony Bensen.

"In recent years the FBI has started to track serial killers, and it seems that there've been periodic sprees all over the country where the victims have all been tall blondes. If it's the same guy, he somehow manages to control himself for a while, and then he starts up again."

Jessica's gaze went back to the sketch the chief held. Her brain was still functioning very slowly, and she wasn't sure she understood what Casey was telling her. "Are you saying that the man who killed my parents could be the serial killer you're hunting now?"

"It's possible," Casey confirmed. "It seems like too much of a coincidence to me, but I can't rule it out. Like one of my partners told me once, coincidences *do* happen."

Jessica picked up the photo again, then asked for the sketch.

"Take away the beard and add some lines and it looks like Joel Matthews to me," Casey said.

"It looks as much like Robert Collins," she countered. "And I'd more easily believe that, since the people at the commune said Bensen was mentally disturbed.

"The truth is that it could be anyone. The pictures aren't good enough and it's been too many years. Besides, you said yourself that it's too much of a coincidence."

She turned away from the pictures, suddenly aware of just how exhausted she was, how much energy it was taking to maintain her self-control. Was the truth worse than her fears? She didn't know. But at least she knew now that her father hadn't been abusive.

She glanced again at the photograph. What might her life have been like if they'd lived? Would she have become a different person if she'd grown up with them?

And what if Casey and the chief were right, and the serial killer he was hunting was in fact Anthony Bensen? She dismissed out of hand the possibility that it could be Joel, but she couldn't quite so easily dismiss Robert Collins.

Casey was talking to the chief about their search for the killer, but Jessica paid scant attention. She felt so terribly drained, as though not one more drop of emotion could be wrung from her. And suddenly, it all just became too much for her.

She got shakily to her feet and heard herself as though from a great distance thanking the chief for his help, then and now. Then she walked through the house and out the front door to the car, just barely conscious of what she was doing.

By the time she reached the car, Casey had caught up with her. Neither of them said a word as he drove back to the motel, although she could feel his gaze on her, a warmth that barely penetrated the bone-deep chill that had settled into her.

She felt as though she'd split in half. One half of her was sitting there in the car, outwardly calm, while the other half was shattering into a million brittle pieces. She kept thinking irrationally that if she could just hold the two halves together somehow, the nightmare—the *real* nightmare—wouldn't come.

He led her up to her room. She started to fumble through her bag for her key, but he took it from his pocket. She'd left it in the door when she'd run from him earlier.

She walked over and sat on the bed. He slipped her bag from her shoulder and set it aside, then knelt before her and took off her shoes. She felt like a child, but seemed powerless to do anything except sink back against the pillows. He sat beside her and took her hand.

"I can ask the chief to get a doctor to give you something," he suggested.

She shook her head. "I don't want to go to sleep. I'm afraid."

"Jessie, honey, the nightmare probably won't come again. It's over."

"But what if it *all* comes back now? He said I had their b-blood all over me. I must have seen it."

"That was twenty-five years ago, Jessie, and they wouldn't want you to suffer now for it. Think about the good things you learned. That story the chief told you about you and your mother, and about your father. Now you can find your other grandparents, and maybe we can track down some of your father's paintings, too."

She knew he was right, and she was trying to think about all that, but the horror was there still, hovering along the edges of those images, threatening to blot them out.

Casey kicked off his shoes and took off his jacket, then stretched out on the bed beside her and drew her against him. Her curves molded themselves to his long, hard body, and she thought about how safe he made her feel and how she sometimes resented that—but not now. And somewhere in the midst of those thoughts, she fell asleep.

JESSICA AWOKE to the sound of a phone ringing nearby and a male voice speaking in the distance. The ringing phone was beside her bed, but a moment passed before she identified the voice coming from beyond the partially open door to the other room.

And then it all came crashing down on her: the nightmare that was now real. Images flashed through her mind, but she knew somehow that they came from the chief's story and not from her own memories that still lay mercifully beyond her reach.

She started to pull herself across the bed to reach for the phone, but Casey came bursting through the door and grabbed it first. He said hello, then repeated it a moment later as his pale gaze rested on her with grave concern. She sat up quickly, remembering those other phone calls. But it couldn't be another one of them! It couldn't be the killer! How could he know that she was here?

"Who were you calling?" Casey asked, then after a pause, said, "Just a minute." With those last words, his tone had changed to something considerably less pleasant. He put his hand over the receiver.

"It's your grandmother. Do you want to talk to her?"

She started to shake her head, then put out her hand for the phone instead. Her grandmother must have called the chief again and gotten the number from him. Knowing Gran as she did, Jessica was sure that if she refused to talk to her, the chief would get another call.

"Hello, Gran," she said tonelessly. This was not a conversation she wanted to have just now.

"I've just spoken to Chief Waters, dear. I tried to spare you this and I'm very upset with him for telling you."

"You could have avoided that by telling me yourself," Jessica responded icily, even as she tried to remind herself that this was an elderly woman who had sincerely believed she was doing the right thing.

"You were only a child, Jessica, and—"

"I haven't been a child for a long time, and I gave you one last opportunity to tell me the truth. Instead, you called the chief and tried to get him to join in your lies."

She knew just how harsh her words had been when they were met with complete silence. Then her grandmother insisted again that she'd been trying to "spare" her.

"And were you trying to spare me from my other grandparents, as well?" Jessica demanded.

The silence was even longer this time, and when her grandmother spoke, it was in that peremptory tone Jessica had occasionally heard in the past.

"They weren't our kind, Jessica, dear. They had nothing whatsoever to offer you."

"Except for love, and memories of my father. And that was the real reason you kept them away from me. You didn't want me to find out anything about my father because he wasn't 'our kind,' either. Instead, you made me believe that he dragged Mother down with him. It's not true, Gran. I saw a picture of them. They were *happy*."

"I'm very worried about you, Jessica, dear. Is there someone there with you now?"

"You know very well that there is, since he answered the phone." Jessica looked up at Casey. "His name is Tadeucz Seamus Casimiricz. He's a cop, and he certainly isn't 'our kind,' either."

She dropped the receiver back onto its cradle without waiting for a response. Casey smiled at her and she found herself smiling back.

"Let her think about *that* for a while," she said with satisfaction. "She told me that she kept my other grandparents away from me because they weren't 'our kind.' Can you believe that someone would actually say that?"

"From what you've told me about her, I believe it," Casey said, chuckling. Then he sat beside her and took her hand.

"How are you feeling?"

"I don't know. I don't seem to know from one minute to the next how I'll feel. And I'm still afraid that some gate is going to open and it'll all come pouring out." She paused for a moment. "But I *am* glad that I know the truth now."

"That's a good start," he said. "Now, how about some food? Do you feel up to going out, or should I bring something in?"

She didn't want to go out because she was afraid she'd lose control of her emotions, so he went out, warning her that it would probably be either pizza or burgers. The town didn't seem to have much else to offer.

The moment he was gone, Jessica felt almost paralyzed by fear: an irrational fear that he wouldn't come back and an all-too-rational fear that her memories would assault her.

I can't let myself become so dependent on him, she told herself over and over as she stood in the shower. But she no longer understood why she was so concerned about that. If he hadn't been here for her...

She let that thought hang as she suddenly burst into tears: tears for that fragile child who'd been covered with her parents' blood, tears for a woman who'd grown up being told that she must be self-reliant and who'd taken that message to heart—perhaps too much.

And what about Casey and her? Now that she understood why she had been so drawn to him, she no longer quite trusted those feelings. And neither could she believe in his feelings for her. The role of protector came so easily to him. But how would he feel when she no longer needed his protection?

Her tears stopped, subsiding into occasional sobs. She got out of the shower and began to dry herself. Her mind seemed to be leaping from thought to thought, never remaining on anything for long. Now she veered from thoughts of Casey to thoughts of Anthony Bensen, the man who had murdered her parents, and to Casey's belief that the serial killer he was chasing was also Bensen.

Why? she wondered. It seemed rather improbable to her. Was there something he hadn't told her?

She thought about that sketch and the blurred photo. She assumed that Casey had them, and knew she should look at them again, but she could not believe that Joel Matthews could be Anthony Bensen. Neither, for that matter, did she believe Robert Collins could be the killer, although she was somewhat less certain about that, given his history of mental illness.

Then she remembered that she'd been expecting a call from Joel about the ladder he was making for her, so she picked up the phone and dialed her home number, then punched out the code to activate her machine.

The first message was from Susan, who sounded very concerned. Jessica remembered that she'd promised to call her. And then Joel's voice came on.

"It's Joel. Your ladder's finished and I wanted to bring it over. I'll call back later."

Casey walked in just as the machine clicked off. His gaze went from the phone to her questioningly.

"I was just checking my machine," she told him, hoping he wouldn't press the issue. But, being Casey, he did.

"Has Matthews called?"

"No," she lied. "Only Susan. She knows I'm here and I promised to call her, but I forgot."

There was no table in the room, so they both sat on the bed to eat the pizza he'd brought. The lie began to weigh heavily on her. Shouldn't she, of all people, know how wrong it was to lie?

"Joel did call," she said, breaking the silence between them. Casey nodded. "You don't lie very well. What did he say?" She told him. "He *can't* be the killer."

"Then let him prove it. When we get back, you make arrangements for him to bring over the ladder—and I'll be there."

She turned away from him as she felt tears welling up. "Joel and I spent some time talking about the sixties while he was working for me. He made me feel closer to my parents than I'd ever felt before. He's *not* a killer."

Casey knew just how close to the edge she was right now, and he began to regret accusing Matthews. It was true that any resemblance to Matthews in that photo and sketch was minor at best, and he probably wouldn't have thought about it if it wasn't for the fact that something about Matthews raised his hackles.

He wanted to ask her what she'd told Matthews about herself, but it would have to wait. "Okay," he said placatingly. "You're right. There wasn't much of a resemblance. Maybe I'm just jumping to conclusions because I'm frustrated."

"Why do you think that the man who murdered my parents is the serial killer?"

"Just a hunch," he admitted. "But it's backed up with some facts. The FBI records on serial killings turned up clusters going back more than ten years, back to when they started to keep records on them. And Chief Waters mentioned those killings in Portland not long after your parents' deaths. They're all the same—tall blondes killed by multiple stab wounds. And none of them was ever solved."

She lapsed into silence again. He could feel her withdrawing from him and he wanted to take her into his arms and hold her and never let her go. But he didn't, because he couldn't face her rejection, and he was certain that she would reject him.

If they'd already become lovers, it would be a lot easier, he thought. But as it was, he feared that any move on his part would be misinterpreted.

They finished the pizza—or, rather, he finished the pizza. She didn't eat enough to fill a sparrow, and she seemed almost unaware of his presence as she sat there, her gaze unfocused, or focused on some inner place where he couldn't go.

He thought about the killer he was supposed to be hunting and wondered if his judgment was clouded. It *was* a stretch to think that it could be the same man, and he had to admit that he wanted that because then he could play the knight and avenge the deaths of her parents.

His life had sure as hell gotten awfully complicated in a big hurry. But as he looked across the bed at her, Casey decided that he could live with that for a while. What he couldn't live with was the thought of losing her.

She stifled a yawn and he gathered up the pizza boxes and soda cans, then told her he was going to his room to make some calls. She merely nodded as though she'd only half heard him. He gave her a chaste peck on the cheek and left, hoping all the way out of the room that she'd suddenly throw herself into his arms and tell him she wanted him to stay.

Chapter Eight

Jessica heard the door between their rooms close with a soft click and slowly came out of her reverie. She'd been trying to reach back more than twenty-five years, trying to grasp memories that must be there in some form. After all, what she'd felt when she'd driven up the hill to look down on the commune must surely have been a memory. And she desperately wanted more of that, to buttress herself against the terrible onslaught of the memories she feared. She was convinced that the nightmare would come again. And this time, the veils of darkness would be lifted.

The room felt achingly empty without Casey's presence. She wanted him to come back, to stay with her. But what she wanted from him was the wonderful closeness of lovers, and they didn't have that. How could he possibly be expected to understand that?

She undressed and got back into bed, then lay there drifting in that strange place between wakefulness and sleep, wanting to slip into oblivion, but fearing what awaited her there.

SHE AWOKE SLOWLY, moving lethargically from the deeper regions of sleep to an almost-awareness of her surroundings. She was lying on her back and she rolled over, her hand reaching out to Casey. Her still-dozing brain was slow to tell her that he wasn't there.

She sat up groggily, staring at the empty spot beside her where she'd imagined him. It must have been part of a dream, one that lingered even now, enveloping her in a voluptuous warmth, although the details eluded her, teasing along the edges of her memory.

She got out of bed, wide awake now, even though her travel alarm told her it was the middle of the night. It must be the result of that nap she'd taken earlier.

A pale, silvery light poured through the crack in the heavy drapes. She walked over and opened it wider, then stared at the full moon, so bright that it obliterated most of the stars. The warmth of the dream remained. And when she turned away from the windows she saw that the connecting door to Casey's room was slightly ajar. He must have checked on her at some point, then left it that way in case she had the nightmare again.

She was suddenly consumed by a need to see him. So she went to the door and opened it just wide enough to allow herself to slip through.

The same moonlight was streaming through an opening in his drapes, too. He lay on his back, bare from the waist up. He'd kicked the covers free from the foot of the bed and his ankles and feet protruded. She smiled. Poor Casey. The world just wasn't made for people his size.

The air conditioner breathed softly as she stood there staring at him, trying to get her mind around her thoughts about him. Did she love him? Did he love her? Were they both still trying to get beyond some doubts, to accommodate themselves to a new reality in their lives?

He didn't awaken slowly. One moment he was lying there and the next instant he was sitting up, staring at her, an unspoken question in his eyes as he switched on the bedside lamp.

"It wasn't the nightmare," she said, answering his silent question. "I think I just woke up because of the nap earlier. I'm sorry I woke you."

Her voice had become slightly husky as she became aware of her skimpy attire—a short, silk nightshirt—and of the probability that he wore even less.

"I'm sorry I shut you out earlier," she went on, feeling a great urge to talk in order to restore some normalcy to a scene that threatened to overwhelm her with its intimacy.

"You've had a lot to deal with," he said, his own voice husky, as well.

"It's ridiculous, really," she said, crossing her arms and taking a few aimless steps around the small room. "I came here to learn the truth, and now I'm afraid that I might remember it."

"I called Susan before I flew out here, and told her the whole story. She said it's impossible to predict. Sometimes it all comes back when you hear the truth, sometimes it's only images your mind creates from what you've heard, and other times, bits and pieces come back over a period of time."

She was touched by his thoughtfulness, although it didn't really surprise her. Part of it was certainly his concern for her, and part of it was his nature, his need to know and understand everything. He'd written about that in his novels, projecting onto his protagonist a trait that she knew was his own.

"Thank you for thinking of that. I was going to call her in the morning."

He put out a hand to her, beckoning her to the bed. "The important thing now is to accept it and move on, Jessie."

She took his hand and seated herself on the edge of the bed—close, but not too close. "That's not so easy to do when I know that the man who killed my parents is still out there, and could even be after *me*."

"You're safe. You know I won't let anything happen to you."

She merely nodded.

"But you don't much like it, do you—feeling vulnerable, I mean?"

She actually managed a smile, wondering if he'd intended it the way she interpreted it: a double vulnerability.

"No, I don't. As Susan would tell you, I'm something of a control freak." She hesitated, thinking for a moment about that. "And now I know the reason."

He nodded. "Susan mentioned that. You weren't able to control—to prevent, that is—what happened to your parents, so you've compensated for it by insisting on controlling everything you can since that time."

She said nothing as they sat there, his big hand wrapped around hers. And at some level she realized that she was indeed moving on, reexamining her own life in the light of these revelations. So many things she'd never understood about herself, things she'd never tied to her parents' deaths, now made sense. And finally, she felt ready to talk about it.

"I've, uh, I've never. . . ." She stopped, embarrassed that it seemed so difficult to say.

"You've never slept with anyone," he said quietly.

She stared at him, recalling a time when she'd wondered if he might have guessed. Then she nodded.

"It makes sense, doesn't it? I was afraid of losing control."

"Making love isn't about losing control. It's about giving up something and getting something more in return."

She lowered her face quickly so he wouldn't see her smile. Would this man ever stop amazing her? She shook her head ruefully.

"Who is the real Casey—the tough cop or the tender romantic?"

He chuckled. "It's probably the Polish-Irish mix, helped along by all those arrows."

"Arrows?" She frowned.

"Yeah. The little guy with the wings seems to have shot his whole quiver into me."

She smiled. "Are you saying that you're smitten?"

He nodded. "Smitten, besotted and probably certifiably insane. It feels pretty damned weird."

She lifted their entwined hands and pressed her lips to his knuckles. He searched her face carefully for what seemed like a very long time, then slid the covers from beneath her and drew her down beside him.

"Are you sure you're ready for this?" he asked as he propped himself up on one elbow and stared at her. "We could just sleep together."

Was it only a few hours ago that she'd thought she wanted only that? She met his gaze and nodded. "I'm sure."

The moment his lips touched hers, Jessica felt the urgency begin to build within her, as though the dam of her pent-up desire was filling rapidly, threatening to burst into a raw, roaring passion. The sheer force of it both excited and frightened her. And she could sense, too, the barely controlled passion in him, the taut, heavy leash by which he restrained his own desire.

He slid an arm beneath her, drawing her still closer as their lips and tongues entwined, then sought new territory to conquer: ears, eyelids, the curve of a neck, the hollow at the base of a throat.

Time stretched out as they held each other, separated only by thin scraps of cloth. Jessica felt ready to explode, then became certain that she would melt instead from the molten fire that flowed through her body. She pressed herself to him ever more tightly, thrilled by the sensation of hard muscles fitted to soft curves and the contrast of smooth skin against bristly hardness.

He was so slow, so careful, when she wanted him to unleash his passion so that she could bask in its heat. The gossamer barrier of her nightshirt became unbearable as his lips and teeth gently teased her achingly sensitive nipples. Impatient now, she began to struggle to free herself from it. He flung back the covers and drew it slowly over her head. The soft silk rasped harshly against her fevered flesh that grew still more fevered as he trailed kisses over it, moving with soft, gliding caresses from her throat to the shallow well of her navel, just above the lacy band of her panties.

She arched to him, moaning, and he covered her with himself as they moved into an erotic rhythm, pressed against each other, yearning flesh chafing against the remaining barriers.

"Please," she whispered, her fingers groping for the waistband of his briefs.

Blue flames leaped in his pale eyes as he lifted his head and stared at her. A tender smile curved his wide mouth as he touched her lips again, seeming for a moment to ignore her plea.

Then they were both struggling with a clumsiness born of suddenly unleashed raw passion, arms and legs tangled up with scraps of cotton and lace, both of them laughing at their eagerness, their awkwardness. And of all the memories Jessica would cherish of this night, this moment, when they both acknowledged the pure joy of it with their laughter, would remain one of the strongest.

The laughter died away into smiles as their eyes met again. No words were necessary now. They'd been living in each other's fantasies for weeks, approaching this from the moment they met, knowing it would happen, and knowing, too, that it would be far more than a sweet, fierce coupling.

Casey slid his hands beneath her, lifting her slowly as he continued to watch her. And then he was sliding into her warm, welcoming softness, moving rapidly beyond that brief pain to fill her with his huge hardness that felt so alien. And so right.

Suddenly she was shocked to feel tears coursing down her cheeks. He became immediately still inside her.

"Am I hurting you?"

She shook her head quickly, smiling through the tears that he kissed away as he drew them both into a slow, building rhythm that pounded through every fiber of her being and left her aware of nothing but the sheer joy of being joined with this man.

The night spun out into magic as Casey held on to the final threads of his control, waiting until she, too, was ready to give herself up to the mindless, blinding moment of ecstasy when they lost their separate identities and shuddered together in the searing, golden flames.

They held on to that moment long after it had passed into mere aftershocks, knowing it must end, but wanting it to linger, wanting to stop time itself—wanting, finally, to deny the limits of their bodies because surely they had touched each other's souls.

But it finally slipped away from them, drifting slowly into a dreamscape of caresses and murmured words and small tremors that glided seamlessly into sleep.

THEY AWOKE to the insistent ringing of the phone beside the bed. Casey picked it up and then made a sound that was more like a growl than a greeting.

"Wake-up call," he muttered as he dropped the receiver back into its cradle, then fell heavily beside her again and slid his arm beneath her to haul her to him for a slow, lazy kiss.

"How are you feeling this morning?" he asked after lifting his mouth from hers.

She smiled, sensing that the question was a very serious one. "The way I've wanted to feel from the moment I met you."

He arched a dark brow. "Is that so? You mean that I've played the perfect gentleman all this time for nothing?"

She laughed. "If that was your idea of a perfect gentleman, I don't think I want to know where you studied gentlemanly behavior."

Then she grew suddenly serious as she began to trace the outline of his lips with a finger. "You guessed from the beginning, didn't you?"

He seized her hand and pressed his lips to her sensitive palm. "Yes and no. I knew something was wrong, but I figured there was an old lover you hadn't gotten over. And I didn't really mean for it to happen last night, either. I wanted to wait, to give you time to get over this."

"I didn't want to wait," she stated firmly, staring down at him and wondering how she could have waited this long. Could it really have been as wonderful as her memory told her, or was she mixing up memory and fantasy? She had a powerful urge to find out.

Their eyes met in that secret communication of lovers, and within seconds she knew that it *had* been as good as she remembered. The urgency seemed to build slowly within them at first, then rose to a fever pitch. The need flowed between them as they both discovered with more certainty now the ways to each other's pleasure.

It was a wild coming-together—less gentle and more demanding, but with the sureness of a perfect understanding. Casey drove himself deep within her and she opened to him, wanting it all, and wanting it to never end.

But the aftermath had a pleasure all its own: murmured words of love, gentle caresses, slow, lingering kisses. It was a long time before they left the bed to face the day.

"ARE YOU SURE YOU WANT TO go back out there?" Casey asked with concern.

"Yes, I'm sure. If I'm ever going to remember all of it, surely it would be there, where it happened." She saw his doubtful look and hurried on.

"I don't want to go on living with this fear that I'll remember at some point. I want to face it now."

So they drove out to the old commune. Casey peered through the broken window. "It isn't safe in there."

"Maybe not for you," she agreed. "But I was in there before."

"The whole damned place looks ready to collapse," he grumbled.

"Then you stay here while I go inside." She hoisted herself over the windowsill and started purposefully across the dining room to the kitchen, stopping as before just inside the doorway. Behind her, she could hear him climbing over the sill.

Nothing. It was just an old kitchen. She knelt on the floor as she'd done before, and still felt nothing except for the distant echoes of the chief's story and Casey's silent presence behind her. She walked through the kitchen to the hallway and stopped outside the closet.

"This was where he found you?" Casey asked.

She nodded, certain that she was about to be engulfed by that icy terror. But once again, nothing happened—and now she knew that it never would. Twenty-five years of uncertainty had been erased by the truth, a truth that had somehow burned away her fears, leaving only a deep sadness that she knew she would always carry with her.

"It's gone," she said, turning to Casey.

"Good," he replied. "Now let's get the hell out of here."

After they had climbed back out the window, they walked around the weed-filled yard for a while. Then she told him that she wanted to go up to the lookout, and they drove there. Clouds were moving in as they stood there, staring down at the ruins, and their shadows drifted over the scene.

She had hoped to recapture that feeling she'd had there before, but instead she found herself thinking about her parents, and then about Casey and herself. But it felt confusing, because the parents she envisioned were both younger than she and Casey were. She hoped they would have approved of him, and told herself they would. It was Casey, after all, who had unwittingly brought her here.

"I've been thinking about your father's paintings," Casey said as they drove back to town. "If we leave for Eugene now, we'll have time to check out some galleries. I know those places tend to come and go, but there's always the chance that someone can tell us something."

THE TRIP BACK TO EUGENE forced separation on them, since they had two rental cars. Jessica was both surprised and rather embarrassed at how much she missed him, and she kept looking in the rearview mirror, but he was only a shadow beyond the windshield.

They dropped her car at the airport, and the moment they were together again, they were in each other's arms, needing the closeness—even a closeness inhibited by a lack of privacy.

"We could look for a motel that rents by the hour," he teased softly as they noticed several people staring at them.

"The galleries," she reminded him huskily, wondering when this constant, all-consuming hunger would lessen, then wondering if she wanted it to stop.

They had no success, but had perhaps a prospect of future success. One gallery owner, himself an artist, had sold his paintings years ago through a gallery no longer in existence. But he was sure he could locate the owner of that gallery, who'd been a prominent figure in the local art scene for more than thirty-five years before he'd retired to Arizona. He also knew a few people still in the area who'd been part of the scene for many years. Jessica left her name and phone number, and he promised to get in touch if he had any information.

It was both more and less than she'd hoped for. She'd known that the chances of finding paintings at least twenty-five years old were slim at best, but filled with the joyous optimism of the newly in love, she'd let herself think they would walk into a gallery and find one of her father's paintings.

JOEL MATTHEWS SHOWED UP at Jessica's office late the next day, a day that had been a nonstop blur of client appointments, court hearings and preparations for three upcoming trials.

She was surprised when she looked up and saw him standing there in her doorway. Their receptionist never permitted clients to get past her. But then she glanced at her watch and realized that it was just past quitting time.

The moment she saw Joel, Jessica also saw that sketch in her mind. There was no similarity at all. How could Casey believe there was?

"Hi," he said with a slight frown. "Is anything wrong? The receptionist wasn't there, so I decided to check to see if you were still here."

She motioned him inside as she shook her head. "Nothing's wrong, except that it's been a long day. How are you, Joel?"

"Getting by," he replied as he took a seat. "Did you get my message?"

She nodded. "I was out of town for a few days. You didn't leave a number, so I couldn't call you."

"I don't have a phone at my new digs yet." He shrugged. "I've got the ladder out in my truck, so I thought I'd try to catch you here and see if you want me to bring it over now."

"Fine. I'm ready to leave. And by the way, I'll need your new address. Your probation officer will need it, too."

He gave it to her and she jotted it down. Then she put some files into her briefcase and they left the office. Jessica was very much aware of the promise she'd made to Casey, but there was no opportunity to get in touch with him now, with Joel here, and since he'd given her his new address, it didn't seem quite so important. Besides, *she* knew that Joel wasn't a killer, even if Casey didn't yet believe that.

"Where are you parked?" she asked as they left the building.

"Over in the garage," he said, gesturing to the far side of the park.

"Fine. I'm over there, too."

They started in that direction, talking casually. Jessica was tempted to tell him about her trip to Oregon, but didn't because she really didn't want to talk about her parents' deaths. Instead, they talked about folk music. Joel said that a local jazz club was thinking about having one evening a week devoted to folksinging.

"They're trying to get the Kingston Trio as an opening act," he told her.

"Good heavens! Are they still around? I've heard their music, but they go all the way back to the fifties, don't they?"

"Yeah, and they're not all that authentic, anyway. But they did bring folk into the mainstream, like Peter, Paul and Mary. I think there's one of the original members left. Would you like to go if they do it?"

She was caught off guard by the invitation, but nodded quickly. "Yes, I'd really like that. Are you going to perform there, too?"

"Maybe—if they'll have me. I need to get some work done on my Martin first." He went on to talk about his guitar, which was apparently quite old and valuable.

They were parked on different levels and Joel insisted on escorting her to her car. The huge garage was virtually deserted at this time of day.

"You gotta be careful," Joel said as they got into the elevator. "You know about those killings, don't you? They all looked kinda like you, you know."

"Yes, I know, but I *am* careful. Besides, there must be hundreds of women who fit that description." At least, that's what she'd been telling herself regularly since her return from Oregon.

"Yeah, that's true, I guess," he said, lounging against the wall as the elevator clanged and groaned its way upward. "I see they put Casey the cop in charge of finding him, but he doesn't seem to be getting anywhere."

Jessica shot him a quick glance, thinking that he sounded rather pleased about that. Then she felt compelled to defend Casey.

"Serial killers can be really hard to catch."

"Right." Joel nodded. "Because they're smart. *They* call the shots."

They had reached her car and she thanked him and said she would meet him at her house. She thought about his statement as she watched him walk away in that unique, gliding gait she'd noticed before. It had almost sounded as though he was praising the killer.

She shook her head in annoyance as she started the car. Of course he wasn't. He hadn't said anything that Casey himself hadn't said. The killer *was* calling the shots. And he might have been getting in a subtle dig at Casey, as well, by saying that the killer was smart.

When she turned onto her street she saw Joel's truck behind her. She pulled up in front of the garage and he parked behind her, then got out to remove the ladder that was chained to the truck's bed.

"It looks perfect, Joel," she exclaimed. "I'm so glad you recommended it."

Her upstairs neighbors drove up at that moment and soon they, too, were admiring the ladder. Jessica invited them in to see the work Joel had done, and they all trailed along after her. He set the wheels in the top of the ladder into the grooves along the top shelf, then climbed it and sent it whizzing along the row of shelves.

The Stevensons were impressed and showed an interest in seeing what she'd done with the rest of the place, so she showed them through, with Joel following along, as well.

"As soon as I can find some time, I want to repaint the place," Jessica said. "I can't stand all this white. Actually, I'd like to put up some wallpaper. I saw some really beautiful Victorian reproductions, but I've never done any wallpapering."

"Don't try," her neighbors groaned in unison, then laughed. They'd tried it themselves, with disastrous results.

"I'll do it for you," Joel announced. "I've done wallpapering before."

"Really?" Jessica immediately imagined on the living-room walls the one print she'd especially liked. "Are you sure you have the time?" she asked, worried that he might be feeling compelled to do the work because she was representing him for nothing.

"No problem. I'll check with you in a couple of days, after you decide what you want."

She thanked him and he left with the Stevensons. She saw them talking in the driveway before he climbed into his truck and drove off. She was glad that she hadn't been able to call Casey and hoped that he'd find a suspect and forget about Joel.

She watered her plants and dispatched some dust, then gathered up some clothes and left for Casey's house, eager to relax in the pool. He'd told her he wouldn't be home until late, so that gave her some time to decide if she should tell him about seeing Joel. She certainly couldn't lie if he asked her a direct question, but that didn't mean she had to raise the issue herself.

She felt a strange need to protect Joel from Casey. She knew that the two of them already disliked each other, and she didn't doubt for one minute that Casey could be very unpleasant, even though she preferred not to think about that side of him.

Besides, she thought, it would certainly destroy her friendship with Joel if he found out that she'd sicced Casey on him. And she liked Joel. Even with her new knowledge of her parents, she still saw Joel as a sort of link to them.

As soon as she reached Casey's house she went for a swim, then fed Howard and tried to ignore Adolf's imploring look. She knew he'd been fed this morning, even if he was doing his best to convince her otherwise. So she gave him some treats to lure him away from Howard's dish, then fixed some dinner for herself.

After she'd cleaned up, it occurred to her that it would probably be a good idea to let her neighbors know that she wouldn't be home overnight for a while. So she found their number and called them. She explained that she would be staying with a friend for a while, and wanted to let them know in case there were any more problems with intruders.

"To be honest with you, Vicki, it's possible that it could be one of my clients. The police are already looking for him. He's mentally disturbed, but I don't really think he's dangerous. So if you see or hear anything, call 911 right away. But I'd appreciate it if you'd call me, too, because if it *is* him, I want to be sure he gets the help he needs." She gave her Casey's number.

After spending some time working on her upcoming court appearances, Jessica finished another of Casey's books. In this story the murderer turned out to be the one she'd least suspected: the victim's brother, who'd been portrayed throughout the book as being both concerned and outraged by his sister's death.

The story left her feeling slightly uneasy, but after a few moments' reflection she decided that Casey had probably just been using a literary device to hold his readers' attention. It seemed highly unlikely to her that a vicious murderer could present himself as a nice person in real life.

Reading about killers probably wasn't the wisest thing for her to be doing at the moment, either. She still didn't really believe that the killer now stalking the city could be the man who had murdered her parents, and even Casey admitted that it was a long shot—but what if it *was* the same man?

She shuddered, thinking about that and about the possibility that he'd already found her and knew who she was. Then, with a sound of disgust, she dismissed the whole matter. She wasn't going to read any more of Casey's books until the killer was caught. Instead, she spent her free time catching up on the ever-mounting pile of legal journals.

She walked out onto the terrace that was bathed in the light of a still nearly full moon. The everpresent Adolf padded out behind her and flopped down at her feet. She stared at the shimmering strip of the pool and decided that another swim was just what she needed to drive out her crazy thoughts.

She went back into the house to get a fresh towel, then grimaced at the thought of putting on her wet suit. What a pleasure it would be to swim without it, something she'd never before done. So she stripped off her clothes just inside the glass doors, wrapped herself in the big towel, then walked to the edge of the pool, where she cast off the towel and jumped in quickly.

It was heaven. The water temperature was perfect, just cool enough to make her skin tingle slightly as she slipped through it, glorying in the freedom of her nakedness. It was amazing how different it felt, even though her suit fit like a second skin and weighed only a few ounces. She thought she had probably spoiled herself forever.

She swam slowly back and forth, changing strokes several times before rolling over to float. She wished Casey was here, but she had no idea what time he'd be home. And even as she thought about him, her body began to feel warmer, her skin more sensitive.

In truth, she was still unnerved by what she felt for him—the passion he'd so quickly aroused in her and how easily she'd cast off any inhibitions. And there was as well a certainty in her that none of this could have happened with another man.

She was floating aimlessly and thinking about the implications of that when she heard a splash. At first she thought it must be Adolf. Casey had told her that he sometimes jumped into the pool. But when she had rolled over to tread water, what she saw instead was Casey himself.

"Finding a naked woman in my pool ranks right up there with my favorite things," he said with a grin.

"I couldn't resist," she replied, her voice suddenly husky as he swam toward her.

From the moment their bodies met, the night dissolved into a silvered passion beneath the moon. Treading water quickly became impossible as their bodies slipped and slid over each other. Gasping, they made it to the edge and tumbled onto the grass, wet and hot with need.

Casey rolled them both over until she was astride him, then arched to drive into her, filling that emptiness she hadn't known existed. With her head thrown back and her body bathed in the glow of the moon, Jessica felt her world explode with the fiery brilliance of a thousand suns. Casey's chest heaved as he drew in some ragged breaths. Then he swept her wet hair from her face and kissed her with the tenderness that had been forgotten until now.

"So how did your day go?" he asked with a wry grin.

She laughed and slid off him to sit in the grass. "Rather badly, until now. How about yours?"

"Well, I sat in meetings, thought about you, ran away from reporters, thought about you, wrote reports, thought about you some more, went to a singles' bar, then came home to follow a pile of discarded clothes to its unlikely source."

"Unlikely source?"

He nodded. In the moonlight his eyes had become silver. "Once upon a time, and not so very long ago, I met this very cool and proper lady. Being the jerk I am, I had to see if I could get past all that. So now I come home to find this woman who obviously threw all caution to the winds and jumped in my pool stark naked. It's very confusing.''

"You didn't seem very confused to me. I thought you knew exactly how to handle the situation, no doubt from long experience.''

He groaned and flung an arm dramatically across his face. "Here it comes. The questions about my sordid past.''

"I don't care about your past, but I *am* interested in why you went to a singles' bar.''

"All in the line of duty, m'dear. Believe me, you wouldn't catch me in one of those meat markets otherwise. I can't stand the smell of desperation. And as someone once observed, why go looking for hamburger when you have steak at home?''

She smacked him and he held up his hands to ward her off. "Just carrying along the analogy. Don't get violent. You know I can't stand violence.''

"And don't you change the subject. Did it have something to do with the latest murder?''

" 'The latest murder.' Now you sound just like the reporters. Yes, it had to do with that. The victim was there the night before she was killed. We just found out today.''

"So?''

He shrugged. "So I don't know. We might have ourselves a suspect. Several people recalled seeing her leave with someone, and no one had seen him there before.''

"You sound doubtful.''

He didn't respond for a moment, but stared off into the darkness. "I don't know. After a while you get a feel for situations, and this one doesn't feel right. There's no indication that he let himself be seen with any of the others.''

"You can't know that for certain,'' she observed.

"Yeah, you're right,'' he admitted. "Anyway, I've got two of the people who saw him leave with her coming in tomorrow to work with the computer sketch artist.''

"How did they describe him?''

"It didn't fit the description of Anthony Bensen, if that's what you're wondering. This guy was short and muscular and blond, probably in his early thirties.''

Jessica hoped that Casey's instincts were wrong, and this *was* the killer. Certainly she wanted Bensen brought to justice, but she wanted even more to put it all behind them.

THE SKETCH OF THE SUSPECT appeared in the newspapers and on TV and Casey's squad was quickly overwhelmed by calls from people who thought they recognized him. Jessica knew that Casey himself still had his doubts, but it was clear that the focus had shifted to the unknown man, and away from both Robert Collins and Joel Matthews.

Jessica remained convinced of Joel's innocence, and of Robert Collins's, as well, but she continued to worry about Robert because he so clearly needed help.

She had no real expectation of finding Robert when she returned to the park several days later. She'd told the police about her belief that he frequented the aviary and assumed that they'd been keeping an eye on it. But she was still haunted by the torment his sick mind must be causing him, so she decided to give it one more try. It was a splendid day, and she thought perhaps the women she'd spoken to earlier might be there.

The women weren't—but Robert Collins was. Jessica saw him the moment she came through the fringe of trees that surrounded the aviary. He was standing at the railing around its perimeter, his back to her as he watched the birds flutter around inside the tall structure.

She hesitated, scanning the area for any sign of police. None was in sight, although there were perhaps a half dozen other people around. So she walked toward him, then decided that it would be better if she stayed some distance away and allowed him to recognize her first. She was cautious, aware of the possibility that this man could be a killer, but she was unwilling to go find a phone and call the police, since he might very well disappear in the interim.

She moved up to the railing about fifteen feet away from him. No one was between them, and if he turned his head in her direction he would certainly see her.

He continued to stare at the birds as she stared at him. She could see that his lips were moving slightly and she noted that he looked dirty and unkempt. He also had a scraggly beard that made him look even more menacing and brought to mind the sketch the chief had given them of her parents' murderer.

Still, for all that, some inner instinct told her that Robert was not a killer, that she would somehow have known if this was the man who'd killed her parents.

She was trying to decide if she should approach him directly when he turned in her direction, giving her no more than a brief glance before turning his attention back to the birds again. She didn't know if he'd seen her and failed to recognize her, or if he hadn't really seen her at all because he was too lost in his own tormented world.

She began to move toward him slowly, then stopped when she was about five feet away. "Hello, Robert," she said with a smile. "How are you?"

His head jerked toward her and he stared at her with a frightening intensity that caused her to take a few steps back.

"I'm Jessica Aylesworth, Robert. Do you remember me? I...."

He drew away. "Are you going to arrest me?"

"No, Robert. I'm not a police officer."

"I like to come here. I'm not doing anything wrong." His voice had taken on a belligerent tone as he glared at her.

"I know that," she said. "You told me that you like to watch the birds."

He continued to stare at her, his dark eyes smoldering. "Are you one of them?"

A chill shot through her. Could he be talking about his victims? Was he killing them because he believed they were out to get him?

"One of whom, Robert?" she asked, trying to keep her voice calm and checking at the same time to be certain there were still other people around.

"They don't like me," he said, his tone shifting from anger to self-pity. "They want to hurt me."

"*I* don't want to hurt you, Robert," she assured him. "Tell me about the people you think are trying to hurt you."

"They laugh at me. But I can make them stop laughing."

Jessica felt ice form in her veins. Her earlier certainty that this man couldn't be a killer evaporated. "How do you make them stop laughing at you?" she asked, hoping he wouldn't notice the slight tremor in her voice.

He stared at her in silence for a long moment, during which she envisioned him drawing a knife from the pocket of the shabby jacket he wore in spite of the day's warmth. Every word of caution that Casey had issued now echoed through her brain.

"*You* know," he said, then suddenly turned away from her and after a few stumbling steps began to run, disappearing into the park within seconds.

Jessica leaned for a moment against the railing, waiting for her heart to stop pounding. How on earth could Casey live this way? Then she roused herself, ran to the phone booth she remembered seeing not too far away and called 911. After giving the dispatcher her name and the information, she hung up and walked back to her car.

She no longer knew what to think. As she calmed down and thought more rationally about the encounter, she realized that she could have misinterpreted his words. Robert was clearly paranoid, so it wasn't surprising that he would believe people were laughing at him. And in point of fact, some probably were, given his appearance and behavior. Neither was it surprising that he would think she "knew." Susan had said that part of his illness was a belief that others possessed magical powers: reading his thoughts, for example.

Still, she was badly shaken, and not the least of that discomfort was acknowledging the possibility that she could be wrong about him being essentially harmless.

When she returned to the office Jessica called Susan and told her about the encounter. Susan confirmed what Jessica had already begun to suspect: that she'd misinterpreted Robert's statements because of her preoccupation with the killer or killers. Susan repeated that she still could not believe Robert to be capable of planning or executing such crimes, but she refused to rule out completely the possibility that he could become violent.

Jessica hung up with a grimace. If she sometimes thought that the law was too imprecise, she was beginning now to see that psychology was even worse. Casey's Law of Human Behavior was looking more and more true.

SEVERAL HOURS LATER, following an appearance in juvenile court, Jessica walked into the office and saw the receptionist hold up a hand to stop her.

"Call for you on line two. It's Casey."

Jessica rolled her eyes, wishing that she'd delayed her return for another minute or two. There could be only one reason he was calling. She went back to her office and picked up the phone, then began to defend herself before he could start haranguing her about playing detective.

"I was only trying to find him to get him some help, and there were people around. He was—"

"Could we rewind this conversation and start again?" Casey interrupted. "I seem to have missed something."

"Oh. Why were you calling?"

"I'll get to that in a minute. Who were you trying to find? Collins?"

Silently she called herself a few choice names. What did it say about her that she was now thinking he was omniscient? The police department was quite large, and he wasn't even involved in the search for Robert Collins.

"Yes," she admitted. "I found him in the park." Then she told him the whole story.

"I'll bet you read Nancy Drew when you were a kid," he said with a chuckle when she'd finished.

"What? No lecture on how I was placing myself in danger?" she asked incredulously.

"I reserve my lectures for those who just might pay attention to them. Basically, I don't see him as a serious suspect, either. Maybe because I'm getting overburdened with suspects."

"What do you mean?"

"We've got a probable ID on the blond guy. And if we're right, he served time for rape. And our escaped burglar has a history of roughing up women."

"But you were so convinced that neither of them could be the killer," she protested.

"I've been known to be wrong on occasion. It keeps me humble. Would you like to hear why I called, other than for the pleasure of hearing your voice, that is?"

"Yes, of course," she replied somewhat distractedly. He was right. There *were* too many suspects. She wondered if detective work was always this frustrating.

"Chief Waters called me. He's been checking around to see if he could locate any of your father's paintings and he found someone who has one."

"He did?" She promptly forgot all about suspected murderers. "Will they sell it?"

"No, but according to the chief, they'll be happy to give it to you. He told them the story. Here's the name and phone number."

Jessica wrote it down. "Oh, Casey, this is wonderful news! I can hardly wait to see it!"

"Well, I'm glad that I made your day, because mine sure hasn't been much fun, and it's far from being over. I've now got twelve guys out combing the city for two suspects, and the chief is breathing down my neck because the mayor is breathing down *his* neck because . . . Well, you get the picture."

"So you won't be home early."

"The way I figure it, I *might* get to see you again before we both start drawing Social Security. But as ol' Willie says, 'You're always on my mind.'"

Jessica hung up with a smile that drained away slowly as she thought about Casey's list of suspects. It began to seem less and less likely that she herself could be in danger, or that the serial killer could be the man who'd murdered her parents.

Then she smiled again as she thought about his news. She'd almost given up hope, since she hadn't heard from the gallery owner. Now, thanks to Chief Waters's kindness, it appeared that she would have something of her father's, after all.

Chapter Nine

A black rage swarmed over him when he spotted her among the crowds in the huge mall. What was she doing here? Had she come here to torment him because she knew he hadn't decided what to do about her?

He'd come here because malls were good places to search for victims. There were far more women than men and there were never any cops around, except for the rent-a-cop variety. And he liked the anonymity, too—people hurrying around, preoccupied with their shopping and not paying any attention at all to him. It made him feel nearly invisible—and powerful.

Even though he didn't want her to be here, he still followed her. He'd been watching her house at night and she was never there, so he knew she must be spending her nights with Casey. The thought of the two of them together made him start to grind his teeth, an old habit of his since childhood.

She moved out of the flow of people and peered into a shop window. He slowed down and pretended interest in a sporting goods display. Then she went into the shop and he walked over to a bench not far away.

He started to drift off into his thoughts, a mixture of disjointed memories and half-formed plans. He was doing that more often now, separating himself from reality. A woman got off the nearby escalator and walked past him. Her expensive perfume wafted in his direction, drawing his attention to her. She glanced his way and then looked away quickly. People often did that now.

She was older, probably in her forties, but she had that look. A look of money and upper-crust snobbery. It was a look that never failed to send him plummeting into his memories. He watched her as she moved through the crowd to the entrance of one of the big department stores. Then he shifted his gaze back to the store where Jessica had disappeared. He was torn, wanting to try to follow Jessica when she left to see if she went to Casey's house because he hadn't yet figured out where he lived. But he also wanted the other one.

WEIGHTED DOWN WITH the results of too much shopping, Jessica started toward the mall garage. Shopping wasn't one of her favorite pastimes, so she tended toward binges, followed by long periods of no shopping at all.

She smiled, thinking that Casey would be amused at the string bikini she'd bought. She'd deliberately selected the skimpiest one she could find. And then she'd bought some sexy lingerie, as well—things she'd never owned before he came into her life.

The truth was that she'd just never paid much attention to her body before. Now, however, she found herself glorying in its power to arouse him. He was amusingly simple and direct in his appreciation of her charms, and as a result she was quickly giving up any lingering inhibitions.

She reached the elevator and tried to remember where she'd parked—7B, she thought. She got in, pushed the button and found herself thinking again about Robert Collins. The police still hadn't found him, although they assured her that they were watching the park.

It had occurred to her this afternoon that he might very well be homeless at this point, and she'd begun making calls to the city's shelters, still hoping that she could do something before the police found him. So far, she'd had no luck, but she still had a few more shelters to call tomorrow.

Mostly, she wanted to find him in order to help him, but she had a more selfish reason, as well. She needed desperately to end the confusion in her mind about whether he could have been the one who'd called her and sent the letters and prowled outside her house. None of those things had happened again, but she felt as though she was always waiting for the other shoe to drop.

The elevator doors opened at level 7 and she got out, then walked to the B section. Her car wasn't there, and she belatedly realized that the color splashed on the pillars was wrong. Muttering a curse, she turned toward the elevator, then decided that it would be faster just to walk down the ramp to level 6, which had been her second choice.

The ramp proved to be longer than she'd expected, and partway down she began to realize just how deserted the garage was at these upper levels. She tended always to drive to the top levels, knowing that the lower ones were more likely to be filled.

She breathed a sigh of relief when she reached level 6 and discovered the pillars to be painted bright orange as she'd remembered. But 6B, instead of being directly under 7B, was all the way across the garage. She wondered what kind of idiot designed these things and why someone hadn't standardized them long ago.

A car pulled out as she got off the ramp, but no one else was in sight. Her footsteps echoed eerily under the low ceilings as she hurried across the huge space, and she involuntarily cast a glance back over her shoulder.

Someone was there! Just as she turned, he ducked behind a minivan. Fear crawled along her spine. She was too loaded down with her purchases to run very fast and her shoes weren't made for running, in any event.

She kept moving as fast as she could toward B section, which still seemed to be half a mile away. Perhaps he'd just been headed toward his own car. She listened, expecting to hear an engine start up at any moment. But the only sounds were her heels clicking on the concrete floor.

She turned again. Some of the lights were out, but she was sure she saw a shadow moving between cars, much closer this time. The stairwell was too far away, the elevator would take forever to come and the entrance into the mall was behind her, back in the direction of her pursuer.

Fear-induced adrenaline coursed through her and she ran awkwardly, trying to clutch her shopping bags and at the same time dig through her purse for her car keys. She did not turn again, concentrating instead on finding her car as quickly as possible.

Two rows from the wall, she told herself, close to a pillar. It didn't help at all that her car was lower than most and therefore easily hidden. She risked another backward glance, and this time saw nothing. Then, with one final burst of speed, she sprinted for the row where she hoped she'd find her car, and there it was. She unlocked the door, tossed the bags inside, jumped in and immediately hit the automatic door lock.

Off to her right the elevator doors opened and several people got out. Jessica sat there, her heart still thumping noisily, and waited to see if anyone got on. But the doors closed. She started her car, then turned to be sure the way was clear and saw someone open the doors that led directly into one of the department stores. She had only a quick glimpse of someone dressed in dark colors, and then the door closed behind him.

She didn't know what to do. It seemed pointless to call the police. The mall was enormous and she couldn't even describe him. She tried to fix that fleeting image in her mind, but found that she couldn't even guess his size.

She drove out of the garage, wondering if she could have overreacted. The more she thought about it, the likelier that seemed. If the man had been pursuing her, he certainly could have caught her. He was probably just someone else looking for his car.

Still, she was annoyed with herself for her carelessness, especially since she'd assured Casey that she didn't take chances.

She was nearly to the freeway ramp when she remembered that she needed to stop by her apartment to pick up her mail and some clothes. So instead, she turned off onto an unfamiliar street, then got lost for nearly half an hour before she finally found her way to her neighborhood.

Her home had that stale, musty smell that spoke of abandonment, so she opened some windows before she sorted through her mail. There were no more threatening letters. Then she checked her machine. The first two messages were from her grandmother, whom she was still avoiding. That situation would have to be dealt with soon, she supposed. It was actually rather surprising that Gran hadn't called her at work.

Jessica knew that, in the end, she would forgive her grandmother, who had certainly acted out of misguided love. But she was still angry enough to let her wait, and hope that she would at least admit to herself that she'd been wrong.

The only other message was from Joel, who wanted to know if she'd chosen wallpaper yet. She hadn't. She had been planning to do it over the weekend, but she was here so little now that it seemed less urgent.

Listening to Joel's voice reminded her that she hadn't told Casey that she'd seen him. On the other hand, Casey hadn't asked about him, either. She hoped that meant he no longer considered Joel to be a suspect. She knew that he was concentrating on finding the other two suspects, who had managed thus far to elude him.

She went into her bedroom and began to sort through her closet, trying to decide what to take with her. But something began to nag at her, and she found herself staring at the two boxes on the top shelf.

One box contained old financial records, preserved for the benefit of the IRS, and the other was filled with an assortment of memorabilia, including old photos and scrapbooks from her childhood and teen years. They were sturdy cardboard boxes with fitted lids, one brown and the other a mottled black and white, purchased at an office supply store. And as she stared at them, she became somehow certain that they'd been reversed.

Uneasiness settled over her like a scratchy cloud, prickling her skin. Why would she think that unless it was true? Why would she have even noticed them unless they were different?

On the other hand, she might still be suffering from the aftereffects of that incident in the garage, and her mind could be playing tricks on her.

Still, she went to the kitchen and got her small ladder, then took down the boxes, telling herself all the while that she was really losing it. What on earth had happened to the calm, levelheaded woman she used to be?

She opened the first box and saw that the files of financial records appeared to be undisturbed. But the box of memorabilia was a different matter. It hadn't been all that well organized to begin with, but it seemed even less so now. Still, she hadn't opened it since her move and it could certainly have been tumbled around then.

She sorted through it quickly and decided that nothing was missing, then put both boxes back up on the shelf and went to check the windows and the front door, since she'd come in through the kitchen entrance.

The windows she hadn't opened were all locked, and so was the front door, where the chain was still in place, as well. But now she couldn't seem to rid herself of that creepy feeling that someone had been here, so she walked through the entire apartment, looking for any missing items.

She was about to leave when she thought about her jewelry. Telling herself that she was wasting her time, she still went back to her bedroom and opened her lingerie drawer, then felt beneath it for the two soft leather pouches where she kept most of her jewelry. They were right where she'd left them and she could feel the jewelry inside.

She closed and locked the windows, gathered up the clothes she was taking along and left the house, really annoyed with herself now for her overactive imagination.

CASEY WASN'T HOME when she reached his house, and she was disappointed, since he'd told her he would be home early. Of course, "early" for him could well mean anytime before midnight, and it wasn't quite eleven yet.

She felt tense and decided that the perfect way to relax would be to try out Casey's big tub spa. Swimming was out because she could hear thunder in the distance. So she turned on the taps and began to undress, hoping he would come home soon to join her. They hadn't used the tub together yet because they'd been swimming every evening.

She picked up the bottle of bath salts she'd bought and poured them into the swirling waters. A delicate floral scent filled the air. She smiled as she thought that he'd probably have a few choice words to say if he came home and found that she'd turned his masculine paradise into a feminine flower garden, even though he'd seemed to appreciate the bouquets of fresh flowers she'd brought home.

Home, she thought as she slipped into the scented, swirling waters. His home, not hers. She needed to keep reminding herself of that. More than once she'd found herself mentally rearranging furniture, adding some of her favorite pieces, making small changes here and there. The house was so unrelentingly masculine, just like its owner.

When this is over, she told herself, repeating a by-now-familiar phrase, we can sort it all out. *Love* was a word that hadn't been mentioned yet by either of them, but she knew they both saw it in themselves and in each other. How could they not?

And yet there were so many troubling questions: his irregular hours, his tendency to be overprotective of her, her need to be independent, to not let herself be dominated by him.

She began to relax as the water churned around her, and then wished that she'd thought to pour herself some wine. So she climbed out of the tub, wrapped herself in a towel and went to the kitchen. Tacked to the refrigerator door was a hastily scrawled note. "Might not be home till morning. Sorry."

She frowned, wondering when he'd written it. Obviously he *had* come home early, and then been called out again. Could there have been some development in the case, or perhaps another killing?

She glanced at the kitchen clock. It was too late for the TV news and when she turned on the all-news radio they were just beginning their lengthy sports coverage. She poured herself some wine and went back to the tub, disappointed that she wouldn't be sharing it with him. Whatever had happened, she just didn't want to hear about it tonight.

THE BEDSIDE CLOCK READ 5:12 when a sound awakened Jessica. Fear turned quickly to relief as she identified it: the automatic garage door. A moment later she heard the distant, muted sound of the door between the garage and the house opening and closing. When several minutes passed and Casey didn't appear in the bedroom, she got out of bed to find him.

He was in the kitchen, fixing himself two large sandwiches. "Is this dinner or breakfast?" she asked as he turned toward her.

"It's a meal. I've given up on defining them."

She sank down at the small kitchen table. His attempt at humor was halfhearted and his expression was grim. She knew the answer even before she asked the question.

"Another one?"

He nodded as he took a carton of milk from the refrigerator. Casey, she'd discovered, was a walking advertisement for the dairy industry. He took a long swallow from the carton, then poured a tall glassful before joining her at the table, dropping a quick kiss on the top of her head as he passed by. He took several bites of sandwich before responding.

"She was older than the others, but the same type. He's moving around. This one was at Woodside Mall."

Jessica felt her world spinning. She was so stunned that she couldn't speak for a moment, and she could actually feel the blood draining from her face. He didn't notice because he'd gotten up again to add some pickles to his meal.

"Wh-when did it happen—exactly?" she asked.

"The medical examiner estimates it was around nine o'clock, an hour before the mall closed. The security patrol found her in the garage near her car at ten-twenty." He had sat down again and was staring at her intently. "Why did you want to know?"

"Oh, my God," she whispered.

"Jessie, what is it?" he demanded impatiently.

"I was there, Casey. I left just before nine, and someone was following me in the garage."

She swallowed hard, then told him all of it while he sat there ignoring his food, his expression becoming grimmer and grimmer. When she had finished, he slammed his fist against the table, nearly spilling his milk.

"Dammit, Jessie! How could you be so stupid? Even if there wasn't a killer on the loose, those damned garages are a mugger's paradise!"

She recoiled, not because she feared him but because she'd never seen him so angry. Immediately his expression softened and he reached out to take her hand.

"I'm sorry, honey, but how do you expect me to react when you do something that dumb?"

She couldn't very well argue the point. "Do you think it could have been the same man?" she asked in a strangled tone.

"We have to assume it could have been. Try to remember. Was there anything at all that stood out about him?"

She shook her head. "I already told you everything I know. If I'd gotten a better look at him, I would have called the police." She stopped and caught her breath with a sob.

"If I'd called them, that woman might not have been killed."

"No, don't blame yourself, Jessie. In a place that size we could have had a couple of squad cars there and he'd still have gotten her. What level were you parked on?"

"Six."

"She was killed on four. She had a couple of shopping bags with her so we're going to check the stores in the morning, to see if we can retrace her route."

He picked up his sandwich again and began to eat, his expression thoughtful. "It might not have been the killer you saw," he said after a few moments. "In fact, it probably wasn't."

"What do you mean?"

"Simple logistics. If the man following you was the killer, then he couldn't have had enough time to find another victim and follow her, unless he got awfully lucky and discovered another tall blonde right after you saw him."

"Then the man I saw could have been just an ordinary mugger?"

"Yeah, but I sure hope that you're not taking any comfort from that."

She wasn't. And somewhere deep inside, in that part of her that operated purely on instinct, she was sure that the man she'd seen *was* the killer, even if the logistics suggested otherwise.

Casey finished his sandwiches in a brooding silence that continued as they went into the bedroom. And he was still silent as he dropped heavily into bed beside her and reached for her, fitting them together and kissing the bare curve of her neck. Within moments he had fallen asleep.

Sleep eluded Jessica for a while longer as she lay there, virtually surrounded by the solid warmth of his body. There were too many patterns in the mosaic of her life at the moment: the revelations about her parents' deaths, the possibility that their murderer and the serial killer were one and the same, the phone calls and letters and the prowler outside her house that might or might not be Robert Collins, the man who'd had the opportunity to grab her but hadn't taken it.

And then, of course, there was Casey and her, struggling to carve out some time for themselves amidst all of it. Everything was so new between them, and even though there were many times when they seemed to have known each other forever, their feelings were still very fragile.

She wanted desperately to do something—anything—to end this. And if the serial killer *was* the man who'd murdered her parents, something she still found impossible to accept, then she wanted even more to be a part of bringing him to justice.

THE NEXT DAY, in between court appearances and client appointments, Jessica resumed her calls to the city's various shelters. And when she reached the next to last one on the list she finally got an affirmative response.

"Yes, he's been here the past four or five nights," the social worker told her. "We're very worried about him. We have a consulting psychologist who's spoken to him briefly and he feels that Robert should be hospitalized."

"Can't he have him committed?" Jessica asked.

The social worker sighed. "No, not at this point. The law governing involuntary commitments are very strict. Basically, he has to pose a threat to himself or to others, and he just doesn't fit that criterion yet. In fact, the courts have ruled in the past that coming to a shelter is proof that a person is unlikely to harm themselves. It's very frustrating.

"I suppose I could call the police and let them know that he's here, but I know from past experience that he'll just end up in jail. It's up to them to decide if he's bad enough to warrant hospitalization instead, and if they do decide that, the cost of his stay in the hospital ends up coming out of the criminal justice budget and, well, you know how *that* is. Jail's expensive, but hospitalization is even more so."

"Maybe I can persuade him to enter treatment voluntarily," Jessica suggested. "Is he there now?"

"No, everyone has to leave during the day, at least from this shelter. We only take single adults and we expect them to get out and look for work during the day. But in Robert's case that's ridiculous. No one would hire him. He'll probably be back when we start to serve dinner at five."

"Fine. I'll come over then and try to talk to him." Then, after she had hung up, she realized that she didn't have her own car. Casey would be picking her up at five. She really wanted to see Robert alone, to make one last attempt to get him some help before giving up and letting the police take him off to jail. Perhaps she could convince Casey to wait outside.

"NOTHING DOING," he told her when she suggested it two hours later. "I'm going in with you. But I'll keep my mouth shut and you can try to talk to him first."

"A lot of good that's going to do," she grumbled. "He'll probably freak out the minute he sees you."

"Was he there from five o'clock on last night?"

"I didn't think to ask, but from what the social worker said, I assume he must have been." She realized what he meant. If Robert had been at the shelter, then he couldn't be the killer.

She thought again about that shadowy figure she'd seen in the mall garage. "I don't think the man I saw last night could have been Robert. He seemed thinner. But the last time I saw Robert, in the park, he was wearing an old, bulky jacket."

"I talked to our shrink about him, and based on what I told him, he doubts that Robert could be the killer. He agrees with what Susan and Todd told you—that he's too disorganized."

Jessica hoped they were all right, but if they were, then she had to face the increased possibility that the serial killer was stalking *her* and taking his time for whatever reason.

WHEN THEY ENTERED the shelter, Jessica saw Robert seated in a corner of the big dining room by himself, eating his dinner and talking animatedly to the empty space across from him. Jessica didn't know if he'd chosen to be alone, or if the others were just staying away from him.

The man in charge of the shelter told Casey that he was fairly certain Robert had been there the previous night and the two of them went off to the office to check the records, giving Jessica a chance to speak to Robert alone.

She made her way past the long tables and sat across from him. He looked up at her and she smiled. "Hello, Robert. Do you remember me?"

"Are you going to arrest me?" he asked, as he had before. But his tone seemed more curious than hostile.

"No, Robert, I'm not a police officer. I'm a lawyer." But she was beginning to realize that in his own way, Robert *did* recognize her, at least to the extent of connecting her to the charges brought against him.

She reminded him gently that he had a court appearance and had failed to show up. He said nothing, and she wasn't sure that he'd even heard her. He kept glancing around him as he sat hunched over his tray.

"What are you afraid of, Robert?"

"Them," he said, continuing to glance around.

"You mean the police?"

He shook his head with an odd, jerky movement. "The ones with needles. They want to stick me."

Considering her earlier observations of the other shelter residents, Jessica at first thought he meant drug addicts. Then she recalled that a psychologist had talked with him.

"Do you mean nurses in a hospital?"

He nodded, then began to attack his food.

"They could help you, Robert. Don't you think you need some help now?"

He said nothing, and once again she wasn't sure he'd heard her. She watched as he stabbed at a chunk of meat loaf, wielding his fork like a dagger. The unmistakable violence of his movement made her blood run cold.

And then he suddenly leaped up from the table, bumping against his tray in the process and sending it crashing to the floor.

"No!" he shouted, his eyes wild as he stared at her. "You're one of them!"

Jessica had risen from her seat as well, and was very grateful for the fact that the long table was between them. But then he turned and ran toward the doorway, only to collide with Casey and the shelter director as they hurried into the room.

Jessica cried out as she realized that Robert still had the fork in his hand, but even as the cry left her lips, Casey had succeeded in getting it from him and turning him so that his arms were pinned against his back. Robert struggled and shouted and swore and tried to kick Casey, and then he just seemed to crumple.

By the time Jessica reached them, Casey was urging Robert out the door and speaking to him quietly. She followed them, determined to get Robert to a hospital instead of to jail. But when they reached the sidewalk a patrol car was just pulling in, and the moment Robert saw it, he began to struggle again.

"Just stay calm, Collins, and no one will hurt you," Casey said as he wrapped himself around the writhing man.

Whether he was heeding Casey's soft words or had simply given up the fight, Robert once again became still, and Casey got him into the back of the patrol car, then turned to the two uniformed officers.

"Take him over to Riverview. I'll call them and let them know he's on the way."

"Why Riverview?" she asked after they had gone. As far as she knew, it wasn't a psychiatric hospital.

"They have a small, locked psychiatric unit. That's where we send anyone who's too crazy to be put in jail. The department doesn't like it much because of the expense, but I can justify it on the basis of his being a suspect in the serial killings. He'll be evaluated by their people tomorrow."

After he called the hospital, they left the shelter to go to dinner. Casey told her that the shelter's records showed that Robert had definitely been there the previous evening.

"They lock the doors at eight o'clock and he had signed in before that. The fire exits are all alarmed and no one left that way. So that eliminates him as the killer."

"But if you knew that already, how can you justify sending him to Riverview?"

Casey turned to her briefly with a grin. "I guess I won't get to see the shelter's records until tomorrow. Would you rather he went to jail?"

"No, of course not." She leaned across the seat and kissed his cheek. "Thank you. But what if the hospital won't keep him?"

"Something tells me that the arresting officer, who's known far and wide for ignoring his paperwork, just might forget about him. I'll call the shrink tomorrow and tell him or her about those letters and phone calls, and see what they have to say about that, too."

"But if Robert wasn't responsible for them, then they must have come from the killer," she said with a shiver.

"Maybe," he admitted, reaching over to squeeze her hand before turning his attention back to his driving.

She continued to mull over the situation as they ate seafood in a small place that more than made up for its lack of ambience by the quality of its food.

"Casey, if the killer has made me his target and I stay out of his reach, you'll never catch him and he'll just go on killing other women." She was thinking about that incident in the mall garage, though, when surely he could have gotten her.

"I think I know where this conversation is headed, and the answer is no."

"If it was anyone else, you'd agree to it," she challenged.

"Maybe I would, but we're not talking about anyone else. We might try using a female officer as a decoy, though. There are a couple of them who are tall enough, and with a blond wig, it might work, especially if he stays at the mall. He might do that, because it's a good hunting ground. More women than men, and most of them are young."

"That sounds pretty iffy to me, especially since he's been finding them all over the city."

"I know that, but the answer is still no."

"Casey, listen to me! I could go back to the mall and you could have some of your men follow me around. Or I could move back to my apartment and you could hide someone there. I want to *do* something!''

They argued, but she knew it was pointless. She even threatened to go to his superiors and offer her assistance. He said she was free to do whatever she wanted, but it wouldn't make any difference. He was in charge of the investigation and he wasn't going to put her at risk.

"You're a male chauvinist pig!" she stated angrily.

"Don't try to lay that one on me. I already said I was willing to use a policewoman as a decoy. It isn't a question of gender. It's a question of being trained to handle the situation."

"If I were a policewoman, you'd still be unwilling to let me do it."

"You're right," he admitted, though far from sheepishly.

"So you admit it!" she said triumphantly.

"The only thing I'm admitting is that I'm unwilling to put the woman I love at risk."

They stared at each other in charged silence. Then she shook her head ruefully.

"I'll say this for you, Casey, you're very good at diversionary tactics. You'd probably have made a very good trial lawyer."

"What are you talking about?" He frowned.

"Did I or did I not just hear you say that you love me?"

"So? Is this new and startling information?"

"You never said it before."

He shrugged. "It didn't seem necessary."

The waitress approached them, a bit warily, Jessica thought, wondering if they'd been providing unintentional entertainment for the other patrons. She glanced around and saw several people avert their gazes a bit too quickly. They were smiling, too.

Casey asked for the check and gave the waitress a credit card. As soon as she was gone, Jessica leaned toward him keeping her voice low.

"I suppose you think I love you, too?"

"I don't think it. I know it."

Their eyes met in a silent clash of wills that was quickly buried beneath the memories that flowed back and forth between them, memories of lovemaking that lent credence to his statement about words not being necessary.

They left the restaurant and drove to her place so she could pick up her mail and some more clothes. Leaving Casey to prowl around the apartment checking windows, Jessica gathered up what she needed, then remembered just as she was about to leave that she wanted the heavy gold chain she usually wore with the blouse she'd selected. So she returned to the bedroom and opened her lingerie drawer, then took out one of the leather jewelry cases.

After removing the chain she wanted, she started to put the pouch back into the drawer, then stopped as something tickled her mind. Not quite sure what was bothering her, she opened it again.

When she realized what was missing, she felt a sudden chill. But she fought it off and got the other case, certain that she must have accidentally put it in there.

She hadn't. In fact, she hadn't taken it out in ages—and now it was gone. She searched through both cases again, desperate now to dispel the truth that was clutching at her with icy fingers. Could she have put it somewhere else?

No, she couldn't have. She hadn't worn it for years—not since her teens—but she'd always kept it here.

She sank onto the bed, horrified. The impossible had now become the only answer. She thought about that shadowy figure following her in the mall garage and about the letters and phone calls. And then she remembered the boxes on her closet shelf that she thought had been moved.

"Jessie?"

Casey's voice was tentative, barely impinging upon her consciousness as she sat there, staring into the deep, dark abyss of the past.

She got up and walked over to the dresser. She'd taken the photo of her parents and her and their fellow commune members to a photographic studio, where they'd enlarged it and then airbrushed out all the others. It was still in a bag, since she hadn't yet found a suitable frame.

She slid it out of the bag and stared at it, feeling that same bittersweet tug of a past she couldn't recall. Casey peered over her shoulder at it.

"They did a good job," he commented. "Jessie, is—"

"Do you—" She stopped to clear her throat. "Do you see that necklace she's wearing?"

He leaned forward to examine the picture. "Uh-huh. It's a peace symbol, isn't it?"

"Yes. Gold on a gold chain. It's gone."

"What do you mean?"

"I had it, and it's gone. It was in that jewelry case." She pointed to the two leather cases on the bed.

Casey picked them up and dumped out the contents, then began to sort through it. She just stood there watching him, hoping absurdly that he'd find it. But of course he didn't.

"Are you sure it was here?"

"Yes. I've always kept it there."

"When did you last see it?"

She thought. "Last week, when I took out some silver chains. I'm not sure what day it was."

"Where are the pearls you wore to the ballet?"

"I don't keep them here. My good jewelry is in a safe deposit box at the bank."

"Are you sure it isn't there, too?"

"Yes, I'm sure," she said impatiently. "Someone was here."

Then she told him about the boxes. "I checked the jewelry cases then, just to be sure they were here. But I didn't open them. And when I didn't see anything missing, I just assumed that I'd been wrong about the boxes."

"Could anything be missing from the box of memorabilia?"

She sank onto the bed. "I suppose it's possible. I didn't look that carefully."

"Was there anything in there that belonged to your mother?"

"No, but there were some pictures of her," she said dully.

He asked which box it was, then got it down and opened it. She didn't want to look, because she was now certain what she'd find—or *wouldn't* find. And she was right.

"There was a smaller version of her college graduation picture. That one." Jessica indicated the framed photo that sat on her night table. "It's gone."

She looked away from him, struggling to control her tears. "Casey, you know what this means?"

He drew her into his arms and kissed her. "Yes. It means I was right about the serial killer being the same man who murdered your parents. I didn't want to be right, Jessie. I've been hoping I was wrong."

"But how did he get in here?" she asked plaintively. "What about Matthews?"

She drew away from him. "It couldn't have been Joel," she protested. "And anyway, I was here every time he came to work."

"When did he bring the ladder?"

She explained. "It *isn't* Joel! Don't you think I would know if he was the man who killed my parents? There has to be another explanation."

She gathered up her things and left the bedroom. Casey followed her.

"Where does that door lead?" he asked, pointing to a door at the end of the hallway.

"It just goes out into the stairwell that leads upstairs."

"It's not a dead bolt. I could slip it easily."

"What are you saying now? That the Stevensons broke into my apartment?" she asked angrily.

"No, but do they ever leave the outside door unlocked?"

"No. They even lock it when they go out to the backyard. I remember because Ted was teasing Vicki about being overly cautious. And I'm sure they've been even more careful since we had that prowler."

"Then we're back to Matthews."

"No, we're not. I don't want to talk about this anymore."

Casey drew her into his arms. She resisted for a second, then wrapped her arms around him and buried her face in his chest. Despite what he'd said earlier, he hadn't really believed that the two killers were one and the same, and he didn't want to believe it now, either. But the evidence that it was indeed the same man could not be ignored.

Somewhere out there was a psycho who'd been killing the same woman over and over for twenty-five years—and one who had now set his twisted mind to completing the cycle of violence by killing the daughter of his original victim.

Casey had hunted killers before, but he'd never had such a personal stake in the search.

Chapter Ten

Casey stopped just inside the glass doors that led to his terrace. Jessica was stretched out on the big chaise longue, her body golden and glistening with suntan oil. She was wearing only the bottom half of her string bikini.

This past week had been difficult for them both. He was frustrated by his failure to capture the killer and she was searching the face of every stranger for the man who'd killed her parents and was now out to get her. He thought wryly that if they were in this "for better or for worse," they sure as hell were getting the "worse" right now.

They hadn't yet discussed marriage, but it was obvious where this was headed. Already he couldn't imagine coming home to an empty house, even though he'd been doing just that for years and had liked it that way.

He shook his head ruefully. One woman, one chance meeting—and, pow! Shot right through the heart by that little winged guy with the arrows. He was even starting to wonder what kind of father he'd be.

He slid the door open and stepped out onto the terrace. Adolf had found himself a shady resting place and lifted his head briefly, then lowered it again. He'd come out to greet Casey at the garage, then returned to his guard duty. Somehow the dog had caught on very quickly, understanding that Jessica was very important to his master.

Jessica didn't move. She was lying on her stomach, one arm flung up to cover her face. He smiled, guessing that she needed some sleep after he'd awakened her at three in the morning. He knew it was selfish of him, but after eighteen hours straight of dealing with various and assorted lowlifes, he'd needed her warmth and softness.

He ran his gaze slowly over her body, a body he knew better than he knew his own—perhaps better than she herself did. She'd reminded him a few times about his streak of possessiveness, but it just wasn't something he could control.

But he *did* understand how she felt, despite what she thought. He knew she was going through a bad time that left her feeling very vulnerable and dependent on him, and that both those things were alien to her nature.

He left her to her nap and jumped into the pool. As he swam his laps he wondered if he should tell her about one of the two surprises he had for her. In retrospect, maybe it hadn't been a wise move on his part. She might accuse him again of trying to take over her life.

JESSICA AWOKE TO SEE Casey climbing out of the pool, his dark hair plastered to his head and his body glistening wetly. She smiled lazily as she felt a thrill of possession run through her. Of course, she'd never admit to him that she felt that way, too.

He walked over and dripped onto her as he bent down to kiss her. "Late night?" he inquired with a chuckle.

"It didn't start out that way," she replied, smiling at the memory of her interrupted sleep. "Did you stop by my place to see if the painting arrived?"

"Uh-huh. It's inside."

She leaped up from the chaise and hurried inside, eager to see it. True to the chief's words, the couple who owned it had refused her offer to buy it and had instead given it to her. Jessica had already decided that she would try to find something similar to give to them as a replacement.

The multiple layers of protective wrapping were cut and peeled away and they both stood staring at it. Jessica was fighting tears as she reached out to trace her father's signature at the bottom.

It was a beautiful impressionistic work, obviously influenced by Monet's paintings from Giverny. There was a field of pastel flowers and a soft gray, weathered fence in the foreground. Jessica recalled the chief's story about seeing her mother and her in such a field and wondered if it could be the same one.

"Well?" Casey asked, leaning close to it.

"Well what?" she asked, still half fighting tears.

"Is it any good—or shouldn't I ask?"

"You probably shouldn't ask, but yes, I think it's good. I didn't know what to expect, really. I guess I thought it might be political in some way."

"Maybe some of the others are."

"What others?"

"The ones your grandparents have."

She tore her eyes from the painting with difficulty. "What are you talking about? I don't know if they—"

"They do. I talked to them."

"You *what?*" She stared at him in astonishment.

"Uh, well, I thought I'd sort of check them out first. They could have died or moved or—"

"You really called them?"

He nodded. "I talked to them both. They seem like nice people, and they're really looking forward to hearing from you. I told them we'd come to visit soon." He gave her a wary look. "Are you mad at me?"

She had to smile at his expression. "No, I'm not mad at you. I'm glad you did it." She sighed and turned back to the painting.

"I've been putting it off because I was afraid they wouldn't want to hear from me. I thought they might blame me in some way for the fact that Gran kept them away."

"I explained all that to them. I think they feel guilty that they didn't push harder to see you, but apparently your grandmother made a pretty formidable barrier."

"I don't doubt that," she said sourly. "So they have more paintings?"

"Uh-huh. Including their favorite. It's a portrait of you and your mother. You were two years old at the time."

"Oh." She felt tears stinging her eyes again.

"They also said you have an aunt and an uncle and a couple of nieces and nephews to meet. They all live nearby."

"Oh, Casey," she said, wrapping her arms around him and burying her face in his chest. "For once, I don't mind that you took over my life."

He kissed the top of her head. "Can I store up some points this time so you don't yell at me the next time I do it?"

"SHE SAW HIM?"

"No, she didn't get a look at him. There are some big bushes next to the door of her condo. Those places never think about security when they do their landscaping," Casey added in disgust. "He jumped out at her as she was unlocking the door. She kneed him in the groin just like they taught her in her self-defense course, and then she ran inside and called 911. Of course, he was long gone by the time the patrol car got there."

"So she didn't seem him at all?"

"The only thing she could tell me was that she thought he was about six feet tall and kind of skinny, but still strong. It was dark because the light over her door was out. She thought it had burned out, but we discovered it had been unscrewed. She fits the general description—about your height, hair a little darker than yours, but still blond. She was pretty shaken up, so I told her we'd talk some more tomorrow."

Jessica frowned. "If he unscrewed the light bulb, that must mean that he'd followed her before, to find out where she lived."

"Right. She hadn't received any calls or letters, but she'd been at the mall the evening before for most of the evening."

"Does she know if he had a knife?"

"He had something. She didn't see anything, but when she kicked him, something fell onto the sidewalk. We didn't find anything."

She envisioned the scene. "But if she turned around to kick him, she must have gotten at least a glimpse of him."

"You have to see the place. It was seriously dark, and raining, to boot. Plus she was terrified. He was wearing dark clothing and a black baseball cap with the visor low. There's a chance she might remember some more when she calms down, but I doubt it. When you're in a situation like that, you don't think ahead to how you can describe him to the police. Still, I think it was him."

"Casey, I want to go back to the mall, and I should move back to my place, as well!"

"Don't start with that again," he growled.

"How many more women are you going to let die before you let me help?" she challenged angrily.

"Dammit, Jess, that's not fair!"

THE NEXT AFTERNOON Jessica walked into the small meeting room at police headquarters. Nearly a dozen people were present and all of them seemed to appreciate her presence, with the exception of one very large and very disgruntled detective leaning against the wall. She ignored him as a compact, gray-haired man introduced himself as the chief of detectives and thanked her for coming.

"I don't like using civilians for decoys, Ms. Aylesworth," the chief said. "But if Casey's theory is correct, you might be our only hope."

"If his theory is correct, then this is the man who killed my parents, Chief, and I want to see him caught as much as all of you do. Even more," she added softly.

Jessica was then asked a number of questions she knew were designed to determine her ability to handle the situation. At one point a dark-haired, bearded man spoke up, introducing himself as the department's psychologist. "He might not really intend to kill you, Ms. Aylesworth. If he *is* the man who killed your parents, what he might actually want is to take you as a replacement for her. From what Casey has told us, it appears likely that he killed her only because he couldn't have her for himself.

"That would explain the first letter, when he said, 'You are the one.' What he might have meant is that he intends for you to be the replacement for your mother."

"But what about the second letter?" she asked, glancing toward the still-scowling Casey.

"That's a little harder to interpret, but my guess would be that he was letting you know that he knew about your relationship with Casey and intended to stop it."

"Or it could mean that he intends to kill us both," Casey said, folding his arms across his broad chest and glaring at the pyschologist. "And in that case, what we should be doing is having me stay at her place, where he'd have a chance of getting us both."

"I don't think he'd go for that," the psychologist said. "The chances are good that he'd guess right away that he was being set up."

"So what?" Casey challenged. "The guy's a psycho and he'll feel compelled to try sooner or later. You said yourself that these creeps think they're invincible."

"I *did* say that," the psychologist acknowledged. "But I didn't mean to imply that he's stupid. If he's responsible for series after series of killings for twenty-five years, he's not taking many chances. And right now, he's able to keep control. He's venting his rage by taking other victims while he waits for his chance."

Jessica could see that this argument had been going on for some time. The others in the room all looked from Casey to the psychologist with amused expressions.

"If he was the one who followed me in the mall garage, why didn't he come after me then?" Jessica asked the psychologist. "He certainly had the opportunity."

"He could have simply wanted to be near you," the psychologist said with a shrug. "Sometimes these psychopaths operate in patterns known only to them."

"Or he could have been waiting until he could get the two of us together," Casey put in, still glaring at the psychologist.

"Casey," the chief said placatingly, "we've all agreed that however sick this guy is, he's not stupid. And to go after you, he'd have to be damned stupid." He turned to Jessica and introduced her to the only other woman in the room, a lanky, athletic-looking redhead.

"This is Officer Dianne Lawson. She's going to be your houseguest. And your neighbors directly across the street have agreed to let us set up shop in their second-floor guest room that faces your house. We'll have two men there around the clock, and they'll have infrared goggles.''

"Infrared goggles?'' Jessica echoed, frowning uncomprehendingly.

"The military developed them. It gives you night vision. Your street and your house aren't very well lit.''

"What about the park in the back?'' Jessica asked.

"The problem there is that it's a private park, as you know, and only the people in your neighborhood have keys. If it was a public park we could plant someone there disguised as a homeless person. But we got a key and we'll have some people there as much as possible. We checked out your upstairs neighbors and the attic, but the trees in the back block the view from those windows.''

The chief smiled at her reassuringly. "You'll be as safe as we can make you, Ms. Aylesworth. Let's just hope it works.''

Jessica felt a twinge of guilt when the chief mentioned her neighbors. She hadn't spoken to the Stevensons, and she thought that at this point they couldn't be too happy having her as a neighbor.

"What about the suspects?'' she asked the chief. "Have you found either of them?''

"As of late this morning, there are no suspects left,'' he told her. "Last night we caught the one who escaped from jail, and his alibis check out. And the blond guy from the singles' bar finally came in. It seems he's married and had no business being there, so he was afraid to get in touch with us. He's clean, too.''

"I talked to the people at Riverview about Robert Collins,'' Jessica said, "and they just don't think he could have sent those letters. Of course, we already know he couldn't have been responsible for the last murder.'' She sighed.

"So it could be anybody.''

"I'm afraid so.''

The meeting broke up and Jessica was discussing Dianne's arrival at her home that evening when Casey walked past her without a word and left the room. Dianne saw the look on her face and laughed.

"He'll get over it. We all think it's pretty funny, actually. It's the first time any of us have ever seen the man blow his cool. Someone's already started taking up a collection for a wedding present."

Jessica laughed, too. "Right now it feels more like a divorce."

"I'd say he's got it bad." Dianne grinned. "And if that old saying about the bigger they are, the harder they fall is true...."

They both laughed again.

"Casey and I went through the academy together," Dianne went on. "Then we worked together on the Sex Crimes Squad for a while. He was so incredibly good with the victims. They really responded to him. It was like he was proving to them that not all men are scum."

Jessica nodded. She certainly knew how gentle and caring Casey could be, but it helped to be reminded of that right now.

They made their plans. Dianne would arrive shortly after Jessica herself got home. She'd be bringing a lot of luggage with airline tags and driving a car with rental plates. And she'd dress up and go out regularly as though she was going on job interviews.

"It isn't likely that he could be spying on the house without being seen, but we want to make it look as authentic as possible," Dianne told her.

"But do you think that he'd try to break in if you're there?" Jessica asked.

"We think he might if he's getting desperate. As a woman, I wouldn't pose as much of a threat to him as a man would, and certainly not as much as Casey would. It's worth a try—that and your trips to the mall."

"But what about Casey? Is he going to stay away?"

Dianne smiled. "That's the game plan. We'd like the killer to think you split up with him. Need I tell you that he didn't like the idea very much? That's why he favors his own theory, that the killer wants to get both of you."

"IT ISN'T WORKING, Dianne," Jessica said glumly as she kicked off her shoes. "It's been four days now, not to mention three trips to the mall. I never did like malls, but now I hate them."

"It must be getting expensive, too." Dianne grinned, glancing at her shopping bags. "Maybe you should ask the department to reimburse you."

"I've already taken some of the things back. But at least most of the stores have their fall merchandise and good sales on summer things."

"Has Casey called you?"

"No, I think I'll try him now. He's been sulking long enough."

"Don't tell *him* that."

"I fully intend to. He needs someone to tell him off occasionally, and I've gotten to be very good at that."

"Ah, I see." Dianne nodded sagely. "Now I understand why you've hit a home run when the rest of them didn't get past first base." She glanced at her watch. "And speaking of baseball, the game should be coming on."

Dianne got up and headed for the TV set. Jessica smiled. Dianne was a baseball fanatic. The two of them were very different in every way, but Jessica liked her. They'd spent a lot of time talking about law school, because Dianne would be starting night classes in the fall and hoped eventually to become a criminal prosecutor. It amused them both to think that they might end up facing each other in court someday.

Jessica picked up the phone and punched out Casey's number. He answered on the second ring.

"I think you've sulked long enough," she said without preamble.

"Excuse me? Who is this? I don't recognize the voice. Are you one of my former girlfriends?"

"You're behaving like a little boy who didn't get his way," she said, undeterred. "Maybe I *will* become one of your former girlfriends."

"Ah, yes, Jessica what's-her-name. I remember you now. I'd put you completely out of my mind. It's a defense mechanism."

"A defense mechanism?"

"Yeah. Either I forget that I know you or I come over there and tear off your clothes and make love to you right there on the living-room floor in front of Dianne."

The image dangled temptingly in her mind—minus Dianne, of course. "I don't think that would be a good idea. Dianne likes you."

"If she likes me that much, maybe I can persuade her to take a walk."

"Maybe we could meet somewhere," she suggested, knowing that she should be keeping her mouth shut.

"Is that your subtle way of letting me know that you miss me, too?"

"I'll stop being subtle, then. I miss you. I want you. And it's driving me crazy."

"Hold on," he said. "I have to go turn up the air-conditioning. It's getting damned hot in here all of a sudden."

"You could always take a cold shower," she teased.

"We could meet at a motel, if you're careful to make sure you're not being followed."

She smiled. The idea was irresistible. "Tomorrow night?"

"I'll call you at work and tell you where and when."

JESSICA KNOCKED at the door of the motel room. This clandestine meeting was adding an element of excitement that wasn't really needed. She'd been unable to think of anything else all day as she struggled to be lawyerlike in court. The five days they'd spent apart felt more like five months or five years.

Casey opened the door. The powerful aura of his maleness jolted her, actually causing her knees to go wobbly. His gaze raked her, then went past her.

"I was careful. I'm sure I wasn't followed."

At that moment she heard a car pull in behind her, and whirled around to see a man who looked vaguely familiar stop only long enough to give them both an "okay" sign with his thumb and finger before pulling out again. Then suddenly she realized where she'd seen him before and glared at Casey as he took her arm and drew her inside.

"You had him follow me!"

"Just playing it safe," he responded as he reached for her.

She pushed away from him. "This is embarrassing! It'll be all over the police department by tomorrow!"

"No, it won't. Jeff's a friend and he knows when to keep his mouth shut. Anyway, what's the difference? Everyone knows you've been living with me."

"I was *staying* with you," she insisted, knowing how foolish she sounded. "There's a difference."

"If you say so. If all you wanted to do is argue, we could have done that over the phone."

Their eyes clashed, setting off a shower of sparks that filled the space between them with a sensual heat. If the bed had been more than a few feet away they probably wouldn't have made it. They tumbled onto the mattress, then tore off their clothes, arms and legs entangled as they struggled to free bodies that demanded satisfaction *now*.

Afterward, Casey rolled onto his back with a dramatic groan. "Woman, what have you done to me? I used to be in control of my life. I used to be my own man."

She laughed, recalling Dianne's remark. "The bigger they are, the harder they fall."

He pushed himself up on one elbow and stared down at her. "If there's one thing I can't stand in a woman, it's gloating. Of course, *you* remain completely in control, Ms. Poised and Sophisticated."

"I love you," she murmured, raising her mouth to his.

He held her to him with sudden fierceness. "I love you, too, Jessie. That's why I've been such a jerk. I'm so afraid of losing you."

They held each other, feeling insulated from the threatening world beyond the small room. And then they made love again, far more slowly this time, savoring every nuance along the way, enjoying the slow buildup of the force that bound them together.

THE NEXT EVENING Jessica was back at the mall, trailed by two plainclothes police officers who parked next to her in the garage, followed her into the mall, then split up to keep her under observation from a distance.

She spent another evening traversing the huge, multistoried mall, trying to behave like an ordinary shopper and trying not to see a potential killer in every man who glanced her way.

They had agreed to stay until an hour before the mall closed, a time they'd discovered when the garage was most deserted. Early shoppers had already departed and latecomers would be staying until closing time.

Retracing her earlier steps, Jessica paused at a shop she'd noticed before but hadn't yet visited—probably the only one in the whole place, she thought disgustedly. So she went inside and began to look through the sales racks of casual summer wear. A pair of pleated, flowing trousers caught her eye and she carried them into the dressing room. They fitted perfectly and she already had a top that would look good with them.

When she left the dressing room she realized that the shop had a circular stairwell that led to the lower level. She decided to have a look down there, as well. And then, just as she reached the bottom of the stairs, she saw Joel.

He was walking past outside, just beyond the doorway that opened onto the mall's lower level. He was even carrying a shopping bag from one of the men's stores. She smiled to herself, thinking that she'd never figured him for a mall rat. But she was sure it was him, even though she hadn't really seen his face. Joel had a distinctive, loose-limbed, gliding sort of walk.

She'd been feeling somewhat guilty about Joel. He'd left two messages some time ago about the wallpapering, and then she'd heard nothing more from him. And she was wondering, too, if he'd gotten the folksinging gig he'd mentioned.

She hesitated briefly. The officers hadn't followed her into the shop and it was unlikely that they'd realize there was a lower level. But surely she could take a few minutes to speak to Joel before they'd start to worry.

She handed the trousers to a saleswoman and promised to return for them, then rushed out into the mall, threading her way past the other shoppers until she reached Joel and called his name.

He started nervously, then belatedly broke into a grin as she teased him about being there.

"Yeah, well, every once in a while I like to see how the other half lives."

"How've you been?" she asked. "Did you get that folksinging gig you mentioned?"

"Not yet, but I'm still hoping. I'm working, though. They took me on for another house."

"That's great, Joel. Are you still willing to do that wallpapering for me, or are you too busy now?"

"No, I'll do it. I'll give you a call next week."

"Fine. I'd better go now. I have some friends waiting and they probably wonder where I went."

Joel said goodbye and walked away. Jessica stood there for a moment, staring after him, thinking about Casey's suspicions. It bothered her that she should even be thinking about them, because Casey was wrong. They'd brought back that photo and the sketch of Anthony Bensen and she'd examined them several times. Whatever resemblance to Joel Casey saw in them was lost on her. But then, she knew Joel and Casey didn't.

When she returned to the shop she found the two officers hurrying down the stairs and looking very worried. She apologized to them and explained that she'd spotted a friend outside in the mall.

They split up again as they all headed for the garage, but no one followed her. Her frustration grew. She'd been so certain that she could lure the killer into the arms of the police.

As she drove home Jessica began to wonder if they could be wrong about the killer's being after her. But how else could she explain the missing necklace and photograph? It still bothered both her and Casey that they hadn't been able to figure out how he'd broken in to her house.

Chapter Eleven

He was frustrated. Rage festered inside him like a suppurating wound. People had begun to eye him suspiciously and move out of his way. But he was only marginally aware of this, because he was retreating more and more into himself, and into the past.

He knew he could get to her, and maybe he could get to him, too. But he wanted them together. He *had* to get them together. It would be meaningless otherwise.

He no longer had any desire to kill others, although he continued to stalk them. Every fiber of his being was now concentrated on finding a way to get the two of them, to make them pay.

But he was cunning. He hadn't survived this long without an almost preternatural instinct for sensing danger. He didn't really know if they suspected him, so he had to play it safe. He had to wait until those instincts told him the time had come.

JESSICA LOOKED UP from her desk, drawn from her work by that uncanny sense of him, a sort of electrical connection that vibrated within her. For a long moment they simply stared at each other. She hadn't seen him for nearly a week, except for one brief, tantalizing glimpse out on the plaza as she'd been hurrying off to court. His gaze felt like a caress, arousing her as surely as if he'd touched her.

"We're calling off the stakeout," he said, coming into her office and taking a seat. "Either he's figured it out or he's moved on."

She nodded, not really surprised. Dianne had told her that the commissioner was complaining about the cost. It had now been nearly three weeks since the last death, and if they were dealing with the same killer it was possible that he'd moved on. His past pattern had been clear: a string of deaths over a several-month period, and then nothing.

"Do *you* think he's moved on?" she asked curiously.

"No. I think he's lying low for some reason, despite what our shrink says about his lack of control. My guess is that he knows our 'breakup' was staged and either knows or has guessed that we're staking out your place and sending you to the mall." He finished with a sound of disgust.

"Everyone agrees that the guy is no dummy, but then they refuse to believe that he's capable of figuring out our game. But if you look at it from his point of view, it's pretty damned obvious."

"If they think he's just moved on, then they must not believe that it's the same man who killed my parents," Jessica observed.

"According to the chief, that connection was always tenuous at best. Despite what the shrinks have said about Robert Collins, he could have made those calls and sent the letters."

"But what about the missing necklace and photograph?"

Casey heaved a sigh. "I've made that point ad nauseam, believe me. But it's a tough case to make in light of the lack of evidence of any break-in. You have to see their point of view, Jess—a necklace that you never wore and could have misplaced or lost somehow, and one photo from a box that could have gotten lost when you moved."

"Is that what you believe?" she asked angrily.

"No, but I can't make a strong enough case to convince them otherwise."

"So what do we do now?" she asked in frustration.

"I want you to come back to live with me. You'll be safe there."

She smiled.

"All right, I want you to come back, anyway."

"Be careful, Casey. You wouldn't want to get too romantic."

He chuckled and got up, then walked around her desk and bent down, bracing himself on the arms of her chair. His lips touched hers in a hard, brief kiss.

"I'll be home about eleven. Then I'll show you how romantic I can be."

After he left, Jessica sat there staring into space, thinking. She wanted so badly to believe that it was over, that they could get on with their lives. And she might have accepted that if it hadn't been for the missing necklace.

She was willing to admit the possibility that she could have lost that picture of her mother. After all, it was only a duplicate of the one she'd had framed. But she couldn't accept the possibility that she'd lost that necklace.

Instead, she felt as though they'd been left in limbo, making a pretense of normality while they waited for the killer to strike.

"WHAT IS THIS?" Jessica stared at him in amazement.

"Just what it looks like." He set down his burdens. "Flowers, chocolates, champagne and oh, yeah, this, too." He reached into his pocket and pulled out a tiny jeweler's box. "Jewelry, too. That should pretty well take care of it."

"Take care of what?" she asked, laughing.

"Didn't you complain that I'm not romantic?" He waved a hand at the gifts. "I think this should take care of any earlier lapses."

"I see." She smiled as she opened the florist's box and sniffed the large bouquet of long-stemmed roses. "You just decided to get it all out of the way at one time, is that it?"

"More or less. If you count the roses, you'll see that there's one for every day I've known you. I thought that was a pretty nice touch," he added smugly.

She thought so, too, but she wasn't about to tell him that. Instead, she turned to the chocolates while eyeing the jeweler's box nervously. Knowing Casey, he might just have slipped an engagement ring into the middle of the gifts and she wasn't sure she was ready for that. She popped a chocolate into her mouth and picked up the velvet box. Of course she was ready! She couldn't face life without this often exasperating but always fascinating man.

"Oh!" she exclaimed when she opened it to discover a pair of earrings. She didn't know whether to be relieved or hurt. Maybe a bit of both.

"They're black pearls," he told her. "Personally, I think they look like ball bearings, but the jeweler assured me that a woman of taste would appreciate them."

She certainly did, since she knew how rare and expensive they were. "They're lovely," she said, stretching up to kiss his cheek. "Thank you for everything."

"You're welcome. Now let's get naked and swill champagne."

They did just that, and a few other things, too. The night was sultry and they went for a swim while the champagne chilled, then retreated to the tub spa when thunder began to rumble in the distance. By the time the storm arrived they were in the midst of their own private love-storm. The power went off and they made love in his big bed, their bodies illuminated by the flashes of lightning outside the floor-to-ceiling windows.

It was after midnight by the time their hunger for each other had been satisfied. The barrenness of his refrigerator drove them out to a Chinese restaurant where he ate everything from both column A and column B, while she contented herself with lemon chicken and fried rice.

Afterward, the waiter brought them a plate of fortune cookies. Casey grabbed one, broke it open and stared, frowning, at the slip of paper.

"What does it say?" she asked, reaching for one herself.

He passed it to her. "If I'd gotten this earlier, I could have saved myself some money."

She read it. "Love is the greatest gift of all."

"You already have that, you know," he said softly, the proof glittering in his eyes.

She smiled and nodded. "And so do you."

But her smile faltered slightly when she pulled the strip of paper from her own cookie. "Beware the calm before the storm."

Casey took it from her and read it, then crumpled it and tossed it aside before reaching for her hand.

"There isn't going to be any storm, Jessie. Either I'll get him or I won't, but he isn't going to touch you."

ANOTHER WEEK PASSED. There were no more killings. The public lost interest. Casey's special squad was disbanded, although he continued to work on the case with a smaller group of detectives from homicide. But there were no leads to pursue and all of them had the usual burden of crimes to deal with.

The newspapers did a recap of the story, including the recounting of earlier murder sprees believed to have been perpetrated by the same man in other parts of the country. The public breathed a collective sigh of relief.

Casey and Jessica settled into the hectic life of a couple with two demanding careers. Summer invariably brought an increase in crime as people spent more time outdoors and left windows open. For both of them this meant an extra burden at work, which in turn made them cherish even more their time together.

Jessica made peace with her grandmother—a fragile peace, though, since she intended to take Casey with her to Gran's eightieth birthday party a little more than a month away.

She also contacted her father's parents and made plans to visit them early in the fall. Their warmth and love touched her deeply and were at least in part responsible for her being able to forgive her grandmother.

They had both stopped talking about the killer, and Jessica was beginning to wonder if she *could* have lost that necklace, as well as the picture. The link between the serial killer and the man who'd murdered her parents twenty-five years ago began to seem more and more unlikely.

One evening Jessica stayed late at her apartment, researching some cases while Casey prowled the streets of the District. Her work load was especially heavy at the moment because two staff were on vacation. Busy at work in her library, she was startled by a sudden insistent pounding at her door. When she started toward the front of the house, she realized that the sound was coming from the door that led into the Stevensons' stairwell.

"Jessica, it's Vicki!"

She unlocked it quickly to confront her pale, nervous neighbor.

"Someone was outside the house! We saw him run away when we drove up. Ted is calling the police."

The effect of this news on Jessica was shattering. In the space of a second the calm and happiness of the past weeks was swept away.

"Where did you see him?" she asked, suddenly thinking about the long windows in the library. She'd begun working in there before dark and hadn't yet closed the windows or drawn the drapes.

"He was outside your window—your library, I think. The light was on. That's how we knew you must be here."

Jessica ran back into the library and quickly closed the windows and drew the drapes. Other windows were open, as well, and she belatedly closed them, cursing herself for her foolishness and at the same time fighting her anger that such precautions should be required. By the time she had checked all the windows and doors, a patrol car was pulling in to the driveway.

She listened as the Stevensons described the man they'd seen. They hadn't gotten a good look at him, but thought he was fairly tall and rather slim with dark hair. One officer left immediately to begin checking the neighborhood while the other stayed to continue taking information. When Jessica gave him her name, he frowned at her.

"Aren't you Casey's girlfriend, the one they thought that psycho was after?"

She nodded unhappily, still almost unable to believe that she was back in the midst of the nightmare. The officer went back to his car to use the radio.

"Oh, God, Jessica, do you think it was him? I thought they said he'd left town." Vicki stared at her in shock.

When the officer returned, they went to the side of the house to check for footprints. Jessica thought about the hours she'd been in there, poring over law books, completely alone in the house, with windows open all over the place. She began to hope that it might have been only a Peeping Tom.

Directly beneath the library window they discovered footprints in the flower bed, sunk deep into the damp soil. Jessica hugged herself miserably, hoping desperately that it was anyone but the killer.

Then two cars pulled into the driveway, one right behind the other. The first was another patrol car, and the second was Casey.

They stared at each other in a silent understanding that the nightmare might not yet be over. Casey's hand slid over her shoulder and around her neck in a brief caress before he turned his attention to the Stevensons. She suddenly recalled that fortune-cookie warning. The calm before the storm was over.

"You were working in there?" Casey asked her after the Stevensons had told him their story.

"Yes. I was there all evening."

He stared at the window. "Was it closed? Were the drapes drawn?"

She hesitated, then shook her head. "No. I was busy and just didn't think about it."

Casey stared at her for a moment, then turned to one of the officers. "Get someone over here to take casts of those prints and dust the windowsills. Check the other windows, too." He turned back to Jessica. "Were there other windows open?"

She nodded miserably.

The first officer, who'd checked the neighborhood, returned and they all gathered to discuss the situation. Yet another squad car arrived. Casey ordered a door-to-door search to see if any of the neighbors had seen or heard anything. Many of them were already outside or peering out through their drapes.

Then a van arrived bearing the logo of a local TV station and Jessica quickly invited the Stevensons inside, so they could all avoid the pushy reporters. When she closed the door behind them she saw the TV crew descending upon Casey.

They were sitting in her kitchen drinking coffee when Casey appeared.

"Do you still have the boxes your law books were in?" he asked.

"Yes, they're in the basement," she replied, nonplussed. "Why?"

"Get them packed up so we can take them to my place. I'll be back in an hour or so. Someone will stay here until then, but he isn't likely to come back."

He turned to leave and she followed him to the door, seething inwardly. Mostly, she was angry with herself, but she couldn't quite prevent a small resentment at his high-handedness.

"You'll get over it," he said, bending to kiss her.

"Get over what?"

"This notion that I'm trying to take over your life. I'm a cop, Jessie, and what you're mixed up in now is *my* business. And don't blame yourself for what happened tonight. You're just behaving like any normal civilian who believes that crime is something that happens to someone else."

"It's him, isn't it?" she asked plaintively, hoping he would deny it. "I was really beginning to believe it was over."

He drew her into his arms. "I knew you were. You needed to believe it."

"But you didn't," she said, making it a statement and not a question.

"No. I hoped it was, but I didn't believe it."

Jessica locked the door and fastened the chain after he had gone, then returned to the kitchen and apologized to her neighbors for the problems she seemed to be causing them. They commiserated for a time, and then, as they were about to leave, Vicki asked if she'd seen Joel recently.

"No, I haven't," Jessica replied, recalling that she'd thought about him earlier this evening, when she'd remembered about the wallpaper she hadn't yet chosen. "Why?"

"He was building some bookshelves for us, and he didn't come back to finish them," Ted told her. "We don't have any way of contacting him."

"I don't think he has a phone yet, but I should be hearing from him soon. I didn't realize he was doing work for you."

"We really loved those bookcases he made for you," Vicki said. "So we asked him to make some for us. He seemed really reliable, so I was worried that something might have happened to him.''

"Well, as soon as I hear from him, I'll remind him," Jessica promised as they left.

Then she went down to the basement and brought up the crates for her law books. But somehow, as she began to pack them, she found that she couldn't get Joel out of her mind. Something was nagging at her, and the more she tried to deny it, the larger it loomed. By the time Casey returned, she had reached a very reluctant decision.

Casey carried the crates out to his car and she followed him to his house, already beginning to second-guess her decision. Casey wouldn't be objective. He didn't like Joel and, furthermore, his frustration at not being able to find the killer could easily influence his judgment.

By the time she reached his house, she had amended her decision. She had Joel's address at the office. Tomorrow she would go there after work to see him and to leave a message if he wasn't there. She told herself that she owed him the benefit of the doubt—and in any event, one more day wouldn't matter.

IT WAS NEARLY FIVE-THIRTY when she left the office and just past six when she finally found Joel's address: a small, nondescript apartment building. She didn't see his old truck around, but there was a driveway beside the building and she thought it might be parked in back.

His name wasn't on any of the mailboxes, but two of them bore only apartment numbers. As she was standing there uncertainly, a couple with a baby walked into the small foyer. She asked about Joel and was met with blank stares.

"There's no one here by that name," the man said.

"He hasn't lived here long," Jessica replied. "Could he be in one of the apartments without a name on the mailbox?"

They both shook their heads. "One of them is empty. The super's doing some plumbing work in it. And we know the people in the other one."

Jessica fought down a growing concern and asked if the super lived on the premises. The couple pointed out his apartment, at the rear of the first floor, and she knocked on the door.

His response was the same. No one named Joel Matthews lived there. Jessica described him and the man shook his head. She thanked him and returned to her car. Could she have gotten the address wrong, perhaps transposed the numbers? She was certain that she'd gotten the street right, but she might have made a mistake with the number.

Then she remembered that he would also have given the address to the probation officer who was acting as his bail supervisor. She decided she would check with him tomorrow. In the meantime, she drove several blocks in both directions, looking in vain for his truck.

"MR. WILLIAMS, THIS IS Jessica Aylesworth from the P.D.'s office. One of my clients is on supervised bail in your caseload and I need to check his address. The date has been set for his trial, and I've been unable to reach him. His name's Joel Matthews."

As she spoke, Jessica stared at the paralegal's note informing her that the trial date had indeed been set for two weeks from now.

"The address he gave me is 2572 Worrick," the probation officer replied. "But he's not there."

"How do you know that?" It was the same address Joel had given her.

"I sent him a letter reminding him that he failed to keep his last appointment, and it came back marked Addressee Unknown. I was planning to call you to see if I might have gotten it wrong."

"I have the same address," she said unhappily.

"Well, it isn't likely that we both got it wrong. I gave it to a detective a couple of days ago, too."

"What detective?" she asked. "Did he say why he wanted it?"

"No, he just called and said he needed it. I don't remember his name."

"Was it Casey?"

"No, I'd remember him. I think his name was Travis. He said he was from homicide. What's going on?"

"I'm . . . not sure," Jessica replied, then thanked him and hung up.

Jeff Travis was Casey's friend, a homicide detective who was part of the special squad set up to find the serial killer. The fact that he was now trying to find Joel must mean that Joel had become a stronger suspect. And it occurred to her that if Casey had indeed unearthed some evidence that could link Joel to the killings, he might not have told her. The man continued to be a sore subject between them.

She tried to think of a logical explanation for the incorrect address. Perhaps Joel had simply gotten it wrong. After all, he'd just moved there.

That makes sense, she told herself, then wondered if she might not be as bad as Casey was. Casey suspected him on the basis of a blurred twenty-five-year-old photograph and a poor sketch, plus his personal dislike of Joel, while she was defending him on the basis of a very limited relationship, plus the tenuous link he provided to an era and a life-style that fascinated her.

An hour later, after appearing at an arraignment, Jessica went to police headquarters. She had no idea if Casey would be there, but if he wasn't, perhaps she could talk to Jeff. In fact, given the arguments she and Casey had had over Joel, it might even be better for her to talk to his friend.

The desk sergeant obligingly rang Casey's office, but received no answer. "He was here earlier, but either he's gone out or he's got his phone unplugged again. Do you want to go down and check?"

She hesitated, then shook her head. "Is Detective Travis in?"

He was, and she followed the sergeant's directions to the homicide division. She found Jeff in the hallway with a cup of coffee.

"Looking for Casey?" he asked after greeting her.

"Well, actually, I was looking for either one of you. Joel Matthews's bail supervisor told me that you called and asked for his address."

"Uh-oh," Jeff said. "We're getting into sensitive matters here."

"What do you mean?"

"What I mean is that you'd better talk to Casey about that."

"Is he here?"

"No, but I'll have him paged and tell him you want to see him."

"Come on, Jeff. Stop playing games with me. All I want to know is why you were looking for him. He's a client of mine."

"I know, but I still think you'd better talk to Casey. I'm not going to get in the middle of this."

"What you're not telling me is that Casey still thinks Joel could be the serial killer. Don't bother paging him. I'll be in court the rest of the afternoon. I'll see him tonight."

"WHY DID JEFF TRAVIS call probation for Joel's address? Do you know something you haven't told me?"

"Suppose I go back outside and come in again and you can kiss me and ask how my day went?" he replied as he shrugged out of his jacket and shoulder holster.

"I want an answer, Casey—and I know Jeff must have told you that I asked him about it."

His pale eyes bored into her. "What's wrong, Jessie?"

"I . . . Answer my question first."

He stared at her for a moment longer, then shrugged. "I can't rule him out as a suspect, that's why. Jeff called probation because I was trying to avoid a hassle with you if I asked you for his address."

"Why do you think he's a suspect? Is it still just those pictures or is there something more?"

"What makes you think there could be more?"

"Dammit, Casey, stop answering my questions with more questions! And don't play cop with me!"

"I don't know if there's more. The problem here is that you're thinking like the defense attorney you are and I'm thinking like the cop I am. You don't want to hear about anything but hard facts, while I spend most of my time operating on hunches and guesswork."

She nodded with a sigh. "You're right. Then tell me about your hunches and guesswork."

"I'll admit that they're pretty thin, but I keep thinking about those things missing from your apartment with no sign of a break-in. That's bugged me ever since it happened. And the only person I can think of who could have taken them is Matthews. I know you said you were there the whole time, but it's a big apartment and if he knew you were occupied with something, he might have taken the risk."

She opened her mouth to protest, then stopped. She'd promised herself that she would look at this objectively. Still, her tone was both defensive and begrudging.

"I fell asleep one time he was there—in the living room. I probably slept for at least an hour." She paused. "And that's not all."

Then she told him about Joel's work for the Stevensons. "But I don't really see how he could have gotten in then. He would have been taking a big risk to go down their stairs and then take the time to slip the lock on the door into my apartment."

"Were the Stevensons home while he was there working?"

"I assume so. I didn't ask, but I can't see them giving him a key." Still, she was thinking about what they'd said—that Joel seemed "so reliable."

"Call them and ask them."

She nodded and went to the kitchen to make the call. This is all purely circumstantial, she told herself, then remembered what Casey had said about the difference between defense lawyers and cops.

Vicki answered and Jessica explained that she needed to know if there'd been any time that Joel had been alone in their apartment. In the brief silence that followed, Jessica felt very guilty. The Stevensons were nice people and she hated dragging them into her nightmare.

"Yes, he was, for maybe an hour or so," Vicki told her. "Ted was out to dinner with a client, and after Joel arrived, I remembered that I needed some things from the supermarket. Why? What's wrong, Jessica?"

"I'm not sure that anything is wrong, Vicki. You haven't heard from him, have you?"

"No. But what should I do if I do hear from him?"

Jessica glanced at Casey, who had followed her into the kitchen. "Call me right away. Do you have my numbers?"

Vicki said she did, and Jessica hung up, then related to Casey what she'd learned. She hugged herself miserably.

"And there's something else I haven't told you. I saw Joel at the mall. Not the night that woman was killed, but one of the nights I was there with the officers."

She expected an angry outburst from Casey, but what she got instead was what she really needed now: his strong arms around her. He kissed her, then stared down at her, shaking his head with a sad smile.

"We're a real pair, aren't we? We're both so damned emotionally involved in this. I want to play the knight in shining armor and slay the dragon who killed your parents, and you want to protect someone who made you feel close to them. One of us is wrong about him, Jessie, but we won't know which one it is until we find him."

ANOTHER WEEK PASSED. Casey and his team were searching the city for Joel and also trying to trace his background. There didn't appear to be much to trace. In fact, Casey became more and more convinced that the man called Joel Matthews simply hadn't existed prior to his arrival here, which, of course, made him even more suspect in Casey's eyes.

Following all this through Casey, Jessica was stunned to realize all the many ways in which a person's background could be traced. And she was shocked, too, at how easily someone could vanish and then reappear as someone else.

Casey had also run the name Anthony Bensen through his various computer sources. Several men of that name turned up, but none of them fit the age and description of the man who'd killed her parents.

To Casey's way of thinking, the disappearance of Anthony Bensen and the lack of any background on Joel Matthews was yet another reason to believe that the two could be one and the same. Jessica, however, remained skeptical, as yet unwilling to confront fully the possibility that a man she knew and liked could have killed her parents and was now after her. Instead, she waited and hoped that Joel would turn up and be cleared.

Early one evening Jessica was out on the lawn at Casey's, playing a game of Frisbee with Adolf, whose graceful leaps to catch the bright red disc were a pleasure to watch.

The property had a thick fringe of trees on all sides that concealed the fence. Mounted on the fence were electronic sensors that would trigger the alarm system if anyone tried to climb over it.

The sun had set and the shadows were lengthening by the time she grew tired of the game. Adolf, on the other hand, continued to catch the Frisbee and trot back to her hopefully.

"Okay, one last time," she told him, then sailed the Frisbee high into the air, where the breeze caught it and sent it off into the woods.

She was already jogging across the lawn, in case it had landed in a tree, when she heard Adolf suddenly begin to bark ferociously.

At first she assumed that he was barking because the Frisbee had landed out of his reach, but as she continued to run toward him, she heard him growl. Worried that he might have cornered an animal and wondering if she could persuade him to leave it alone, she ran into the woods, then spotted Adolf running along the inside of the fence, still barking and growling.

She heard a car start up before she reached the fence, and for the first time, Adolf's frenzied barking sent a chill through her. Dusk was falling, but she caught a quick glimpse of the car before it disappeared around a curve in the street beyond the fence. Adolf continued to bark for a few more seconds as he ran to stand between her and the fence, then subsided slowly into a series of low, frustrated growls. Periodically he'd stare up at a tree, then erupt into barking once more.

Jessica stared, too. There were trees on both sides of the fence. The one that interested Adolf had a sturdy branch that came within six feet of the fence, and on the other side of the fence, another tree branch came slightly closer. It certainly wouldn't be easy, and she'd never try it herself, but she guessed that someone with athletic ability might be able to make the ten- to twelve-foot leap.

Especially if he was desperate enough, she told herself with a shiver.

It didn't occur to her until they were on their way back to the house that the sensors could be activated even by someone passing over the fence without actually touching it. But as they started across the lawn she could hear the wail of the burglar alarm at the house. Adolf stopped growling and began to whine.

She ran into the house and switched off the alarm, then studied the instructions for how to reset it. When Adolf suddenly began to bark again, she froze for a moment, fearing that there'd been more than one intruder and he'd actually gotten onto the property. But then she belatedly remembered that the alarm system was tied in to the nearest police station. When she went to the front door she was greatly relieved to see a patrol car coming up the driveway. Casey had told her they had the code for the gate.

She explained what had happened and described the car. "I remember the first part of the license number, too," she told them, and gave it to them. One officer got back into the car to check on the license number, while the other followed her back to the fence. By now it was nearly dark. He played the beam of his flashlight over the fence and the trees while she told him what she thought might have happened.

"Yeah, I suppose it's possible, but it's a long jump. Casey'd better get one of those branches trimmed."

The officer turned the flashlight beam on the ground outside the fence. "There's a footprint!" he exclaimed.

Jessica saw it, too: a single print in the one spot where the ground was dusty, rather than hard packed. She told him about the print they'd gotten from her place.

"We'll call in the Crime Scene Unit and get one here, too."

"Has Casey been called?" she asked.

"Yeah, he's been paged, but something's going down in the District, so he's probably tied up."

Jessica felt a renewal of her fear. Most of the time she was able to keep her mind away from the dangers of Casey's job, but the officer's casual words did little for her already shattered peace of mind.

They returned to the patrol car to discover that the car she'd seen had been reported stolen the night before from a suburban area. Then the radio began to squawk again and one officer reached in and pulled out the mike. Casey's familiar voice identified itself and Jessica relaxed.

The officer told him what had happened. Casey asked to speak to her and he handed her the mike.

"Are you okay?" he asked. "I can't come home right now, but I'll get someone to stay with you."

"I'm fine," she assured him—even though she wasn't. "Your system worked and Adolf certainly made his presence known."

"HE'S GETTING DESPERATE," Casey said flatly when he came home several hours later. "I drove around to have a look at those trees. I'll get one of the branches trimmed tomorrow."

"Do you know yet if the sneaker print was the same as the one they found at my place?"

"Yeah, but it's a popular brand. They canvased the neighborhood, but no one remembered seeing that car. A couple of people weren't home, so we'll check again tomorrow. But with the houses set back so far from the street, our only hope is that someone was out walking or running."

"I just want it to be over," she said with a catch in her voice.

Casey drew her into his arms. "So do I, honey. What worries me most now is that he has to be getting really desperate. And if he can't get to you, or us, he's probably going to start killing again."

CASEY CALLED HER AT WORK the next day. "Someone *did* see the car and the driver. Two of my neighbors were just coming back from a bike ride and he went past them about a block from the spot where you saw him. They went out after that, which is why we didn't get to talk to them till this morning."

"Did they get a good look at him?" she asked, holding her breath as she awaited his answer.

"Yeah. They said he had dirty blond hair, kind of long and curly. They only caught a quick glimpse of him in profile, but they estimated his age at between thirty and thirty-five and said he seemed short and stocky, although that's hard to judge when someone's sitting in a car. And he was wearing a dark Windbreaker."

"None of that sounds like Joel," she said with unconcealed relief.

"No, but it could be a wig, or maybe he bleached his hair."

Jessica said nothing, but she thought that Casey was still too eager to pin it on Joel. She couldn't blame him, because she knew how frustrated he was, but she hung up with considerable relief.

Before long, however, that relief drained away, to be replaced by a gnawing anxiety. Which was worse: a killer she knew and liked, or a stranger who could be anybody she saw on the street?

Chapter Twelve

He could just barely contain his excitement. He was sure that this must be the chance he'd been waiting for. They were leaving the city!

He'd studied a map of the area where Casey lived and had quickly discovered that all the winding streets in that neighborhood fed into one main artery. Then he'd begun his surveillance, parking in the crowded lot of a shopping center. For days he'd been watching them come and go—her in her expensive sports car and him in his Wagoneer.

He'd been stealing cars and then abandoning them, never keeping the same one for more than a day. The cops would probably chalk it up to joyriding kids. And while he sat at the busy intersection he'd conducted his own survey to determine which color and model of car was most common and therefore least likely to draw attention.

Yesterday he'd gone out to the airport and had stolen a silver Honda from the long-term parking lot. The stamped ticket was inside, showing that the owner had parked it there only hours before he'd stolen it. That was Thursday, so he figured that he was probably safe through the weekend.

But he'd done something else, too, and he smiled now at his cleverness as he followed them. He'd bought two magnetized transmitters and a receiver. Putting one on her car had been easy enough. She parked in a big municipal garage during the day. But he hadn't managed to get the other one on Casey's Wagoneer until yesterday. The lot at police headquarters was too risky, with cops coming and going all the time and lots of windows overlooking it. But last night he'd found the Wagoneer parked down in the District and had finally managed to attach the device.

He had them in sight now, a safe enough situation on the busy interstate that bisected the city's western edge. For a while he worried that they might be headed for the airport, but they passed that exit and continued on. Obviously they were going off for a long weekend somewhere. And wherever it was, it had to be easier for him to get to them than that fortress of his.

He smiled to himself and reached up to touch the chain he was wearing around his neck. His fingers slid down to grasp the peace symbol hidden beneath his shirt. Yes, he had a very good feeling about this. It was all coming together at last.

For more than an hour he trailed them along the interstate, staying well behind them, but not so far that he couldn't keep the Wagoneer in sight. Traffic was still heavy and there were a lot of trucks, so it was easy to disappear from view for a time.

The Wagoneer had been traveling steadily in the left lane, but now it signaled and moved over into the right lane, where some trucks blocked it from his view temporarily. A big green-and-white sign announced an approaching exit. He stayed in the right lane, well hidden behind a truck.

He was debating whether or not he could risk getting off at the exit as they must surely be doing. Then the problem was solved for him as the truck put on its turning signal and began to slow down for the exit. He couldn't see the Wagoneer, but he figured that the worst that could happen would be that he was wrong about them exiting, and he'd have to get back on again.

The exit ramp curved downhill and he tried to see around the truck. There it was! He let out a shout of pleasure. The Wagoneer turned right and so did the truck.

But his luck ran out about ten miles later when the truck turned off and the Wagoneer continued straight. He was directly behind them now, keeping a safe distance back, but getting worried. It was a rural area with little traffic in either direction.

A few miles farther on they came to another intersection and he turned right, then drove just a short distance and pulled over. His receiver was beeping steadily, but he knew that its range wasn't all that great. After waiting impatiently for five minutes, he pulled out again and returned to the intersection, then continued in the direction they'd taken. They were no-where in sight, but the receiver indicated that they were still within range.

He picked up speed a bit in his eagerness, but after another four or five miles he still didn't see them, and the signal began to fade. He pulled over, did a U-turn and started back. He'd seen only one road that turned off this one: a narrow gravel road that disappeared into the thick woods.

When he reached it, the signal became stronger, so he turned onto it, then stopped again. His heart was thumping noisily in his chest. Sweat broke out on his face and hands. He was tak-ing a big risk here. He could come upon them at any bend in the narrow road.

But he was so close! He could feel it all coming together at last. He could make her understand how he'd suffered, how long he'd waited. When he got rid of Casey and she saw that he wasn't such a big man after all...

He waited, checking his watch every couple of minutes. The signal was getting weaker again, but he was still reluctant to follow them on a road like this. There was nothing around. He hadn't seen a single house since well before he'd turned off the main road.

He got out his map. At first he thought that the damned road wasn't even on it, but then he finally saw the thin blue line that ended abruptly near a series of small lakes. No towns, no nothing. He couldn't believe his luck now. It must be a cot-tage.

The transmitter continued to work, although it was getting steadily weaker. He kept expecting it to stop any minute and was wondering how many cottages there could be. But after a time he realized that the beeps remained steady. They must have reached their destination.

He consulted his map again and saw that there was a town not too much farther on along the main highway, so he reluc-tantly turned around and drove there. After wasting an hour or so getting gas and something to eat, he went back to the gravel road, where the receiver once again began to beep.

He decided to risk it and continued on the gravel road, the signal once again growing stronger as he drove cautiously. And then the road ended abruptly. Beyond it lay a maze of narrow dirt roads with wooden signposts. There was one large sign that said Private Roads and what looked like a dozen smaller ones with names on them. All of them vanished into the thick woods, no doubt leading to the lakes.

He scanned the names. Thomas, Hardesty, Travis, Hanrahan, Jacobsen.... No Casey. Some of the signs were clustered together beside a single driveway, while others were separate.

Then it occurred to him for the first time that Casey could be a first name, not a last. He hadn't thought about that before, since everyone just called him Casey.

No, wait a minute! He *had* seen another name in the newspaper. Some Polish name, he thought. He studied the signs again, searching this time for something familiar. But he didn't recognize any of them and began to wonder if they could be borrowing a cabin.

Worried about staying long in such an exposed place, he turned around and headed back to the highway. It might take him a while, but he knew he could find them. The receiver was small. He could come back tonight and hide the car somewhere, then carry it with him and start checking the maze of roads. He'd find them.

He smiled the smile of a man who has finally hit the jackpot. Now he could do some serious planning.

"THREE DAYS WITH NOTHING to do!" Jessica exclaimed happily as they got out of the Wagoneer.

Casey smiled. It felt good to see her happy. They both needed this little vacation. She'd been so withdrawn lately that he'd begun to fear that he was losing her—an irrational fear, he knew, but there nonetheless.

"Well, actually," he drawled as they began to unload the Wagoneer, "I *did* have a few things in mind for us to do."

She grinned. "You mean, fishing, or swimming in the lake?"

"That, too." He looked up at the deep blue sky. "I wouldn't object to a rainy day. I'm sure we could find some indoor activities to occupy our time."

"To make the observation that you have a one-track mind would be rather like observing that the sun rises in the east," she responded dryly. "So I won't do it."

As they carried everything into the cabin Casey admitted to himself that he needed to relax, too. When she'd suggested that they spend a long weekend up here, he'd been reluctant at first. It was an isolated spot, and if the killer was still after her, it could be dangerous for that reason.

But he'd agreed to it because that was what she wanted, and now he was satisfied that they hadn't been followed. It had been impossible to be sure of that while they were on the heavily traveled interstate, and he'd been wary when he'd seen a car exit behind a truck that had followed them off the interstate. But then the car had turned off and he'd seen no more of it. They were safe now. The area was a veritable maze of private roads leading to cottages, and his name wasn't even posted since he'd never seen any reason why it should be—any friends of his knew how to get to his place, and no one else needed to know, as far as he was concerned.

He looked around the cabin, thinking about the other time they'd come here: how he'd made an exception by bringing her here, and how he'd left knowing that something big was happening.

What continued to surprise him most was how easily she fit into his life, as though she'd always been there. He hadn't expected that, and sometimes he still worried that it would all come crashing down on them, and when the dust settled they'd both look at each other and wonder how they'd let themselves get involved.

He had also begun to worry about his own vulnerability, definitely a new and unpleasant experience for him. Every once in a while this little voice inside his head would start whispering to him that he actually needed her—maybe more than she needed him, although of course, she did need him now, with the killer still on the loose.

They put away the groceries and unpacked their belongings, then went for a walk in the woods to stretch their legs after the long drive, holding hands as they made their way along the water's edge. They circled all the way around the lake, passing the other two cottages that shared this particular lake with his. Both were shuttered, so they had the place to themselves, at least until the weekend.

The sylvan peace of the place began to seep into both of them and Casey's guilt over walking away from the investigation lessened. He'd told himself and the others that he needed to back off a bit from the case, and that was true enough. But what he'd really needed was to see her happy again.

As they continued on their way back to the cabin, Casey's thoughts turned to Matthews. He wished he could settle that matter in his mind. She had backed off from her willingness to consider him a suspect, and Casey himself had some doubts, even though he had some people out looking for him. Much as he wanted to capture the killer, he was hoping that they'd find Matthews and clear him, for her sake.

JESSICA STRETCHED and yawned. A pleasant, pinescented breeze blew through the bedroom, carrying with it the noisy joyfulness of birds. Beside her, Casey was still asleep, his arm lying heavily against the hollow of her waist.

She slid carefully out of bed, not wanting to disturb him. She knew just how little sleep he'd gotten these past few weeks as he searched for the killer and still tried to deal with his other responsibilities.

She picked up his discarded T-shirt and pulled it over her nakedness, breathing in the scent of him. Then she padded on bare feet out to the screened porch. Another glorious day. It looked as though Casey wouldn't get his wish for a rainy day they could spend in bed. She smiled. They were wearing each other out as it was. Was there a square inch of her that he hadn't touched, any part of her that he had yet to learn?

She decided to go back inside and make breakfast. If he wasn't up by the time it was ready, she'd serve it to him in bed. He'd like that, but of course she'd let him know that it wasn't going to become a habit. There was always going to be a certain tension between them, a jockeying for the upper hand between two strong-willed people. Some might find that offputting, but she thought it added a spice to their relationship and was probably the chief reason they'd fallen for each other.

Just as she started to turn to go back inside, she caught a brief glimpse of someone walking along the far side of the lake, half-hidden by the trees that grew close to the water over there. For one brief moment her fears returned, but then she realized that it was now Saturday, and no doubt some of the other owners had arrived for the weekend. The man she glimpsed had been carrying fishing gear and he disappeared quickly around the bend in the lake.

Casey hadn't stirred by the time breakfast was ready, so she piled everything on a big tray and carried it into the bedroom to find him just sitting up in bed. A lazy smile transformed his rugged features when he saw her.

"Don't get used to this," she warned him as she set the tray carefully onto the bed.

"Why not? It's my second favorite way to wake up," he responded, his deep voice still husky with sleep. Then he ran his ice blue gaze slowly over his T-shirt, which fitted her like a loose dress.

"Too bad I don't wear a smaller size."

After breakfast they made love, slowly and deliciously, and then Casey got up and announced his intention to go for a swim.

"You might want to put on your swim trunks," she cautioned him as he started, naked, toward the door. "We're not alone here anymore."

"Oh?" He turned to her.

"I saw someone earlier on the far side of the lake. He had fishing gear with him."

"What did he look like?"

She shrugged away that earlier fear, brought back now by a certain sharpness in his tone. She wasn't about to let this day be ruined by their paranoia.

"I didn't get a good look at him. Average size. He was wearing a hat, so I didn't see what color his hair was. Light, I think."

"Probably Neal Jacobsen," Casey said. "He has that little A-frame on the other side of the lake. I noticed he hadn't brought his boat up yet. Come on. Aren't you going to join me?"

"Not until I've put on a suit."

He rolled his eyes heavenward. "How did I manage to get mixed up with a prude?"

She arched a brow. "You, more than anyone else, should know that's not true."

He chuckled. "Not in the bedroom, at any rate. Okay, get your suit and bring some towels."

They swam for a while and Jessica regretted that she'd put on a suit, since there was no sign of anyone. Then they returned to the cabin and showered together, which led to some very inventive, if rather slippery, lovemaking.

"Have I mentioned lately that I'm seriously in love with you?" he asked afterward as he made a halfhearted attempt to dry her off with a big towel.

"Not today." She smiled, amused at how often he "mentioned" that now. He was definitely learning.

"But I *am* getting better at it."

She laughed and kissed him. "Yes, you are. And I love you, Casey. I think I've been in love with you all my life—or with the idea of you, anyway."

They drifted through the day, taking the boat out for some unsuccessful fishing, then playing chess, a game they'd discovered that they both liked. When the game was over she remembered that they needed some groceries. Since he had already settled into the hammock with a crime novel, she went into town alone.

As she emerged from the long driveway onto the gravel road, she saw a car disappear down another of the driveways. They'd walked over earlier to see if Casey's closest neighbors had come up for the weekend, but no one was there. Apparently they'd decided to come, after all.

She drove into town, bought the groceries, then started back. There was one very bad spot in Casey's driveway, where snow melt and spring rains had all but washed out the dirt road, necessitating some very careful maneuvering. She had just reached that spot when a deer ran out of the woods directly in front of her.

Fortunately, she wasn't traveling fast, but as she jerked the wheel to avoid the deer, both wheels on the driver's side slipped off the road and down into a ditch that had been made much deeper by the washout.

She was greatly relieved to see the deer bound off into the woods unhurt, but the Wagoneer was now sitting at a precarious angle. After several unsuccessful attempts to maneuver it back onto the road, she climbed out to survey the situation.

"Damn!" she muttered as she saw the angle at which it rested. Maybe Casey could get it out, but she doubted it. It looked to her as though they'd probably have to get a tow truck.

She started to the cabin on foot, wondering if he'd believe her when she told him she'd swerved to avoid a deer. He'd warned her twice to be careful in that spot, and he'd probably think she was blaming a nonexistent deer for her own carelessness.

She had expected to find him in the hammock, still reading, but he wasn't there, so she went inside, prepared to do battle if he criticized her driving.

But he wasn't inside, either, so she went back out. The boat was still tied to the dock. She scanned the lake, wondering if he might have gone swimming. But there was no sign of him and they'd always stayed within sight of the cabin before.

She glanced back at the empty hammock. The book he'd been reading was lying on the ground beside it, as though he'd dropped it without bothering to mark his place. A can of beer lay on its side nearby, and she saw that some of its contents had spilled onto the book.

For one brief moment a chill slithered through her. It looked to her as though he'd left in a hurry. But then she recalled the car she'd seen earlier. She was getting paranoid again. No doubt he'd just gone over to visit the neighbors. And now that she thought about it, she was glad that they'd arrived. He'd have some help getting the Wagoneer out of the ditch.

The cottage was nearly a quarter mile away through the woods. There was a path of sorts they'd taken earlier, so she followed that. The ground was soft and strewn with pine needles, and as she walked along she saw that the needles had been scattered and the earth beneath dug up somewhat.

She kept walking, but more slowly now, her eyes on the ground as an uneasiness stole over her again. It almost looked as though something had been dragged along the path—something very large. She was sure that it hadn't looked like this earlier.

Stop it, she told herself. But the disquiet remained, gnawing at her as she saw the clearing ahead. Then before she had reached it, she saw a man walk out of the cottage and start in her direction.

She came to a stop without really knowing why, and that uneasiness she'd been feeling now edged closer to panic. Still without fully understanding her actions, she dropped down behind a thicket of blackberry bushes. She hadn't seen the man very clearly, but something about him had troubled her and she struggled to think what it could be.

She was fairly sure that it was the same man she'd seen earlier with fishing gear, but Casey had said that he lived in the A-frame on the other side of the lake.

That means nothing, she told herself. He could be visiting the neighbors, too. What's wrong with me?

But something clearly was. She risked another look, peering through the tangled branches of the bushes. And then she knew what it was that had bothered her: his walk. He had that same unusual way of walking that Joel Matthews had. But he had blond hair, not dark hair like Joel.

Then she remembered the man who'd tried to climb the fence at Casey's had been described as having blond hair. But hadn't the neighbors also described him as being stocky? This man was of slightly above-average height and rather slim, like Joel.

Images whirled sickeningly through her brain: the book, the spilled beer, the signs of something having been dragged along the path. She went numb. The killer had found them!

"Casey!" She started to say his name aloud, then stuffed a fist into her mouth,. She couldn't afford to panic now. She had to believe he was alive and unhurt. And she had to do something.

Staying in a crouch, she backed away from the bushes, and then turned and ran back to the cabin, pausing twice to see if the man was following along the twisted path. She didn't see him, but she poured on still more speed. And all the while, her mind was racing.

She couldn't go for help because the Wagoneer was stuck, and as far as she knew, there was no one else around. As she reached the cabin, gasping for breath, she remembered Casey's gun. He'd put it into a dresser drawer when they arrived.

She ran inside and got it, then peeked out the window that faced the woods between the two properties. She could see him now, even though he was still some distance away. He was definitely headed for the cabin.

Get out of here, she told herself. He won't know you're back because the Wagoneer isn't here. You've got some time.

So she ran out the back door of the cabin and took off up the driveway, knowing she'd be out of sight of the cabin within a few minutes. Still, she didn't slow down until she reached the Wagoneer, and then she sagged against it, trying to ignore the pain in her side and the unfamiliar weight of the gun in her hand.

He might come up the driveway, although that seemed unlikely. But if she tried again to move the Wagoneer he might well hear it, even from the cabin. Better to get away. But away to where?

She stuck the gun in the waistband of her jeans and started off again, jogging until she reached the gravel road. And there she stopped, staring at the maze of driveways. None of the other cottages was close by, and in any event, she knew that she couldn't count on anyone being there.

A sudden thought of Casey jolted her, sending shards of ice through her veins. Could he be dead? She shook her head, denying even the possibility. If the killer had sneaked up on him and killed him, why would he then have dragged him all the way to the other cottage?

No, she thought, Casey isn't dead. I can't let myself even think about it. He must have knocked him out and then dragged him over there because he wanted to separate us for some reason. But there was no doubt in her mind that he intended to kill them both.

The place where she'd stopped was very open, making her feel vulnerable. So she ran across the intersection and plunged into the woods across from the entrance to Casey's driveway. She was now hidden from view if he should come that way, and she could also see the other driveway where she'd seen the car earlier.

She pulled the gun from her waistband and sat down to think. A glance at her watch confirmed that she had less than two hours of daylight left. She judged that she could get to the nearest house out on the main road before dark, but she was sure that the killer would discover the Wagoneer and be out looking for her before that.

Whatever was to be done, she had to do it herself. She stared at the gun she was cradling in her lap. She felt reassured by its solid presence, but she also knew that was a false confidence. She'd never fired a gun in her life, never even held one before.

She examined it closely. She'd noticed some time ago that he didn't carry the kind of gun she usually associated with the police. It was both smaller and slimmer and she thought it must be what was called an automatic. From somewhere, her desperate mind dredged up the fact that most handguns had a safety—a device that prevented them from being fired accidentally.

She wondered if she could try it out, then quickly abandoned that thought. It was so quiet here that it was certain to be heard all the way back at the cabin or the neighboring cottage.

There were two features she didn't understand: a small button and a sort of lever. One of them must be the safety and the other was probably something that allowed the gun to be reloaded. Holding the barrel pointed away from her, she pressed the button. Immediately something slid out of the grip. A clip, she thought it was called: the thing that held the ammunition. She pushed it back in again until it clicked, then flipped the lever. Nothing happened, so she assumed that must be the safety and flipped it back again.

Then she began to feel foolish, hiding in the woods with a gun. What if she'd misinterpreted the situation? Maybe Casey had just gone for a walk and the man she'd seen was his neighbor, coming over for a visit.

But no matter how much she tried to convince herself of that, her instincts told her that it was no more than wishful thinking. The evidence of the book and the spilled beer and the signs of something having been dragged along the path could not be wished away. Somehow the killer had found them.

She wondered if she could capture him just by aiming the gun at him. Surely he wouldn't be crazy enough to charge her when she was holding a gun. But he *was* crazy. They both knew that.

Casey. She drew in a shaky breath and banished his image from her mind as she got to her feet again. He was alive and she had to rescue him, save them both.

She aimed the gun at one of the signs, testing how it felt. Then she remembered the stance she'd seen in movies and on TV and tried to mimic that: feet apart, slight crouch, both hands gripping the gun. She wasn't quite sure how to hold it with both hands and had to experiment a bit until she thought she'd got it right—one hand on the grip and the other steadying the barrel.

Now what? she asked herself, feeling foolish once again as she stood there aiming at a sign.

Now I find Casey, she told herself as an icy knot of dread formed in her stomach.

She crossed the road and slipped into the woods next to Casey's driveway, scanning it for any sign of the killer. The driveway was visible for only about fifty yards before it made a sharp turn and was hidden from view. When she saw no one, she sprinted across the driveway into the stretch of woods that separated it from the neighbor's driveway.

She saw that their driveway had as many twists and turns as Casey's did, which made it too risky to walk along it. So instead, she stayed off to the side in the thick woods, crouching low each time she came to a bend.

She had stuck the gun into the back of her waistband once again, and it pressed unyieldingly against the hollow of her spine as she made her way carefully through the woods toward the cottage, moving in a series of runs and walks and crouches. Blackberry bushes tore at her clothing and scratched her arms.

After a while a bubble of near-hysterical laughter welled up in her and she made a choked sound as she tried to stop it. This was absurd, surreal! A discarded book and spilled beer and scattered pine needles did not add up to violence. And the man she'd seen was probably Casey's neighbor, a tax accountant. Casey had told her that his wife was an attorney with a public interest law firm whom he'd thought she would like.

So why was she behaving like this, sneaking through the woods with a gun she couldn't possibly use? Had she really, truly become paranoid? Now she did laugh, though she stifled it quickly. She was recalling a remark she'd heard somewhere. *Even paranoids have enemies.*

And yet *something* had made her run from that man. But thinking about it now as she continued to make her way through the woods, she wondered about her belief that he'd walked like Joel. She'd caught only the briefest glimpse of him through the trees. Had she thought that only because she was still unsettled in her own mind about Joel?

Please let it all be a mistake, she prayed silently. Please let me get there and find Casey having a beer with the neighbors.

By the time she caught her first glimpse of the cottage through the trees, Jessica was already trying to decide how she could explain herself. Could she hide the gun somewhere and then get it later and return it to the drawer without Casey's knowing she had it? Could she say that she'd just decided to go for a walk, or was simply looking for him?

The silver car she'd seen earlier was parked beside the cottage, which was now directly below her, still partially obscured by the trees and dense undergrowth. She saw now that the wide yard didn't totally surround the cottage. On the side farthest from the driveway and Casey's cabin, the woods came to within a few feet of the white frame structure.

She crossed the driveway at a run, then started to make her way through the woods, staying low to the ground. Finally she was less than twenty feet from the side of the cottage. She dropped to the ground, propping herself up on her elbows as she listened, feeling more and more foolish.

Silence. No voices in relaxed conversation greeted her, despite her fervent prayers. She wondered where the man she'd seen was now. If he *was* the killer, could he be waiting for her at the cabin, or could he even now be walking up the driveway to discover the Wagoneer?

And then the truly terrifying question, the one she'd been trying to avoid. Was Casey in there, only a short distance away, hurt or dead?

A wave of nausea came over her. Cold sweat prickled her skin. A huge knot formed in her throat and tears began to sting her eyes. But she knew that she had to find out if he was there.

There were two windows on this side of the small cottage. One was probably a bedroom and the other would be the living room. She decided to make for the living-room window. She got to her feet before her nerve could fail her and sprinted across the narrow strip of lawn. Then she flattened herself against the wall of the cottage and listened again. Nothing.

With her heart now thudding crazily in her throat and her mouth filled with the metallic taste of fear, Jessica edged along the wall of the cottage until she reached the window. Then she stretched until she could see inside.

The room lay in shadows, and for the first few seconds, as her eyes adjusted, she could see nothing. And then she saw Casey!

Chapter Thirteen

Jessica stood there, paralyzed, unable even to breathe. Casey was lying on his side on the polished wood floor, his arms drawn behind him and bound together with his feet. For several long seconds she was sure he was dead. But then she thought she saw the slight rise and fall of his breathing. Or was that only her desperate hope?

She was about to run in there, regardless of the danger to herself, when she heard a sound and realized that someone was coming up onto the screened porch. A door slammed. She jerked away from the window and scurried back to the cover of the woods.

He's alive, she told herself. He *has* to be alive. But she was shaking all over and her vision was blurred by tears.

Then she heard a man's voice, high-pitched and angry. She couldn't make out the words, but it didn't sound like Joel's voice. Was he talking to Casey? He must be, and that surely meant that he was alive. She strained to hear a response, but there was none, and after a few minutes the shouting ended and a door slammed again.

She rubbed her eyes and willed herself to stop shaking. Casey was alive; she had to believe that. She remembered how Casey had told her that he had to put himself into the killer's mind, and she tried to do that now.

She felt certain that Casey had been right when he'd said that the killer wanted to get them both together. So he must be waiting for her. And the fact that he'd come back here suggested that he already knew she'd returned. So what would he do now?

He'd have to assume that she knew something was wrong. Otherwise, she would have been at the cabin. So he could start searching for her. But there was a lot of area to cover and it would soon be dark. If he thought that she'd started back to the main road for help, then he would surely have gotten into his car and gone after her.

Finally she decided that he was staying here, waiting for her to show up to rescue Casey.

But would he know or guess that she had Casey's gun? And did he have one, as well? And could she really be sure that he knew she'd returned? How likely was it that he'd walked up the driveway and discovered the Wagoneer?

She drew in a ragged breath. Enough about what *he* thought. It was time to decide what she should do.

She peered through the bushes at his car, wondering if the keys might be in it. But if they were and she took it, he might well kill Casey in a fit of rage. She thought about that eerie, high-pitched voice and shivered.

And then she stopped thinking completely as the image of Casey lying there, bound and helpless, filled her mind. For a moment she actually could not believe what she knew she'd seen. Casey had seemed so all-powerful to her, so completely invincible. And although she'd protested his protectiveness toward her, she saw now that in fact she'd been relying on it, counting on him to keep them both safe.

Now it was all up to her. Their lives depended upon the action she took. She swallowed hard and stared at the cabin, praying that she'd been right, that she had seen him breathing.

The shadows were lengthening; dusk was approaching. Her arms stung from the scratches and insect bites. Her muscles felt stiff and she shifted to a more comfortable position. And that reminded her of the painful, twisted position in which Casey lay.

She thought again about Casey's theory that the killer wanted her to see him die, to prove that he was the more powerful so that she would want him instead.

Maybe she should circle around to the other side of the cottage, then simply walk out of the woods toward it, making it appear that she was innocently searching for Casey. Then, when the killer came out to meet her, she could confront him with the gun.

She played around with that idea. It was dangerous, because he could be armed as well, and if he was, he must surely be a better shot than she was. But the killer had always used a knife in the past, and Casey had told her that they tended to stay with the same M.O.

The shadows grew ever deeper. She couldn't come up with another plan. And she was also worried that the longer she delayed in putting in an appearance, the greater the likelihood was that he would kill Casey.

Then, as if to emphasize that point, she suddenly heard the killer's voice again, that strange, shrill, deranged voice. But this time she also heard another voice: Casey's!

She was creeping back to the window again even before she realized what she was doing, lured by the blessed sound of Casey's voice. As she flattened herself against the wall of the cottage and angled toward the window, the killer began to shriek again.

"Where is she?"

"She went back to the city," Casey responded, his voice weak and slow. "We had a fight."

Then she heard a thudding sound and Casey's deep groan. Pain tore through her as though she herself had been struck. For one irrational moment she was ready to step into the open window and fire. But she forced herself to remain still. Casey's life depended on her not taking any rash action.

"You're lying!" the killer screeched. "She wouldn't leave you here without a car. Where is she?"

Jessica put her hands over her ears as the blows and groans started again. She had no time left now. He would surely kill Casey if she didn't do something quickly.

She envisioned herself bursting through the door, gun blazing. It was a very satisfying scenario, but she knew it wouldn't work. He might kill Casey or use him as a shield. And she certainly couldn't count on her shooting skills. She had to draw him away from Casey.

The killer was still screaming and cursing as she ran around the rear of the cottage and across the backyard into the woods. From what she'd overheard, she knew now that the killer didn't know she'd returned.

So she started back toward the cottage on the path that led from Casey's cabin. Then, when she judged that she was close enough to be heard from inside, she began to call Casey's name. She kept her eyes glued to the cottage, willing him to appear and ordering herself to remain calm and act casual.

Suddenly he was there at the door to the screened porch. She couldn't see him clearly as he opened the door and stepped out into the yard, and she didn't know the range of the weapon pressed against her spine, so she kept on walking—walking toward the killer. She could see no weapon in his hand, but she knew he could be concealing something, just as she was.

Now she had reached the big yard and he was still walking toward her. And once again she was struck by the familiarity of his walk.

"Hello!" she called. "I'm looking for Casey. Is he here?"

The distance between them was closing even as she spoke, and now she felt the icy chill of certainty. It shouldn't have come as such a blow at this point, but somehow it still did. She stumbled to a halt.

"Joel!"

He stopped, too. His face was shadowed by several days' growth of dark beard that contrasted sharply with the disheveled blond hair on his head. Even in the dim light she could sense the madness in him. Still, she managed to keep her voice reasonable.

"Joel, what are you doing here?"

"Casey's here," he replied in that low drawl she remembered, so very different from the crazed voice she'd heard earlier. "We were waiting for you. Come on inside and I'll explain."

He turned abruptly and strode quickly back to the cottage. Jessica stood there for a fateful few seconds, feeling the gun press against her spine. She started to reach for it, then stopped.

What if she missed? And a deeper, more frightening thought came to her: could you actually kill him?

Joel Matthews, the gentle hippie who'd brought her parents to life for her. And now she knew that he must also be the man who'd killed them. Yes, she told herself. I can kill him if I must.

He turned briefly as he reached the steps to the porch, beckoning to her as though this were merely a social call. The scene felt surreal, but she started forward as he vanished inside. With dread dogging her steps, she followed him. And at the last moment, as she stepped up onto the porch, she reached behind her and fumbled until she found the safety, then flipped the lever.

She stopped in the living-room doorway. Joel had switched on a lamp and he'd dragged Casey into a half-kneeling position in front of him.

"See?" he cried in that terrible high-pitched voice as he shook Casey viciously. "See what's happened to your big man? He's nothing!"

Jessica saw Casey's head wobble and his eyelids flutter briefly. Joel was holding a long knife against his throat. A thin trickle of blood ran down Casey's neck, staining his pale blue shirt.

"Joel, please don't do this!" she begged. Her thoughts were racing. If she pulled out the gun now, he would surely have time to plunge the knife into Casey's throat before she could fire. She had to try to reason with him. If she could play on his obsession with her . . .

"I thought we were friends, Joel," she said, adopting a hurt tone. "Why are you doing this?"

"It's *his* fault," Joel said, shaking Casey's limp body again. Once more, Jessica saw Casey's eyes open briefly.

"Why is it his fault, Joel? I don't understand."

Joel stared at her and Jessica had all she could do to meet those crazed eyes. The madness she saw in him now, together with his bleached hair, made him seem like the evil brother of the gentle hippie she'd befriended.

"He came between us!" Joel hissed. "He thinks he's a big man, a big, tough cop who can have whatever he wants. But he's *nothing*, see?" He shook Casey again.

Jessica remembered what she'd heard Casey say about a fight between them. "He doesn't have me, Joel," she replied, giving Casey a scornful look. "I told him that before I left."

Some of the mad light seemed to go out of Joel's eyes and her hopes rose. He glanced uncertainly from Casey to her. "You came back!" he accused.

"Yes, because I realized I couldn't leave him up here alone. There isn't even a phone."

She could see that Joel's arms were growing tired from the strain of holding Casey's limp body. If she could just keep talking, maybe he'd let Casey go and she could use the gun. But then she saw Joel's gaze harden again.

"I can't trust you, just like I couldn't trust *her!*" he said harshly. "She said she was my friend, too, but she lied!"

"Who lied, Joel?" she asked as her stomach clenched. She knew who he must mean.

He ignored the question. "She said she wanted to help me. She said she liked me. We used to talk a lot when he wasn't around."

"And what makes you think she lied?" Jessica asked. The muscles in his arms were trembling with the exertion, and he pressed the knife harder against Casey's throat. A fresh trickle of blood ran down into his shirt, but he didn't stir this time.

"She wouldn't leave him. I wanted her to come with me. We belonged together." Joel's voice had become a petulant whine.

"Maybe she thought she couldn't leave because of . . . her daughter."

Joel stared at her. His eyes had a peculiar and frightening glaze. She wasn't sure what he was seeing as he stared at her. Then he sagged to his knees, still clutching the inert Casey with one arm. But the hand holding the knife moved toward his own throat, and for one electrifying moment Jessica thought he was going to stab himself.

Instead, he slid his fingers around a thin chain she hadn't noticed before, since it was mostly hidden by his shirt. Then he suddenly ripped it from his neck and flung it to the floor between them.

"She lied!" he screamed.

Jessica kept her eyes on him, but she still saw the familiar peace symbol, winking in the reflected light from the nearby lamp. Rage filled her, momentarily blinding her to the danger of taking any action now, when he still had Casey as a shield.

The gun had become a hard presence at her back, almost urging her to seize it and use it. She raised her hands slowly, then rested them against the curve of her waist, sliding her right hand around as far as she could without being obvious.

Still on his knees, Joel once again pressed the knife against Casey's throat. It was a position he could maintain without difficulty now, since he basically had Casey propped against himself.

"He's a cop, Joel. You can't kill him. If you do, they won't stop until they find you."

As she spoke, she saw Casey's eyes open and meet hers. She had no idea if he even saw her, but his gaze remained fixed on her. She looked away from him quickly and back to Joel.

"They won't find me," Joel said dismissively. "Cops are dumb pigs. I killed another one once."

The next moments would forever remain a blur to Jessica, a slow-motion scene that in fact lasted only a few seconds. She saw Casey's thigh muscles bulge against his jeans and the muscles in his bound arms tense. Joel lifted the knife from Casey's throat and wrapped his other arm across Casey's forehead, jerking his head back to expose his bloodied throat.

The knife began to descend in a wide arc. The lamplight reflected off the blade of its bloodied tip. Jessica pulled out the gun and gripped it with both hands.

"Stop, Joel!" she shouted as the knife began its downward arc toward Casey's throat.

Joel paused for one brief second, and in that moment Casey was able to lower his head slightly to see her. Suddenly he flung himself sideways—and Jessica fired.

The explosion was deafening in the small room. The shot went wild, chipping plaster from the wall behind Joel. Casey had rolled just beyond Joel's reach and was trying to get up on his knees, his movements sluggish as he struggled against the bonds. Joel lunged toward him and raised the knife again.

Jessica fired, twice this time. And then Joel was staring at her with a surprised expression, all madness now gone from his eyes. He crumpled slowly to the floor as a bright red stain spread across his white T-shirt. He seemed to be trying to say something, but the words were too soft for her to hear as the echoes of the gunshots rang in her ears. Finally he lay still.

Casey had by now managed to get to his knees, but he was wobbling, and before she could reach him, he had toppled over onto his side.

"No!" she cried, dropping the gun as she ran to him, terrified now that she'd shot him, as well.

His eyes were closed and he merely groaned as she tried to lift him into her arms. But she could see no blood on him other than the slight wound from Joel's knife.

"Knife," she said aloud through her sobs. She had to cut the ropes that bound Casey so cruelly.

Joel's bloodstained knife lay with its blade across the peace symbol, an image that would be forever burned into her brain. Her hand shook as she picked it up. She took several deep breaths to steady herself, then went back to Casey and began to saw frantically at his bonds. He was completely limp now, but when she had freed him at last, he groaned and rolled over onto his back.

"Casey," she said softly, pressing her lips to his ear, "you're safe now. It's over."

He mumbled something, but didn't open his eyes. Jessica held him as she stared at Joel's body, still unable to fathom that she'd shot him. There was so much blood and she could see no sign of life. Reluctantly she let Casey go and got up to check Joel. He lay on his back and his eyes were wide open and staring sightlessly. There was no pulse. She straightened again, swaying slightly as blackness hovered at the edges of her vision.

"It isn't over," she said softly into the silence of the room. She had to get help. She ran through the cottage and out the back door to see if the keys were in Joel's car. They weren't, so she ran back inside again and, fighting down a wave of nausea, dug through Joel's pockets until she found them. Then she paused to kneel beside Casey's unconscious body.

"I have to go for help, Casey. Joel's dead. He can't hurt you." His eyelids fluttered slightly and he made a sound that seemed to be a protest. She kissed him, then got up again.

Leaving him there was the hardest thing she'd ever had to do, in a strange way much harder than shooting Joel, since that had happened so fast. But she knew there was no way she could drag him out to the car. He was simply too heavy. And even if she could, she was by now worried that he might be suffering from internal injuries.

Her mind remained mercifully blank as she drove up the driveway, then flew along the deserted gravel road to the highway. She turned toward town, remembering that there were a few scattered homes along the way. When she saw lights at the first house, she breathed a sigh of relief.

By the time she had reached the top of the long driveway, a porch light had come on. She came to a stop behind a pickup truck and stumbled from the car.

"I need to use your phone," she told the man who came out onto the porch. "I have to call the police and an ambulance."

He led her inside, where a woman and several children hovered, their eyes wide as they stared at her. Belatedly, she realized that she had blood on her. Was it Casey's or Joel's—or both? She felt hysteria welling up in her as she dialed 911—and got a loud squeal, followed by a recording stating that all operators were busy at this time.

The man gave her the number and she punched it out with trembling fingers. A male voice answered on the second ring. Jessica began to speak even before he had finished.

"One man is dead and another is injured. Please get some help here quickly. The one who's injured is a police officer," she added, hoping that would forestall any questions and get them moving.

The man asked his name and she told him. "He's with—"

"We know who he is," the dispatcher replied. "Is it his cabin?"

"No, the one next door. Take the driveway next to his."

She hung up before the man could ask any more questions, then barely paused to thank the couple before running back to the car. She was by now convinced that Casey must be hurt worse than he seemed. He could be dead or dying even now from internal injuries.

She was driving so fast that she nearly missed the gravel road in the darkness, and the Honda lurched crazily as she swung onto it at the last possible moment. By the time she reached the cottage she was sobbing and calling Casey's name over and over, as though by saying it she could guarantee that he would still be alive.

He was still lying where she'd left him. She sank to the floor beside him and took his limp hand, then bent to kiss his brow. She told him that the police and an ambulance were on their way, even though she doubted that he could hear her. Then she shifted his position and hers until she was cradling his dark head in her lap.

She began to stroke his thick, black hair, saying over and over that she loved him. Then her fingers touched a lump at the back of his head and he groaned. A concussion, she told herself. That's all it is. He'll be all right. She told him that, too, but there was no response.

It seemed forever before she heard the distant wail of sirens and then finally the sound of a car's engine. But when she checked her watch, she saw that only twenty-two minutes had elapsed since she had called them. Given the rural nature of the area, it was an amazingly fast response.

She lowered Casey's head gently to the floor and got up as she heard car doors slam. Two state troopers met her at the back door, their guns drawn and their expressions wary. The sight of the guns set her legs trembling and she backed up against the kitchen counter.

"Where's the ambulance?" she demanded. "He needs an ambulance."

They ignored her and went into the living room. She followed them. One of them bent to examine Joel, while the other went over to Casey. Then they both looked at her.

She started to explain, then stopped and sank into a chair. One officer went to the kitchen and got her a glass of water. She heard another siren in the distance and hoped it was the ambulance this time.

"The gun belongs to Casey," she said when she saw them staring at it. "He's a cop. But I'm the one who used it. He's dead, isn't he?" she asked, forcing herself to glance briefly at Joel's body.

One officer nodded. "It looks like he was shot right through the heart."

The hysteria overtook her again and she made a strangled sound. "I'd never fired a gun before in my life. My first shot hit the wall." She pointed to the spot with a shaky finger.

"Looks like you got lucky, then," the officer said carefully. "Who are you and who is he?" He pointed to Joel.

She started to explain, then stopped as the paramedics rushed into the room, carrying their long, unwieldy cases. After examining Joel very briefly, they turned their attention to Casey. One of them went through his pockets and found the leather case with his detective's shield. He handed it to the closest officer.

"Yeah, we know who he is. They've been called."

The paramedics examined Casey and then stood, looking down at him doubtfully. One of them turned to the other. "I hope the stretcher will hold him. Damn, but he's big."

"What's wrong with him?" Jessica demanded, her voice shrill with fear.

"Looks like a concussion to me, ma'am. And I think he's got a couple of broken ribs. But there's no sign of any internal bleeding that we can see. What happened to him?"

"I don't know," Jessica told them. "I think Joel must have sneaked up on him and hit him on the head with something. Then he kicked him and hit him after he was tied up."

She stopped abruptly as she recalled hearing—and actually feeling—those blows. A concussion and broken ribs. He would be all right. Relief flooded through her warmly.

The state troopers began to ask questions again and she tried for a time to answer them, but when Casey had been loaded onto a stretcher, she got up and followed the struggling paramedics out to the ambulance. One officer told her to wait, but the other said to let her go. She climbed into the ambulance, ignoring their argument.

They flew along the road to the hospital, where a flurry of people in white took over, whisking Casey away from her. He remained unconscious, and despite the paramedics' soothing words, Jessica was still worried that he might be seriously injured.

One of the paramedics asked her if she wanted to see a doctor herself, and she shook her head. What she wanted wasn't a doctor but a magician to wave a magic wand and take away the past few hours. The kind paramedic brought her a cup of coffee, then left her alone in the deserted waiting room. It took all the energy she had left to lift the cup to her lips.

Images began to bombard her: the madness in Joel's eyes, and then that look of surprise at the end, Casey lying helpless on the floor, the bloodied knife lying on top of her mother's pendant.

She felt hysteria welling up in her again, and so was less displeased than she otherwise might have been when the police arrived. There was one of the troopers who'd come to the cottage, and another man in plain clothes, who was introduced to her as their criminal investigator.

"You're Casey's girlfriend?" he asked.

She nodded.

"Have you had anything to eat?" he asked gently.

She shook her head, wondering if that was why she felt so light-headed. He got her a sandwich and more coffee from the vending machines, then led her to a small, empty office.

"Will they know where to find me?" she asked nervously. Somewhere in her tormented mind there lurked a fear that Casey would die as a punishment for her having killed Joel.

He nodded. "The doctor should be in shortly, but he's okay. Don't worry about him. I know Casey, by the way. We go fishing together sometimes when he's up here."

Then he asked her to start from the beginning and she did the best she could, though at times she had to back up under his gentle prodding. She felt inadequate. As a lawyer accustomed to asking questions herself, she should be more coherent, more organized. She told him that, and he said that under the circumstances she was doing just fine.

She had just finished and was beginning to worry about Casey again when there was a knock at the door and a dark-haired woman about Jessica's age came in.

"I'm Dr. Jennings. We're just sending him upstairs to a room now. He has a concussion, but he'll be fine. Two ribs are broken and there are some bad bruises, but nothing serious. You must be Jessie," she added, smiling. "He said your name quite a lot. In fact, that's about all he has said."

Jessica got up eagerly. "He's conscious, then? Can I see him?"

"He's drifting in and out and he'll probably be that way for a while." She smiled again. "Why do I get the impression that he's not going to be a cooperative patient?"

The police investigator chuckled. "If I know Casey, he isn't going to be a patient at all as soon as he can walk."

She reached his room just as a nurse was leaving. She was ready for a fight if they tried to tell her that she couldn't stay, and perhaps her expression conveyed that, because the nurse made no attempt to stop her.

Casey lay in the white-sheeted bed naked from the waist up, his feet dangling over the end of the bed. Jessica smiled through her tears of relief. They probably hadn't been able to find a gown large enough for him, not to mention a bed long enough. As he'd so often grumbled, the world was made for midgets.

She walked over to the bed and picked up his limp hand and held it to her lips. Her tears trickled over his bronzed skin. How she loved this man, and how close she'd come to losing him.

His hand twitched and his dark lashes fluttered slightly. She said his name softly. Then, suddenly, his pale blue eyes opened.

"Jessie," he murmured groggily, a smile flickering over his rugged features.

"It's over, Casey," she replied. "We're safe now."

He stared at her for a moment, frowning, and then his eyes closed again. She sat on the edge of the bed for a while, but when he didn't awaken again, she finally went over to a big, comfortable chair and collapsed.

SHE AWOKE WITH A START to the same question she'd been asking herself when she'd fallen asleep. Was there anything she could have done differently, any way she could have avoided killing Joel? But now, as then, no answer presented itself.

It's over, she told herself as she stared at the sleeping Casey. And you had no choice. He killed your parents. He would certainly have killed Casey. And sooner or later he would have killed you, too. And then there were all the others who'd died simply because they had borne some resemblance to her mother.

Still staring at Casey, she recalled how he'd disliked Joel from the beginning, and how she herself had defended him. Had Casey known instinctively what she hadn't seen until the end?

She belatedly realized that she'd been awakened by low voices out in the hallway: men's voices. And now the door opened slowly, and Jeff Travis put his head around its edge. Then he came into the room, trailed by Casey's boss, the chief of detectives. Both men stared at Casey, then gestured for her to follow them out of the room.

She got up reluctantly, knowing she was going to be forced to tell the entire story once again. The police had an insatiable appetite for such things. It was part of their training and allowed them to catch inconsistencies in a suspect's story. But she wasn't a suspect, and she resented being forced to confront again the horror she now wanted to put behind her.

Both men were solicitous, but they clearly wanted to hear it all. So they sat in a deserted lounge area and she told her story again. When she had finished, the chief regarded her with open admiration.

"You're one gutsy lady, Jessica. But then, I wouldn't expect Casey to end up with any other kind. He's not going to like this much, though."

"What do you mean?" she asked, perplexed.

He chuckled and shrugged. "It's going to be tough for him to face the fact that *you* saved *him*, instead of the other way around."

THIS TIME WHEN SHE AWOKE from a blessedly dreamless sleep in the big, comfortable chair, it was to find a nurse bent over Casey's bed, her overly loud, overly cheerful voice shattering the stillness in the hospital room.

"I'm fine," came Casey's low growl in response to the nurse's question. "Where's—"

His question was cut off as Jessica stood at the same time he heaved himself into a sitting position and caught sight of her. She smiled tentatively, recalling the chief's warning about Casey's state of mind. Then she realized that at this point he didn't even know what had happened, and knew she would be forced to repeat her story one more time.

Casey stared at her, his expression grim, and she began to wonder if he did, after all, know what had happened. She started toward the bed. His expression didn't change, but as she approached, he put out a hand to her, and as soon as she took it, he drew her down beside him. The nurse moved aside, but hovered nearby.

"Mr. Casimiricz," she began, mangling his name.

"Get out!" Casey growled, not taking his ice blue gaze off Jessica. A moment later the door opened and closed.

Casey lifted a hand to run it through her sleep-tangled hair. "Are you all right?"

"I'm fine, except for some scratches." And some horrible memories, she thought, even though they were vague at the moment.

He drew her face to his and kissed her gently—a surprising gentleness, given the tension she could feel in him. Then he sank back against the pillows with a groan.

"How many ribs did I break this time?"

"Two, and you have a concussion."

"I've had both before," he said dismissively, still peering at her intently. "Are you sure you're okay?"

"Yes."

He seemed to be considering whether or not she spoke the truth, then lowered his gaze. "What the hell happened? I don't remember very much."

The admission came very reluctantly, and Jessica again suspected that he did remember, but didn't like it much. She told him the whole story, wishing as she did that there was some way she could soften it or downplay her own role. But there wasn't, and in any event, it wasn't her nature to try to portray herself as a shrinking violet. She wasn't proud of what she'd done, but she *was* proud of having had the courage to do it.

Casey listened in silence, asking no questions. His expression remained grim, and when she had finished, he swore.

"I'm sorry, Jessie. I promised to keep you safe and I didn't."

"It's done, Casey. It's over. That's what's important now."

He took her hand again, his mouth still set in a hard line. His head throbbed and at times while she had told him the story, he'd been seeing two of her. But none of this mattered to him at the moment. What mattered was that he'd failed her, and dragged her into his own dark, violent world. His job was to protect people, and he'd failed to protect the one who meant the most to him.

Belatedly he realized how tense she seemed and reached out to draw her to him, ignoring the pain in his injured ribs. "You're right, Jessie, it's over now, and we've got each other. I love you."

She flowed into his arms, but very carefully since she was clearly worried about his injuries. He held her silently, kissing the silken tangle of her hair as he continued to curse himself for his carelessness. How the hell had Matthews found them? He knew he had no one but himself to blame for that, and for the horror she'd been forced to live through.

Jeff Travis and the chief of detectives arrived while they were still locked in a careful embrace. Casey glared at them, but at least he didn't tell them to get out. Instead, he sat up in bed like a disgruntled, wounded bear and growled periodically as he talked to them, his gaze straying to Jessica regularly with a mixture of love and pain.

More police arrived. The doctor stopped by and was growled at, as well. The room was filled with men's voices talking in that often indecipherable language known only to the police. They had found the receiver in Joel's stolen car, and that had led them to the tiny transmitter affixed to the Wagoneer. The chief told her there was probably one on her car, as well. Joel Matthews had been one very determined man.

By afternoon, Casey was clearly tired again. Jessica kissed him goodbye, then left with Jeff and the chief to get the Wagoneer, which had been hauled out of the ditch. They returned to the city, and after going to the police station to sign a statement, she checked into a bed and breakfast not far from the hospital.

She was exhausted, but even so, found sleep elusive. The memories kept assailing her, replaying vividly in her tired brain. But most of all, she was worried about Casey and their love. What would happen now? Could he possibly feel so guilty over his failure to protect her that he'd forget that he loved her?

After tossing and turning for several hours, she fell asleep and didn't awaken until the next morning, when she immediately felt guilty for not having returned to the hospital to see Casey. But just as she was struggling out of bed, the phone rang. It was Casey.

"Get me some clothes from the cabin and get over here," he growled, then paused and asked in a much softer tone, "Are you okay?"

"I'm fine. I must have slept twelve hours. Did the doctor say you could leave?"

"I'm leaving."

She sighed and agreed to do as ordered. At least she'd be doing the hospital a favor by getting him out of there.

She was just about to leave when the phone rang again. It was Jeff Travis this time.

"I just talked to Casey and he told me he's declared himself to be discharged," he said with a chuckle after asking how she was doing. "Want some advice?"

She told him she'd be happy to get some at this point.

"Just stay away from him for a while. Take him home and leave him there."

"But he shouldn't be left alone," she protested. "The doctor told me he should stay in the hospital for a few more days."

"He won't. I'll check on him regularly. Right now he's too wrapped up in self-pity and too mad at himself to think straight. Casey's problem is that he thinks he's invincible. He needs to get his head on straight. And he will—because he's in love with you." He chuckled again. "Are you sure that you're ready for a lifetime of dealing with him?"

She actually laughed. Jeff's teasing had a wonderful effect on her. "I thought I was, but maybe I should reconsider."

"Well, I hope you don't reconsider, because you're perfect for him. He's a good guy, Jessie—the best—but he does have a few faults."

She kept his advice in mind as she walked into Casey's room later to find him pacing around, wrapped in a bedsheet. So she handed him his clothes and then went off to find the doctor, who assured her that he'd be fine, but should have someone checking on him regularly.

"I can't exactly say that he's been a favorite patient," the woman said with a smile. "But he's quite a man."

Jessica nodded. She couldn't dispute that, even if he did more closely resemble a wounded bear at this point.

His only concession to his condition was to agree that she could drive. The long trip home was accomplished mostly in silence, with Casey dozing much of the time. Before they went to his house, they stopped at the kennel to pick up Adolf, who'd been sent there for stud service. Casey's only reference to what had happened came when he cast a baleful look at the dog and remarked that none of it would have happened if he'd taken Adolf with them.

As soon as they arrived at his house Jessica went directly to the bedroom and began to pack her clothes. Casey came to stand in the doorway.

"What are you doing?"

"Going home," she stated succinctly.

"What is this?" he demanded. "Look, I know I haven't been very nice, but—"

"Don't argue with me, Casey. I'm in no mood for it. Just call me when you grow up."

"I want you to stay here."

"Well, I'm not. You'll be fine. Jeff said he'd check on you."

He lapsed into a sullen silence as he followed her out to her car. She kept waiting for him to ask her again to stay and wondered if she'd give in. But he said nothing. When she drove away, he was still standing there in the driveway, staring after her.

ONE WEEK LATER Jessica had still not heard from Casey. Jeff called her regularly to let her know he was okay. He told her there were a lot of bets over who was going to make the first move, and he himself was betting on Casey, who was back at work and clearly miserable.

Jeff also told her that they'd found Joel's apartment, and among his things were newspaper clippings going back twenty-five years, including the stories of her parents' deaths. He said that police across the country would likely be closing a lot of cases.

Her mother's necklace was returned to her and she put it away in her safe deposit box. Perhaps someday she'd be able to look at it again without seeing that knife stained with Casey's blood.

The press descended upon her as soon as the story broke, but she ignored them as best she could, then grimaced when she saw the stories that made her sound like a female Rambo. When a co-worker told her that a national tabloid had picked up the story, she called her grandmother and then her father's parents. True to form, her grandmother was more concerned about the "scandal," but her newly discovered paternal grandparents were kind and sympathetic, and she was more than ever eager to meet them.

She caught one brief glimpse of Casey one day as she was leaving the courthouse and he was walking across the plaza toward police headquarters. He didn't turn her way, but she stood there watching until he had disappeared from view.

She didn't know what to do. Was she wrong to have walked out on him like that? What if he thought she didn't love him? Or what if his guilt and anger at himself kept him away from her forever?

But although these questions tormented her, deep down inside she knew he would be back. What they'd found with each other was real, and far too precious to let die.

More times than she could count, she picked up the phone to call him, then put it down again. She wanted him to come to her, and she wanted him to admit that he needed her, as well as loved her. And she would wait as long as she had to.

Her wait came to an end twelve days after she'd returned to her own home. After yet another lonely evening during which she'd been unable to get him out of her mind, she was just climbing into bed when the doorbell rang.

She knew instantly that it must be Casey. Who else would show up at such an hour? Her heart thudding crazily, she put on a silk robe over her nakedness. Her fingers were trembling as she tried to tie the sash.

He stood there on her doorstep with a huge florist's box and a very uncertain look on his face.

"Uh, I know it's late. Did I wake you?"

"No, I was just going to bed," she replied huskily, wondering where he'd managed to find flowers at this hour.

She stepped back and he came in, then paused in the foyer and finally thrust the box at her.

"I got these earlier. There's one there for every day I've known you."

His speech was so stilted and formal that she had to suppress a smile as she took the box and opened it to see it was filled with long-stemmed red roses that indeed looked as though they'd been there for some time.

"I'd better get them into water," she said. "Thank you."

She turned and went to the kitchen. He followed her and stopped in the doorway, watching as she found a vase and filled it with water.

"I can be a real jerk sometimes," he muttered.

"Oh, I knew that the moment I met you," she said, still hiding her smile.

"You deserve better," he ventured.

"You're right. I do." She turned back to him. "But it seems that I'm stuck with you."

"The least I could have done was to be there to help you deal with all of it."

She nodded as she began to arrange the roses in the vase.

"But I was too busy kicking myself in the butt for letting it happen."

She continued to arrange the roses, snipping the ends off some to create the arrangement.

"You're not making this any easier for me, you know," he said.

She finished the arrangement and turned to face him, folding her arms across her chest. "What exactly would you like me to say, Casey?"

He started to say something, then stopped and jammed his hands into his pockets. "Well, you could say that you forgive me and that you still love me." He paused, then looked at her uneasily. "You do still love me, don't you?"

She nodded, but to her surprise the uneasy look on his face didn't go away. He pulled a hand from his pocket and ran it through his thick, dark hair.

"Uh, do you think you love me enough to marry me?"

She nodded and barely managed to say a husky yes as the tears welled up in her eyes. He closed the space between them quickly and drew her into his arms, crushing her against his chest.

"Dammit, Jess, I've been driving around for the past hour rehearsing what I was going to say—how I was going to convince you that you had to marry me even if I *am* a jerk. I love you, Jess, and I need you in my life. It just isn't worth living without you."

She drew back in the circle of his arms and smiled up at him through her tears. "You've just convinced me."

And as he lifted her into his arms and started toward her bedroom, Jessica remembered Susan's remark about staring at the sun and then seeing a spot before your eyes afterward. For better or for worse, she was going to be staring at the sun for the rest of her life.

This summer, come cruising with Harlequin Books!

PORTS OF CALL

In July, August and September, excitement, danger and, of course, romance can be found in Lynn Leslie's exciting new miniseries PORTS OF CALL. Not only can you cruise the South Pacific, the Caribbean and the Nile, your journey will also take you to Harlequin Superromance®, Harlequin Intrigue® and Harlequin American Romance®.

- ♦ In July, cruise the South Pacific with SINGAPORE FLING, a Harlequin Superromance
- ♦ NIGHT OF THE NILE from Harlequin Intrigue will heat up your August
- ♦ September is the perfect month for CRUISIN' MR. DIAMOND from Harlequin American Romance

So, cruise through the summer with LYNN LESLIE and HARLEQUIN BOOKS!

HARLEQUIN®

I N T R I G U E®

Ski through glitzy Aspen with the King of Rock 'n' Roll
for the hottest—yet most mysteriously chilling—
August of 1994 ever!

#285
DON'T BE CRUEL
by Cassie Miles
August 1994

Gina Robinson headed for glittering Aspen to purchase
her uncle's Elvis memorabilia...only to find herself
snowbound with Conner "Hound Dog" Hobarth. The two
built a cozy cabin fire destined to lead somewhere very
special. Unfortunately, the morning after, they found
Gina's uncle dead on the premises and discovered the law
thought the lovebirds had spent the night committing
murder!

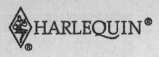

⬥HARLEQUIN®

Weddings, Inc.

THE WEDDING GAMBLE
Muriel Jensen

Eternity, Massachusetts, was America's wedding town. Paul Bertrand knew this better than anyone—he never should have gotten soused at his friend's rowdy bachelor party. Next morning when he woke up, he found he'd somehow managed to say "I do"—to the woman he'd once jilted! And Christina Bowman had helped launch so many honeymoons, she knew just what to do on theirs!

THE WEDDING GAMBLE, available in September from American Romance, is the fourth book in Harlequin's new cross-line series, **WEDDINGS, INC.**

Be sure to look for the fifth book, **THE VENGEFUL GROOM,** by Sara Wood (Harlequin Presents #1692), coming in October.

WED4

This September, discover the fun of falling in love with...

love and laughter

Harlequin is pleased to bring you this exciting new collection of three original short stories by bestselling authors!

ELISE TITLE
BARBARA BRETTON
LASS SMALL

LOVE AND LAUGHTER—sexy, romantic, fun stories guaranteed to tickle your funny bone and fuel your fantasies!

Available in September wherever
Harlequin books are sold.

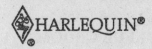

HARLEQUIN®

Don't miss these Harlequin favorites by some of our most distinguished authors!
And now you can receive a discount by ordering two or more titles!

HT #25525	THE PERFECT HUSBAND by Kristine Rolofson	$2.99	☐
HT #25554	LOVERS' SECRETS by Glenda Sanders	$2.99	☐
HP #11577	THE STONE PRINCESS by Robyn Donald	$2.99	☐
HP #11554	SECRET ADMIRER by Susan Napier	$2.99	☐
HR #03277	THE LADY AND THE TOMCAT by Bethany Campbell	$2.99	☐
HR #03283	FOREIGN AFFAIR by Eva Rutland	$2.99	☐
HS #70529	KEEPING CHRISTMAS by Marisa Carroll	$3.39	☐
HS #70578	THE LAST BUCCANEER by Lynn Erickson	$3.50	☐
HI #22256	THRICE FAMILIAR by Caroline Burnes	$2.99	☐
HI #22238	PRESUMED GUILTY by Tess Gerritsen	$2.99	☐
HAR #16496	OH, YOU BEAUTIFUL DOLL by Judith Arnold	$3.50	☐
HAR #16510	WED AGAIN by Elda Minger	$3.50	☐
HH #28719	RACHEL by Lynda Trent	$3.99	☐
HH #28795	PIECES OF SKY by Marianne Willman	$3.99	☐

Harlequin Promotional Titles

#97122	LINGERING SHADOWS by Penny Jordan	$5.99	☐
	(limited quantities available on certain titles)		

	AMOUNT	$
DEDUCT:	10% DISCOUNT FOR 2+ BOOKS	$
	POSTAGE & HANDLING	$
	($1.00 for one book, 50¢ for each additional)	
	APPLICABLE TAXES*	$_____
	TOTAL PAYABLE	$_____
	(check or money order—please do not send cash)	

To order, complete this form and send it, along with a check or money order for the total above, payable to Harlequin Books, to: **In the U.S.:** 3010 Walden Avenue, P.O. Box 9047, Buffalo, NY 14269-9047; **In Canada:** P.O. Box 613, Fort Erie, Ontario, L2A 5X3.

Name: _____

Address:_____City: _____

State/Prov.: _____Zip/Postal Code: _____

*New York residents remit applicable sales taxes.
 Canadian residents remit applicable GST and provincial taxes..

HBACK-JS